THE DOC
WEARS THRE

*Three faces wears the doctor: when first sought*
*An angel's; and a god's the cure half wrought;*
*But when, the cure complete, he seeks his fee*
*The Devil looks less terrible than he.*

ANONYMOUS

Mary Bard

# The Doctor Wears Three Faces

GEORGE MANN *of* MAIDSTONE

THE DOCTOR WEARS THREE FACES
by Mary Bard



First published in Great Britain
by Hammond, Hammond in 1950

First published in this edition by George Mann, 2005

**ISBN 0 7041 0401 6**

Printed and bound in the United Kingdom
by Woolnough Bookbinding Ltd
of Irthlingborough, Northamptonshire
and published by
George Mann Books, PO Box 22, Maidstone
in the English County of Kent

*To*

*MY SISTER BETTY*

*who egged me on*

# 1

# Adequate Medical Attention

DOCTOR: *A doctor is a man who is licensed to practise* medicine.

A HUSBAND IS A MAN who is licensed to come home every night on the 5.10, eat dinner, play with the children, read *Time* and work in the garden.

Combine the two and what do you get? A husband who is licensed to come home every night on the 5.10, eat dinner, play with the children, read *Time*, work in the garden and also to practice medicine? No. You get a draught in the hall, a slammed door, an empty chair at dinner and a voice on the telephone.

If I'd known this, I would have married Jim anyway. It just so happens that at the time I met Jim, the Bards had had practically nothing to do with doctors. Many of the men in our family were professional men, but they ran more to lawyers, ministers and engineers. Their wives were an obedient lot, produced more than the usual number of children and, outwardly at least, accepted the mores of their generations and the edicts of their husbands.

When Daddy married Mother, he, a young Western mining engineer, wrenched her from the reluctant arms of an Edwardian New York family and brought her out to Butte, Montana. In those days Butte was young and lusty. The colour and adventure appealed to every sense of Mother's vital and exuberant self. She loved Butte, the West, wandering all over the country as a mining engineer's wife, and most of all she loved Daddy.

They were very happy and healthy, spent long and joyous hours galloping over the sagebrush when Daddy went on prospecting trips, moved gaily from one wild and unsettled Western town to another, and had no need for or interest in a doctor until Mother was pregnant with me. She was delighted to discover that she was pregnant although it meant staying home while Daddy went prospecting. She refused to go home to New York to be delivered, but, as a sop to her distraught family, chose a woman doctor who was educated in Philadelphia and who turned out to be a homoeopathic physician.

Homoeopathy is frowned on by the medical profession today, but Mother stuck with its theory of 'like cures like' until she had five children. It must have been fairly successful because we're all alive and have most of our faculties. Of course this could also be due to the fact that a doctor to us, whether he was homoeopathic or psychopathic, was somebody who came in, stamped the snow off his feet and went upstairs to deliver another baby.

Because Daddy was a mining engineer, we were seldom in one place longer than six months. This made a family physician an impossibility. We had to get the disease and then find a doctor to match it. When Mother found herself alone with her family in some god-forsaken area, and couldn't find a panacea in her well-worn doctor book, she gave us copious doses of calomel if we were green, milk of magnesia if we were cranky, and occasionally aconite, a hangover from the homoeopathic days, if we had a temperature. Otherwise she did what the most brilliant specialists do today—let nature cure the disease as far as possible.

On the rare occasions when it was necessary, Mother used a technique for getting a doctor in a strange city that I still think is excellent. She called up the largest hospital in town, named the disease or described the symptoms, and asked for a list of physicians. She then chose the last name on the list of five because he was probably young and struggling, wouldn't charge too much, and would have the time and patience to make night calls.

Following Daddy around the country all the time made our education sketchy. In addition it made it necessary for us to adjust ourselves at a moment's notice to new schools, new playmates, new houses, new climates, new Sunday schools and new doctors. This sounds hard but it wasn't—we had lots of vitality and excellent health and we liked to adjust. In fact, we became so eager to accept new things that our method of becoming acclimatized was quite a lot like a person who listens, not very attentively, to a lecture on swimming and then runs home and dives off a twenty-foot board.

When we grew up we didn't move around so much, but we had become so attached to making adjustments that we changed jobs all the time instead. Sometimes the change was our own idea, but more often it was not. First we got bored and then we got fired. Occasionally we got fired before we got bored, but that was due to our other outstanding characteristics.

I met Jim because aspirin, Mother's substitute in adult children for calomel and milk of magnesia, didn't work on my case of flu. We all ignored my condition as long as possible. As a family we were much too busy to be sick, thought that only big bores talked about their operations, and howled 'Big Sicko' or 'Big Saddo' at any member of the family who did not have a temperature to bolster up his complaints. We were far more entertained by my latest job—radio promotion with an advertising agency. I had three large advertising accounts—a department store, a ferry company and an advertising dentist—and the family were much more interested in the myriad details of these new environments than in the fact that my chest was sore and that I coughed all night. When Mother found that I had a temperature of 102 I was judged legitimately sick, and was allowed to stay in bed. The family switched their enthusiasm to illness, discussed the desirability of a complete physical examination, a house call—did anybody know a doctor?—I might have pneumonia or pleurisy—maybe I'd even go to a hospital—they'd always wanted to know what a hospital was like. Mother didn't think so much enthusiasm was necessary, after all I just had the flu and there was lots of it around.

I stayed in bed for three days and my temperature fluctuated between 99.8 and 102. Three days with a temperature and without visible improvement was all Mother ever allowed any disease. She hunted for the homoeopathic remedy book for a while, remembered it had been lost in one of the moves, and then called the General Hospital. She described my symptoms and told them she wanted a doctor. Jim's name was fifth on that list. Mother said a house call wasn't necessary, she just wanted to be sure she was doing the right thing. My sister Betty had been working for an insurance company for two weeks and was an authority on physical examinations. She demanded that I have a complete physical examination—the first, as far as I can remember, in the family.

My appointment with Jim for the physical examination was for five o'clock on a Friday. At a quarter to five I dumped the radio copy on which I was working into a briefcase and took a taxi to his office. The place was a mass of dejected-looking customers, morosely leaning against the walls, sitting in the chairs, or standing and looking sadly out of the windows at the dreary rain. The acrid odour of disinfectant combined uneasily with the rubbery smell of wet raincoats.

Realizing vaguely how busy the doctor was, and much more accurately how busy I was, I gave the calm-faced nurse my name and told her I had to be back at my office not later than quarter to six.

She filed another card, adjusted her cap and said, "Doctor is delayed this afternoon. It will be just a little while I am sure. Sit down, please, and I will call you."

I looked at my watch at six-second intervals, stamped my foot, coughed, and gave the nurse the magnetic eye. Even if all the rest of these Big Sickos enjoyed spending their time being cooped up in a doctor's office, I didn't; and I had some radio copy to get out before I could go home. The nurse ignored me completely, and in a warm, sympathetic voice continued to tell the biggest lies in the world to the patients in the room and the importunate ones on the phone.

"Mrs Morgan—this is Dr Jay's nurse—the Doctor will be just a little late for your dinner party this evening—oh about six-thirty—he has one or two more patients to see before he leaves." We looked at each other to see which were the lucky two and wondered what she was planning to do with the rest of us. A man opened the door, walked briskly over to the reception desk and said, in a deep busy-executive voice, "Mr Jones, North-west Steel."

The nurse looked up at him and smiled absent-mindedly. "Come right in Mr Jones. Doctor is waiting for you." Mr Jones came in fifteen minutes after me and anywhere from ten minutes to two weeks after the other people in the room. From my advertising standpoint, this was the most casual way to treat customers I'd ever witnessed. These people all had appointments and yet Mr Jones was given unexplained preference. This doctor would be lucky if every patient in the room were not at least a potential loss.

'No appointment necessary' was the opening line in all of my advertising dentist's announcements—his offices took care of hundreds of people every day and no one ever had to wait more than five minutes. What this doctor and nurse needed was a little fundamental coaching on customer control. (Later I found out that the nurse was not partial as I had supposed, nor was Mr Jones pulling rank—he was an emergency sent up from North-west Steel. I now know that no doctor has ever heard of customer control.)

There were little irritated coughs and murmurs from all sides of the room. Maybe if I looked like the sickest customer I would be taken into the doctor, if only for sanitary reasons. I blew my nose, coughed three deep, racking coughs, rested my head in my hands and looked out from between my fingers to see how the nurse was taking it.

She merely picked up the telephone, said, “Oh yes, Mrs Talbot, Doctor is almost through, you can come over any time—we were a little busy earlier in the day but most of the patients have gone now—oh about ten minutes.” There was further uneasy rustling among the dejected ones and a sort of musical chair exchange of seats.

The woman crouched on a low footstool next to me sighed. I turned to her. “I have to be back at the office at quarter to six and it’s twenty-five to, right now.” She shrugged one shoulder. “I’ve been here before—I took the afternoon off.” A ‘habit’ customer. But those habits could be broken by well-directed promotion. Hadn’t my advertising dentist built his Coast-wide business on that theory?

The woman next to me began to moan faintly and gather her things together. She was weakening but I wasn’t—I was going to see the doctor if it took a month—if for no other reason than to give him a few suggestions and tell him his furniture was impossible. An enormous roll-top desk, pigeon-holed like a dovecot, took up a good third of the waiting-room. Wet umbrellas stood in an open stand near the door, dripping little puddles of water on the linoleum-covered floor. A row of wicker chairs was broken by a purple velvet armchair, a footstool and a wicker couch on which two patients sat and warily eyed one another. A standing lamp, with a base as thick as a post, had a small shade covered with a gritty beaded substance in three shades of old gold. (The same oak desk reposes in Jim’s study right now and the study is only about half the size of the office waiting-room. The only reason we don’t have all the rest of the stuff in our living-room now is that Jim decided that he couldn’t bear to part with it.)

I shuddered. This doctor not only was unaware of eye appeal, but he thought nothing of the customer’s comfort. I’d like to take him down to the Foley Family Dentist’s main office. Beginning with the concealed speaker in the ceiling of the reception-room, which played semi-classical music from nine until six, their atmosphere was a masterpiece of allure. The walls and ceiling were turquoise blue broken by bands of glass brick behind which hidden lights glowed restfully. The floors were carpeted from wall to wall in honey-coloured broadloom with a pile as luxuriant as pampas grass. The receptionists, nurses and dental assistants wore turquoise blue uniforms and blonde hair.

The first time I'd taken Norman, our sales manager, up to the Foley Family Dentist's main office, he'd been very much impressed. "Looks more like a house of assignation than a bed of pain", he murmured as he gingerly settled back into a tufted chair. He whistled softly as each blonde assistant sauntered into the waiting room, tenderly took the arm of a patient and disappeared through a glass brick door. "And will you look where the spider sits!" He pointed to a circular desk in one corner. The blonde account executive was writing out a receipt for a patient. Her lashes, painted to resemble a dark blue fringed gentian, batted gently with the difficulty of her task. "It would be a pleasure to have her yank your dough or your teeth", Norman murmured out of the side of his mouth. His admiration increased perceptibly after a conference with their promotion manager and a look at their advertising budget.

Maybe Dr Jay couldn't afford to start with anything so elaborate, but it might be interesting to tell him a few cogent facts about dealing with the public. I began by mentally disposing of everything in the office including the nurse, carpeting the floors in soft grey, installing indirect lighting and scattering around a few love seats in subdued jewel tones—the whole *décor* to be built around one GOOD picture instead of those framed diplomas.

The nurse said, "Miss Bard, Doctor will see you now."

The hall down to his office was stark, with brown mottled linoleum and unrelieved white walls. The doctor was at his desk writing when I walked in. A lock of straight blond hair hung over his forehead, giving him an engagingly youthful appearance. Without looking up he murmured, "Sit down, please", and continued to write scratchy hieroglyphics in the blank spaces on a chart. Over his head on a wall hung a motto:

> 'Joy, Temperance, and Repose,
> Slam the door on the doctor's nose.'

I slammed my briefcase down on the corner of the desk, sat down and began, "I've been waiting about three hours to see you and—"

"What seems to be the trouble?" His voice was deep and unhurried as he placed the chart carefully in a folder on his desk.

"I have the flu—was in bed for three days last week—I've got calliopes screaming all over the state, radio announcements blatting on every station at three-second intervals, am spending millions of dollars advertising a damned disinterested ferry company—carrying on the whole thing practically single-handed—and haven't got time to breathe let alone stay in bed—so don't suggest it. I have got a few ideas for your office though—"

He looked up. His eyes were widely spaced and very blue. Then he smiled—a slow luminous smile which lit up his whole face and as far as I was concerned, the whole office. Right then I dropped advertising, customer control and promotion without a backward look, and embraced the cause of medicine.

When I got home that night I announced to the family that I was going to marry a doctor with the most beautiful smile they'd ever seen.

Mother said she was glad he had a nice smile, but what about my chest. I told her that I was to go to bed every night at ten o'clock, which would be all right because doctors required a lot of rest; that he'd given me a prescription for cough medicine, but otherwise I was hale and hearty. Then I settled down to describe the doctor in minute detail. The family were joyfully enthusiastic and recalled everything they had ever read about doctors. It sounded like a wonderful life.

The next morning I put the research department of the advertising agency to work on finding out about Jim. Born in Texas, thirty-four years old, educated in Omaha and Dartmouth. Rush Medical College—internships—residencies—I skipped all that part and rushed to the meat. Unmarried! I called Jim to ask him how much cough medicine it was safe to take—and asked him to dinner Friday night.

Aside from abounding health and immense vitality, the Bards have three other outstanding characteristics. The first, which gets us into the most trouble, is a violent and unquenchable urge to help. '*Poor* little *thing*!' can and does refer to anything from a filing clerk in the office to the president of U.S. Steel. The second is a mania for talk. The third is a catholic taste in literature. Just so it's printed, it's all right with us. From the time I met Jim, all four characteristics were in high gear. At the time I started pursuing him we had all read: *The Story of San Michele; V. V.' s Eyes; District Nurse; Rats, Lice and History; Rich Girl, Poor Girl; Great Physician; A Short Life of Sir William Osler; Country Doctor; Of Human Bondage; Undaunted; Arrowsmith; K.; Noguchi; Young Doctor Galahad* and *Magnificent Obsession*. They were all about doctors and we liked them.

From these books I had gathered that the ideal doctor's wife should be a combination of Hedy Lamarr and Eve Curie. Therefore if I succeeded in trapping Jim, I was prepared to watch him do a very difficult piece of brain surgery—never done before of course—while I, masked and gowned, observed intelligently from the gallery.

Any baby delivering I assisted with would naturally be on a pine kitchen table by the flickering light of a candle, on the hospital lawn, or in the back of a careening car.

In the evening I would loll on down-filled davenports, smoking foreign cigarettes and galvanizing my husband's research assistants by my brilliant offhand suggestions.

"Have you gentlemen thought of using histamine in rabies?"

Occasionally, appropriately garbed in a wimple, I'd float in and call on the patients in their homes.

In between times, of course, I'd be privileged to sit around stroking my husband's long, skilled, surgeon's hands.

The first shock came when I found Jim was an internist.

From then on, I learned the hard way that the would-be doctor's wife could just as well be a totally paralysed Mongoloid. All she ever does is sit and wait!

While we were engaged I waited fourteen hundred and fifty-six hours and twenty-one minutes, in a draughty Chevrolet coupé. I haven't had the heart to count up the time since.

I waited in front of apartment houses on deserted, night-filled streets, holding my breath and listening for footsteps.

I waited on lonely country roads with the wind howling and the rain beating relentlessly on the windshield, and where an escaped maniac could have carried me into the next county before Jim discovered it.

I waited in restaurants where the waiter hovered around filling my water glass and swiping at non-existent crumbs.

I waited in front of hospitals where any sympathy I might have had for the stream of frightened people going in was turned to green-eyed jealousy because they were at least going to be warm.

For six months I worked like a fiend all day getting my accounts out of the way so I could spend every evening waiting in the car for Jim and endeavouring to get his mind off his patients long enough to hear me when I asked him to marry me. By the time the wedding day arrived I was utterly exhausted.

We chose the unearthly hour of eight o'clock in the morning to be married because the boat to Victoria left at ten o'clock. On the boat I entertained Jim with a detailed review of *Noguchi* and he took soda tablets for his ulcer. I asked him if all doctors had ulcers. "Not all of them", he said gulping down two more tablets. "It's strain that makes an ulcer active."

We went to the north end of Vancouver Island for a blissful week of lying on the sand. No matter how carefully I questioned Jim, he refused to divulge any drama in the practice of internal medicine. No emergency operations, no baby delivering, just finding out what was wrong with sick people. He had such a nice profile that I didn't care.

We went back to Victoria at the end of the week. It wasn't until we arrived in the lobby of the Empress Hotel, and were greeted by a mob of cheerful doctors and their wives, that I found we were also attending a medical meeting. Today, of course, it would never occur to me to suggest any trip which did not also include a medical meeting, but at that time I was slightly nonplussed. Jim left for the first lecture before I woke up in the morning. I had breakfast with two or three other doctors' wives and spent the day wandering around Victoria. We joined the doctors at five o'clock for cocktails, the men went on to the dinner meeting if there was one, or if not, we all had a joyful dinner together. I had a golden opportunity to find out from the women exactly what it was like to be married to a doctor. I can't recommend this system strongly enough for that grim procedure laughingly called a 'honeymoon'.

By the time we got back to our house, I was sure I was completely adjusted to being a doctor's wife, and Jim had eaten a whole bottle of soda tablets.

# 2

## For Some Unknown Reason

*PEPTIC ULCERS: Peptic Ulcer is a sharply circumscribed loss of tissue beginning in the mucosa, extending through the sub-mucosa into the muscular layers of the oesophagus, stomach or intestine, and resulting from the failure of the mucosa to withstand the digestive action of acid gastric juice. . . For some unknown reason, males are afflicted about four times more frequently than females . . .*

CECIL: *Textbook of Medicine*

WE HAD BEEN HOME a week, the house was wonderful and marriage was wonderful. I watched Jim finishing his breakfast of kippered herring, gjedost, pumpernickel and a carefully selected Delicious apple, and wondered if his diet had something to do with being an internist or was the accepted diet for duodenal ulcer . . . He took a large bite of the apple, and through it said, "By the way, suppose I ask the Morgans, the Stokes, and Young of California for dinner Friday night—that all right with you?"

Of course it was all right with me—I could hardly wait to begin smoking those foreign cigarettes and giving little dinner parties to impress Jim's confrères in medical research.

"Who are all these people?" Jim identified them for me as only a doctor would. "Tod Morgan you already know—Faith got back yesterday—internist—interested in phthisiology primarily. (I certainly did know Tod—every time I'd seen him he'd said, 'Mary, flee while there is yet time—you're too young to die.') Stokes and his wife—endocrinology—she's an ex-chief surgical nurse—and Young and his wife—thoracic surgery—giving a paper Monday night—from California."

It may have been wispy for purposes of greeting them at the door, but I basked in the sound of those long medical words and felt that surely by Friday night I could do enough research to suggest something even better than 'histamine for rabies'.

Jim went on eating and reading the paper and I got a pencil and tablet and started on my party list.

*Anything but ham or turkey.* (The only way you could tell the doctors' dinner parties apart was by the address and occasionally by the flower arrangements. The guests and the food were always the same.)

*Keep the men and women together.* (The most idiotic thing about the doctors' dinner parties was the caste system—the doctors shunned the wives as though they were unclean.)

Suddenly I had a brilliant idea—instead of taking Tod aside and asking him about Jim's ulcer, I'd memorize an article on ulcers and repeat it word for word, quite casually, of course, to the doctors!

*Medical book.* (Cecil would probably be best.) Just as a starter I asked, "By the way, what does phthisiology mean?" Jim grinned. "Thought you'd like that one. Phthisiology means tuberculosis, and endocrinology is an indivisible division of Internal Medicine having to do with certain glands which secrete specific substances into the blood stream for use by other tissues.

"Thoracic surgery is chest surgery. I'll tell you more about them when I come home tonight. Jean will give you their wives' home numbers—Young is at the Olympic."

*Call Jean at office.*

*Foreign cigarettes.*

*Flowers.*

Jim rose and I followed him out in the hall and hugged him enthusiastically. "I'll have the fanciest party you've ever been to."

He picked up his bag. "Don't have anything elaborate. One of the doctors is liable to get a call you know, might have to eat and run or be served after the others have finished."

He went down the steps and called back as he opened the car door, "Ask Pete and Maggie too; I want to ask Pete about that patient who's eclamptic."

"What's eclamptic?"

"Acute nausea with pregnancy—better make it Friday. There isn't a meeting that night."

He closed the car door and was gone.

I called Mother, told her we were about to give our first dinner party, that the guests were to be dear old tuberculosis, good old gland, chest paper from California and assorted wives, and Maggie and Pete. I asked her what frightfully *soigné* thing she could think up to eat. She said, "Have something you know how to cook—go to Roy."

"No", I wailed. I wanted to serve something fascinating. The main idea was to impress these people.

"Men don't want to be impressed—they want to be fed." Mother was firm. "I presume Yuri can cook frozen vegetables, if she'd deign to."

Mother didn't care much for Yuri, the little Japanese girl who came in after school to loathe me and be a doormat to 'The Doctor'. I thought her rapid, badly done cleaning was a question of being Issei, or first generation, and admired her because she was foreign and beautiful. Mother recognized it for what it undoubtedly was—adolescence with the added disadvantage of Japanese guile.

*Medical Book:* Cecil's *Textbook of Medicine* is a thick book, liberally illustrated. It begins with virus diseases and works doggedly, cell by cell, to treatment of infections. Only the fact that I had to go to the office kept me from settling down to a morning of goose flesh, which Cecil referred to as 'cutis anserina', engendered by each squalid photograph. There proved to be twenty-three pages of fine print on ulcers. Better start with the Definition and go as far as I could in three days.

Jean gave me the wives' numbers: Mrs Morgan was a honey, Mrs Stokes treated everybody like a student nurse, Mrs Young sure liked a lot of service, and Maggie Roberts was her favourite.

*Foreign cigarettes*: I'd see what I could do when I went to see Roy.

*Flowers*: Yuri and 'myfather' could take care of that.

All morning at the office I muttered, 'Peptic ulcer is a sharply circumscribed loss of tissue beginning in the mucosa' as I wrote, 'You too can have beautiful dentures—no appointment necessary—'

Roy did what he had done since I was twelve. He leaned across the counter, handed me a wienie and said, "Why don't you have a nice pot roast cooked in beer, like I taught you?" We'd had pot roast cooked in beer for Roy's benefit six times a month for sixteen years and twice during the week since I had been keeping house. I chose three Muscovy ducks, which Roy would not recommend. On the bus I checked over my list.

*Muscovy ducks* √
*Muscular layers of the oesophagus* √
*Wives' numbers* √
*Foreign cigarettes* √
*Flowers* √

Friday afternoon, when I came home from the office, I found Yuri rapidly smashing dishes and washing, in mounds of soapsuds, the ones that resisted her efforts. There was a strange odour all over the house which was an illusive intermingling of kippered herring and dead rat. As I got out the silver and silver polish, the odour in the kitchen was almost unbearable. Yuri glanced over her shoulder, saw the silver polish and set her lips.

"All the silver must be polished, Yuri."

"With the polish in the pot?" Yuri carefully hung a greasy, spotted dish towel over the clean linen towel on the rack and stiffened. The polish in the pot and washing the window had an equal significance to Yuri. "In Japan—the window is of paper. Japanese people do not use silver. Could I polish the knife and fork with the cloth?"

I told her of The Doctor's pride in his wedding presents and the guests' undoubted disappointment in the Japanese nation as a whole if the silver were dirty.

Black eye met green eye and green eye hung tough. It was disheartening to know that if Jim had casually mentioned that he'd like her to clean the whole outside of the house, shingle by shingle, with a tonsil swab, she would have been honoured to do it. In order to divert her attention from the hated polish in the pot, I mentioned the dead fish and the deader rat.

Yuri smashed a final salad plate and turned and faced me. "It is not The Doctor's fish; it is not the dead mouse—it is my medicine." She reached into the vegetable bin and brought out a sack which she had hidden behind the potatoes. As she came toward me the smell nearly knocked me over. "It is small Japanese dried fish. Myfather say I cannot stay if I do not eat the fish before I eat the American food. American food make Japanese sick."

I wondered about the smell and American guests, decided that the battle of the polish in the pot was more important, and told her to put the little fish in the back part of the cooler so they would get lots of air and keep longer. I opened the back door and the front door so the guests would keep from being anaesthetized, and went upstairs to dress.

While I bathed I went over the ulcer article again—it was difficult to keep my place because Cecil would repeat words like ‘peptic’ and ‘mucosa’. By the time I got out of the tub I was sure I had Definition and Distribution down cold—it was when I tackled Incidence that I got into trouble. ‘For some unknown reason, males are afflicted about four times more frequently than females.’ Their lowered resistance wasn’t surprising if they had to memorize much stuff like this. Checking the pronunciation of ‘hematemesis’ and ‘cholelelithiasis’ in the medical dictionary, I went downstairs.

Yuri was flitting around setting the table. Her winged black brows made a charming V of concentration in her delicate oval face as she hesitated for a moment and then proudly put the knives on the wrong side.

“The knives point at the water glass, Yuri.” I switched them for the twenty-first time. “Japanese-people-do-not-use-silver”, she breathed. “Myfather send you the carnation and the peach blossom for the party.” She pointed to an exquisite flower arrangement on the earth, air and water basis which she had created from two mossy green twigs, a spray of flowering peach, five pink carnations, and a deft Japanese ability.

The silver was grey and spotty, she had not used the polish in the pot, but she had put at each place a ricepaper card with peach blossoms painted in the corner. The odour of dead fish was congenially combined with the spicy fragrance of carnations, the table looked delightfully foreign and the living-room seemed pleasant and welcoming.

I knelt down to struggle with the fire. It hissed wetly and fell apart. I wished that the skill in Jim’s fingers included the ability to build a fire. Yuri’s technique consisted of filling the fireplace with large logs, placing a wisp of paper well to the front, tossing a lighted match over the edge of the fire-screen, and examining her butterfly fingers for splinters.

The telephone rang. Maggie said, “Is Jim there yet?—He will be because he’s not an obstetrician—I could kill Pete. He has one on the nest who’s been hoppin’ in and out of the hospital like a regulah cricket for two weeks. He doesn’t dare leave her because it’s her first baby, and she’d have it in the taxi sure as shootin’ if he did.”

Now this was more my idea of medicine. I wondered how long it would take Jim to study up on obstetrics. Maggie said, "Oh well, honey, I'll come on alone, which is all I've ever done since I laid eyes on that Yankee", and hung up.

I wandered back to the sullen and spitting fire and planned the scintillating conversation. Tonight I would astound Jim with my ability to draw out our guests. My lack of medical knowledge would be more than compensated for by my interested, intelligent, medical questions. I would probe for each detail of every patient, his symptoms, background, probable psychological factors involved—and then—stun them with 'ulcers'!

The doorbell rang and I went to answer it.

"Hello, I'm Lester Young and this is Helen."

Yuri hovered behind me looking beautiful, polite and flower-like. She had changed her air of sullen martyrdom with her uniform and now wore grey sateen and an expression of glowing servitude. I asked her to take Doctor Young's coat. At the word 'Doctor', Yuri's hard little black eyes shone, her delicate pale brown hands deftly took the coat and hung it carefully on the hanger—even going so far as to arrange the shoulder pads. "Thank you, Doctor", she murmured bowing deeply. I thought grimly of how she piled my clothes all on one hook in the closet, kicking what fell off into the darkest corner.

As Helen Young took off her coat she said the inevitable "My, but you are fortunate. Lester and I would give anything to have a little Japanese girl. Isn't she beautiful?"

"Yes, but pretty is as pretty does", I said through clenched teeth. Maggie called from downstairs. "Mary honey, may I come up?" She came in all soft and Southern in a black velveteen suit. "Aren't doctors devils? I don't know when that fiend of a Pete's goin' to get here—if at all." She examined her bewitching face in the mirror. "I sweah I look like a spook—been ironin' since dawn with sparks bitin' at me every minute. As Pete fixed the iron I suppose I ought to be thankful I wasn't electrocuted." She turned from the mirror. "I hope your husband isn't an obstetrician, Mrs Young. I declare Pete's patient's been in labah ever since I can remember."

Helen Young laughed. "No, my husband is a chest surgeon—but it's practically as bad."

The telephone rang. "Is Dr Stokes there?"

"No, he isn't. I expect him however. May I have him call?"

"This is the Medical Exchange. Please have him call as soon as he comes in."

We all went downstairs to find the fire smouldering. Dr Young was eyeing it suspiciously, and obviously wondering who was going to make it burn. He was a fat pompous-looking little man and moved his lips in and out judiciously before he spoke. "Surgery is more in my line than fires, I'm afraid. In Southern California we use fires very little, sunshine keeps us warm, you know." He pursed his lips and looked helplessly down at the fire again.

Maggie fixed him with a large blue eye. "I'll bet you can make that fire roah like a forest fiah. I'm a regulah little match girl when Pete's out—I just light matches and paper until I get warm." Lester Young got down on his knees and began feebly to rearrange the logs and blow ashes all over the room.

"It's the first fire Lester's ever built to my knowledge. I'll be interested to see if it goes", Helen encouraged him.

"Nonsense, my dear, nonsense." He smiled fatuously up at Maggie. "Used to build 'em as a child all the time. Boy Scout, you know."

"So was Pete—as a child", Maggie murmured, and winked at me.

The telephone rang. "Is Dr Roberts there?"

I told them he was on his way to the hospital. "What hospital, please? This is the Medical Exchange." I turned to Maggie. "Is Pete on his way to Maternity?"

"Uh-huh, he should be there now. Give the Exchange Maternity's number until Pete comes here—they'll drive you crazy if you don't." She sighed and turned to Helen Young. "It's gettin' so I just answer every 'phone call with 'How far apart are your pains?' It startles the gas man, but I can always straighten him out latah."

The doorbell rang.

"Hello, Mary, I'm Ed Stokes. Is Edith here yet? I was supposed to pick her up but I forgot. Any calls?" He handed the hovering Yuri his coat. "Am I the latest, as usual?"

"The Exchange is trying to reach you."

"Oh, thanks." He called the Exchange, said, "Be right down", and turned to me—"Sorry, Mary, have to go back to General. Get here as soon as I can", and left.

I closed the front door. This lone relay race from door to

telephone to door again certainly prevented my being anything more fascinating than a cold wind as I dashed by my guests. And how could I ask doctors brilliant medical questions when they weren't there?

Yuri called me. "The open-face sandwich for the cocktail party is ready." I was completely bewildered by this development and followed her out into the kitchen. She had made millions of open-faced sandwiches, when and how I'll never know. She handed me one to taste. "I help at cocktail party many time, I know how to make it." Rows of avocado rings, cottage cheese, peanut butter, and tomato—all perfectly beautiful and perfectly tasteless. It was going to be like eating a patchwork quilt, patch by patch.

"I'd planned to serve potato chips and Roquefort cheese", I said hopelessly.

"The Doctor would not like it. He like the sandwich without the top." I shook salt over the ones I could reach, thought, 'It's a damned good thing The Doctor hasn't told her he likes to pull taffy', and went to answer the door. On the way I had a mental flashback of the day I waited in Jim's office, furious because I had to wait so long, and further enraged by his nurse's apparently irrelevant telephone conversation with one Mrs Morgan, who must have been Faith Morgan. 'This is Dr Jay's nurse—the Doctor will be just a little bit late for dinner this evening—he has one or two more patients to see before he leaves.' I wondered how many patients were still stacked on that wicker furniture.

I opened the door and a tall woman held out her hand and said, "Are you Mary? I'm Edith Stokes." White hair, white coat, white eyelashes and a mighty frosty manner, she looked like a Band-Aid with the wrapping still on. Handing Yuri her coat and brushing past me she said, "Is Ed here?—He said he'd pick me up, but of course he forgot." This was the famous head surgical nurse, still clinging to her sterile white costume.

"Aren't you nice?" She patted me as she walked into the living-room and nodded to the guests. "And what a cunning little house—my, aren't you fortunate!" Lester Young was still vaguely kicking at the fire. "Here—let me fix that—fires are my speciality." She gave the fire three brisk pokes, pushed the lower log back, and it began to glow and snap.

The telephone rang. It was Pete Roberts. "Is Jim home yet,

Mary? Have him call me when he comes in. Maternity—thanks. Magnolia struggle over by herself? Happy dinner, save some for me."

The doorbell rang. Tod said, "Hi, Mary, Jim home yet? That's good—this is Faith—I was so late at the office she thought we'd gum up your party."

Faith laughed. "Not that that would bother him one whit—he's afraid to start a precedent by arriving on time." Faith was even more beautiful than Maggie had said she was—'Tall, sort of like a Madonna with a gleam in her eye'. She'd been a nurse of some kind too, but it didn't show. She put her arm around me. "What can we do to help? Jim isn't here yet, of course. Tod, you go make the drinks for Mary."

As we went into the living-room Faith said, "This is a darling house. Jim told me a grateful patient had leased it to him for a year."

The conversation wove in and out like smoke as I passed the open-faced sandwiches.

"What the dear doctors would do without the Grateful Patients, the G.P.s I don't know. Grateful they may be when the first one is safely born but after the tenth I don't see how they can be to the extent of a silver vegetable dish. Periesophageal hernia must be distinguished roentgenologically from eventration", Dr Young meticulously enunciated each word.

Edith Stokes' cool voice said, "I've always maintained that a doctor who marries a woman without any medical training has three strikes against him."

"I'll show her", I thought lighting an Abdullah.

Tod and Lester Young drifted over into a corner, "—and symptomatically from conditions such as angina—" Lester Young squeezed each careful word through the gate of his clenched teeth.

Maggie and Faith pulled their chairs over closer to Edith and Helen. "So many mink coats I felt like I was out of uniform . . ."

"I told him I'd been to ten parties in a row, alone, and was going to get myself an unemployed Latin . . ."

"The telephone interrupts everything anyway—and I mean everything . . ."

I thought, 'No wonder the men go off by themselves and talk medicine. Chit-chat. Nothing stimulating about it.' Where in God's name was Jim! I picked up a tray of sandwiches, arranged in coloured rows like a spectrum, and walked briskly over to the doctors.

"Periesophageal hernia resembled ulcer—well, well, little lady, what have we here?" Dr Young opened his clenched teeth long enough to insert an avocado ring.

"Speaking of ulcers—try the tomato, it may taste a little less like modelling clay—if a peptic ulcer is a sharply circumscribed loss of tissue beginning in the mucosa—"

Tod patted me. "This wasn't an ulcer—" He turned back to Dr Young who was hovering over the cheese sandwiches. "You know Frank and Hamilton report the successful repair of a hernia of the diaphragm in which there was a penetrating ulcer—"

"In my case", I continued, smiling brightly, "it extended through the submucosa into the muscular layers and—"

"Naturally", Tod said. He frowned and looked vaguely around as though he didn't know quite where to put me. Dr Young bit a pink sandwich whose surface looked like toothpaste (and might have been, for all I knew), pushed his lips back and forth experimentally, said, "Interesting", and turned to Tod, "Periesophageal hernia often—"

Maggie called to me, "Mary honey, where did you say you got that green sweater?"

"Morris's", I answered briefly and turned back to Tod and Dr Young. I wished people would stop interrupting me—now I'd lost my place again. Dr Young was vacillating between a red and a white sandwich. He pinched his lower lip, rocked back and forth on the balls of his feet, and finally chose the red. As he put it in his mouth he stuck his lips out so far the inner lining showed. 'Mucosa—digestive action'—that was it! I grabbed Tod's arm. "You know, gentlemen, I think it's tremendously interesting that ulcers result from the failure of the mucosa to withstand the digestive action of acid gastric juice. For some unknown reason—"

Tod shook his arm free, took my elbows and turned me so that I faced him directly. "For some unknown reason, you've been reading a medical book. For God's sake, Mary—who's got this ulcer and where is it?"

Maggie called me again, "Mary honey, come here a minute!"

"Well, it isn't exactly a patient—that is, it's Jim's ulcer—"

"What's Jim griping about? His ulcer, if any, is unimportant and mighty small. Mine's the size of a teacup and gnawing into the pancreas." He marched me toward the women. "Now go on over there and play with the girls. We're busy."

Maggie patted the arm of her chair and lowered her voice. "Honey, they're talkin' medicine and you can't stay over there. One of the first things a doctor promises when he grabs that little stick with the snake wound around it is, don't ever tell your wife, nor anyone's wife—anything—at any time!"

"Including what time you're coming home for dinner." Faith smiled. "You'll get used to it. I don't say you'll like it—but you'll get used to it."

"I think medicine is interesting, and I'd like to know what they're talking about", I said.

Edith Stokes gave me a long look. "It is interesting, Mary—but it is also dangerous. You might hear something, and not realizing its significance, repeat it in the wrong place. We started the Forlorn Ones for that very reason."

"Tell Mary about the Forlorn Ones, Edith", Maggie said. "I declare, it's the only time I ever heard of women bein' banded together for any reason other than eatin'."

The telephone rang. It was Pete asking if Jim had come in yet. Yuri called me and I came into the kitchen just in time to prevent her from dropping three packages of frozen peas into a five-gallon preserving kettle of boiling water. I explained the steamer again and fixed it for her. "In Japan we do not have frozen pea—"

When I got back to the group around the fire, Edith said that when she and Ed were first married they found that several of the doctors' wives in their age group had had no previous experience of medicine. In order to make them feel less strange, and to provide a safe outlet for medical discussion, they had organized the Forlorn Ones. They met once a month, ostensibly to sew for the Children's Hospital but also to give the new wives a chance to ask questions about medical customs with which they were unfamiliar. She was about to suggest that Maggie and Faith and I organize a similar group called, for instance, the Neglected Ones.

The front door opened and Jim came in. "See what I mean", Edith murmured. "Medical custom. He's about two hours late and doesn't even know it. They're all like that."

There was a gurgle of delighted laughter from the circle around the fire as Jim greeted them. He walked promptly over to Tod and Lester and the two dissimilar conversations continued.

Yuri came over to me. "The dinner is ready. Shall I serve?" I looked instinctively to Edith for procedure, as neither Pete Roberts nor Ed Stokes had come in yet. She nodded. "Might just as well. They'll be in and out all evening and there's no reason why we should eat cold food."

Jim began to carve the ducks. Tod and Lester brought somebody's periesophageal hernia over to the table and trailed it after them as they served themselves. The ducks were tough and not very well done; Roy had been right. I could see a long vista of pot roast cooked in beer down through the years—it kept warm indefinitely.

The telephone rang. It was for Tod. He came beaming back to the table. "How would you like to come down and see that patient with me, Young? Interesting case and I'd like to have your opinion." Dr Young dropped his plate and almost ran to put on his coat.

The telephone rang. It was for Jim. "Excuse me, girls." He went to the telephone. Maggie moved the women's places to one end of the table. Edith continued her conversation with Faith Morgan, "—and you'll find, my dear, that all doctors suspect that they have whatever disease happens to be interesting them most at the time, whether it's cancer, cardiac disturbance or ulcers."

Maggie giggled. "I can hardly wait to hold Pete's head when he's eclamptic." She sniffed. "Mary honey, are you burnin' punk or something?"

I stubbed out my foreign cigarette and joined the Neglected Ones.

# 3

# Inflammatory Matter

APPENDICITIS: *Appendicitis, the most common major surgical disease, is an inflammatory lesion of the vermiform appendix. It may occur as an acute attack, acute appendicitis, which progresses to perforation or subsides spontaneously; as mild recurrent attacks, recurring appendicitis, or, if adhesions or obliteration follow infection, a so-called 'chronic appendicitis'.*

CECIL: *Textbook of Medicine*

AS WE WERE BOTH WORKING, Sunday was our day of rest. We had coffee in our bathrobes, threw Sunday papers all over the living-room and built a big fire in the fireplace so we could have breakfast in front of the fire.

Jim was absorbedly checking over his tackle box, and I was reviewing my lists of things to remember for next week. After so many years in a matriarchy, this pleasant unfamiliar masculine atmosphere was delightful. I scratched off, 'Monday, Yuri wash', and with a resigned sigh, substituted, 'Monday, Japanese laundry'. It was rapidly getting to the place where I could write 'Yuri's schedule for the week as, 'Yuri—arrange flowers and smile', and mine as, 'Mrs Jay, do all the rest of the work'.

"I'm going to give you this Hanson plug." Jim handed over a bitten, paintless treasure from his tackle box. "Might as well start with the best." I prepared to offer my all in return.

"How would you like grilled shad roe with nice crisp bacon on it, corn bread and pink grapefruit for breakfast?"

He whipped at the bookcase experimentally with his salmon rod, peered down its length as you would a gun sight and said, "I don't think I want any breakfast, I'm a little nauseated. Think I'll lie down for a while."

The possibility that a doctor could get sick had never occurred to me. Naturally, with all this free medical care lying around, I'd planned quite a few interesting little diseases for me, the type that required long-stemmed roses with a card attached, 'To me, you're always beautiful.' This development was a blow, but I managed to produce the old family stand-by "Where do you hurt?"

"Kind of a pain in my side, that chicken we had last night tasted funny—probably Salmonella." He drooped toward the stairs. "Call me around one, I have to make rounds. Take the calls for me unless they sound urgent."

Pain in the side! In our family that meant an appendix and you called a doctor even if you were fairly sure it was the result of green apples. If you were married to a doctor, you already had one so to speak. I picked up the papers and fishing tackle and followed Jim upstairs. He was huddled in bed in his pyjamas and hunting jacket, with three pillows bunched under his head in uncomfortable knots. I whisked the pillows out, rearranged them, removed the hunting jacket and substituted his hated bathrobe. Then I peered diagnostically at him, told him he was shivering, and looked quite green, and offered to get the electric pad. He gave two dreadful groans.

"See if we have a hot water bottle, I want that too."

I came back with the electric pad and the hot water bottle, to find the pillows in knots and the hunting Jacket on over the bathrobe. He had pulled the covers off my bed and added them to the lumpy pile on his bed. The groans were regular and heart-rending from under this heaving mound of bedclothes.

"Have we any chicken soup? —I'm freezing."

"Wouldn't you rather have a cup of hot tea? Chicken soup might make you more nauseated."

"Damn it to hell, I haven't had anything to eat but black coffee and orange juice—no wonder I'm nauseated. I want some hot chicken soup, some crackers and hot tea."

He shuddered convulsively, clutched the pad and the hot water bottle, placed them tenderly on his stomach, and pulled the pillows down over his face. The moans were slightly muffled but seemed louder and much oftener.

I wondered as I fixed his tray, 'Are doctors like other men—do they make mountains out of molehills when they are sick just to get lots of attention, or is he really at death's door?' Fear clutched at my stomach. I tried to remember exactly what Jim's office girl had said about his dreadful illness when he was an intern.

Something about four-inch headlines in all the Chicago papers, my dear. "He got empyema—that's an infection, of course—cut his thumb, while doing an autopsy. He dropped down to eighty pounds, absolutely a skeleton. And were the big guns upset! They couldn't have given him more attention had he been one of their very own children. God help him if he ever gets a serious illness, pneumonia, or anything like that—he only has one good lung you know—they did a rib resection."

I carried the tray up to Jim, asked him what Salmonella was, patted the parts of him I could see and reach and asked him if I should call Dr Stokes.

"Hell, no—I have a red-hot appendix, I think. If you have to call someone, and I suppose it would be better than having you twit around like a mourning dove, call Marsh—but not until I tell you to. This tastes good, I'm probably just starving."

Suddenly he made a dive for the bathroom, where he was sick. I waited until he came back to bed, wan and shaking, put the hot water bottle and the hot pad back on his stomach, rearranged the quilts a little more comfortably and reached for the pillows. "Stop patting the Goddamned pillow, I like it that way." He huddled down in the covers and continued to shake, his teeth chattering like a pavement drill. I went downstairs to call Mother.

"Men are always awfully sick—what seems to be the matter with him?" Mother's voice was calm and slightly resigned.

"He's having dreadful chills and he's sick at his stomach. He won't let me do a thing; won't even let me call a doctor."

"Call the doctor anyway; don't discuss it with him."

"But Mother—he's a doctor."

"He's also a man. Call me if you need me. 'Bye."

I called Dr Marsh and described what I thought Jim had and what Jim thought he had. I couldn't remember Salmonella—so I substituted food poisoning.

"Um-hum. Probably ate when he was overtired—don't worry. I'll be right over." Dr Marsh also sounded calm. At a time like this it was certainly dandy to be married to a doctor. I could just see dozens of doctors all straining at the leash to help one of their own, nurses hopping around like crazy—all anxious to further their nursing reputations by giving the sick doctor remarkable care—the best and largest room in the hospital (if he had to go to the hospital). No matter what he had, I certainly didn't have to worry.

Dr Marsh was falsely hearty as he came in the room. "What seems to be the matter with you, don't you know that a vacation makes a doctor sick—and a honeymoon makes 'em both sick?" As he examined Jim he used the paediatric technique. "See the nice shiny gastroenterectomy I did yesterday?" Poke. "I hear Wharton's been appointed to the Board at County—about time they did something." Punch. "What did you decide to do about Maria Di Julio? Getting along all right now?" He stuffed the thermometer in Jim's mouth. Jim mumbled, glared and twitched. "Yep, a diabetic who won't stay on her diet is sure hell, even insulin can't do everything." He looked at the thermometer, shook it down and eyed Jim meditatively. "You may have an appendix all right, but your abdomen is perfectly soft and we won't worry about surgery yet. You have ice bags, haven't you, Mary?" I restrained the desire to snap, 'No, my trousseau was awfully sketchy', and offered to go to the drug store for some. "Don't bother—just pound up some ice—fill two hot water bottles and keep his abdomen packed. Give him one capsule; it's nembutal and call me if his temperature goes up." He turned back to Jim, whose eyes were black with fury. "If Wharton does just half the things he wants to do, we'll get some action at County yet. Suppose we do a white count in the morning when you get to the office. If your temperature goes up and the pain doesn't subside, let me know and we'll go down to the hospital this afternoon. It'll probably quiet down. Call me any time, Mary. I'll drop around tonight on my way home."

It seemed a damned casual way to treat an appendix. Everybody knew about ruptured appendices and operations performed with jack-knives in front of the headlights of cars.

As I went downstairs with Dr Marsh, I ventured a mild "Is it all right just to leave a red-hot appendix to simmer?—won't it rupture or something?"

"I doubt it. Occasionally we miss of course—but not very often—his abdomen's still soft—but he bears watching." He patted me comfortingly. "Cheer up, there are a lot more doctors where he came from. Just give him a little tea and dry toast if he gets hungry. He'll probably sleep most of the afternoon." He drew on his gloves and picked up his bag. “An internist always hates to let the surgeons get a whack at him—give him nothing but bland food, we’ll know more in the morning. You might stay home from that office for a day or so. See you later.”

I winced at that last crack. Doctors’ wives, if they worked, were supposed to do nice appropriate things like being technicians or nurses—not to spend their lives doodling away at interrupting radio programmes with commercials. It was being borne in on me more and more each day that doctors were supposed to marry their own, not stray into foreign fields to mate.

I went into the kitchen and started to crack the ice in a dish towel. It tore large holes in the towel and sprayed all over the kitchen. I got the Japanese laundry bag Yuri had thoughtfully provided, put the contents of three ice trays in it and began to beat on it with the hammer. By the time I had rammed a small portion of ice into the hot water bottle it had melted, and I started all over again. There was a roar from upstairs. “Mary, what in hell are you doing? Welding, for God’s sake?” The urge to rush upstairs and pound Jim on the head with the hammer was almost overwhelming.

“Just filling the ice bags, dear. I’ll be up in a minute.” My self-control was a major achievement in marital adjustment and I glowed with complacency.

When I came in with my soggy offering, Jim allowed one evil eye to peer out from under the covers. “Don’t bother to crack any ice, I won’t have ice bags on my belly. All surgeons are crazy and Marsh is the craziest of the lot. Empty those bags and fill them with boiling water. I want steak and some fried onions, some salad and a cup of *good* coffee, which I’ll probably have to make myself.” He sat up and put his feet over the side of the bed. “Look in my bottom drawer and hand me a pair of wool socks.”

“Shall I put them on for you?”

“No. I’m not paralyzed.” He reached over and carefully and laboriously began pulling on the socks, groaning regularly like a power saw. He tied a blanket Indian-fashion around his loins, pulled the bathrobe down over it, added his hunting jacket and tied them all securely around his middle with the bathrobe cord. As he lumbered toward the door, a grimace of very real pain crossed his face. He wavered for a moment, rocked back on his feet and fell across the bed.

I begged him not to make any effort, to tell me whatever he wanted and I would be more than glad to get it. He got his breath with difficulty and gasped between pains, "Measure the coffee carefully, one heaping tablespoonful to each cup of boiling water—put a pinch of salt in the water before the coffee boils up—heat the cup first—I guess I don't want any fried onions—just steak and salad. Fill those hot water bottles before you go." His coffee instructions indicated that I wasn't the only one who was capable of making marital adjustments.

He got back into bed, and I put the hot water bottles around his abdomen—the way Dr Marsh had said the ice bags were supposed to be placed—and prayed that internists were right and surgeons were wrong.

While I was cooking dinner I thought over my growing problem. I was doubling in brass, pretending each time I changed instruments that the other one was a little old nothing that for some strange reason I whimsically cherished. My entire mind and heart were on Jim and his welfare. Tomorrow, I would have to behave at the office as though my home and my husband were an amusing little hobby that I had found to occupy my spare time.

I put Jim's dinner on a tray and tiptoed upstairs. He was sleeping quietly, so I went back downstairs and ate the dinner myself. About six o'clock Dr Marsh dropped in, checked Jim's temperature and said, "Fine, I thought it would subside. We'll take a white count in the morning. I'll let you know." I dropped thankfully into bed about eight-thirty and Jim and I both slept quietly through the night.

When we woke up in the morning, Jim said, "I feel fine—could lick my weight in surgeons. Salmonella just as I told you." I asked him again if Salmonella was a medical pun for eating too much fish, or if it was the same thing as ptomaine poisoning, and did he want any breakfast.

"Neither—it's in the paratyphoid group. Ptomaine, the word by the way is seldom used now, is caused by eating food decomposed by saprophytic micro-organisms." He walked over and peered in the mirror, pulling his lower eyelids down so he looked like a bloodhound. "Better just make it milk toast and tea, and just a sliver of gjedost", he said as he wandered into the bathroom.

At the office, all hell had broken loose. Norman was calling on God to witness that his staff of employees had arrived *en masse* from a home for mental delinquents. The switchboard girl was bawling, the copy boy was preparing to leave before he was fired, the announcers, distinctly pale, were reading their announcements with more than the usual precise toothy care. 'I hope it isn't one of my accounts this time', I thought as I took off my coat.

"Mary—come here!" It was one of my accounts. I braced myself and walked into Norman's office. "Morris's called this morning—you put on a stocking sale for them. They have screaming women beating the doors down, the police are there and Morris's Department Store wants their little Mary to explain why they are advertising stockings at sixty-four cents a pair which cost them ninety-six cents a pair. Think quickly, dearie—and the answer is wrong."

"I'll have to check, Norman."

The announcement was correct, the copy was correct—the announcer had obviously been sleepy and had misread the seven o'clock announcement.

When I got back to the radio station from Morris's it was almost twelve o'clock. A sheaf of telephone messages was on my desk. 'Call General Hospital.' 'Call Jean at the office.' 'Call Dr Marsh at General.' There were six calls from Jean so I called her first. She said calmly, "Doctor Jay is in General. His white count was fourteen thousand, so they decided to put him in for observation. Dr Marsh is trying to get in touch with you, he's at General now."

I went into Norman's office, told him Jim had gone into General for observation for a probable appendix and asked for some time off. "Sure—sure." He looked up. "I've heard that the mortality rate is fairly low with an appendectomy, so you can stop quivering your lip. Want me to drive you up?"

"I ought to go back to Morris's this afternoon—they're only temporarily calmed down."

"I will call on Morris's. Your accounts will have the supreme honour of having the sales manager call on them while Jim is in the hospital—what more could they ask? Come on—let's get the car."

Miss MacFarlane, the hospital receptionist, said, "Go right up, Mrs Jay. They have surgery all prepared but I think Doctor is still in his room, 603."

Room 603 was empty. They had taken Jim to surgery and I hadn't even seen him. The tentacles of my instinct reached frantically for familiarity and found only strange smells, unaccustomed noises, hushed voices and the hurried, quiet impersonality of the hospital; a sound as sharpening to the ears as the eerie scuttling of rats in the wall.

A brisk nurse walked in, laid something wrapped in a towel on the bureau and said, “He’ll be down in a few minutes. Just make yourself comfortable.” Handing me a magazine and a brief, impersonal smile, she bustled out.

Warmed slightly by her visit I told myself that Jim was a doctor, that he would get every care, that he would get well more quickly because he was a doctor and knew how important co-operation was on the part of the patient.

I opened the magazine. The words persisted in turning into unrelated sounds—‘to-bac-co-to-bac-co-to-bac’. Often, waiting for Jim in the reception-room at General, I had idly wondered why the relatives, in the stiff, uncomfortable chairs, didn’t read or talk but just sat. The reason was now obvious to me. They were in a state of suspended animation while someone they loved was having an unknown thing called ‘an operation’.

Out in the hall, a doctor spoke in a low, judicious voice. Half-heard conversations rushed in on my consciousness: ‘Septicaemia—embolus—anaesthetic pneumonia—autopsy findings.’

For two hours, a slow helpless rage at the matter-of-fact, inconsiderate medical mind alternated with cold fear of the hospital.

Another nurse walked in. “Good afternoon, Mrs Jay, I’m Miss O’Connel. Everything’s just fine—they’re bringing Doctor down from surgery now. Would you like a cup of coffee?”

“No thank you. Shall I go down to the reception-room?”

“No. Just sit still. You’re perfectly all right here.” She turned to another nurse who was wheeling in a machine. “Put the intravenous apparatus on the other side of the bed, Miss Nelson. That’ll be fine. His specials will be here in a few moments.” I gulped. Specials were for very sick people.

“Was the operation just routine, Miss O’Connel? Does he need specials?”

“No use in being a doctor if you don’t get a lot of service.” She ripped the bed to pieces and began to remake it. “He’ll have specials for a few days. Dr Marsh prefers to have his retrocecal patients specialled.”

The door opened and Jim was wheeled in. He was grey, moaning and gasping. I felt the room begin to go around and pinched my legs hard. If I had been an ordinary lay person, someone would have taken the trouble to get me out of the room. But I was a doctor's wife, so they took it for granted that I must be a nurse and therefore thoroughly familiar with the hoarse moans of the patient coming out from under anaesthesia. The sickly, dead-flower smell of ether flowed over me in waves. Jim was lifted off the surgery cart and on to the bed, where he lay, limp and unfamiliar, breathing stertorously, his face mottled and his lips blue. Dr Marsh came in still wearing his surgical cap and gown, his mask hanging around his neck. He motioned to me to come out in the hall.

"The appendix was retrocecal, high up under the ribs—that's why it took so long in surgery. Everything was fine. He'll be coming around in an hour or so. I've ordered three specials. Nothing wrong—just prefer to take precautions, with his case history. Better get yourself a cup of coffee and come back. Don't stay but a minute; he'll sleep most of the afternoon." He put his arm comfortingly around me. "There's nothing to worry about. He just needs rest, quiet and good nursing care. We'll keep him here a week or so—and then you can take him home and spoil him."

A brisk, efficient-looking nurse stopped beside us. "Mrs Jay, this is Miss Wayne." I nodded dumbly. They walked down the hall, Dr Marsh giving directions while he untied the strings of his surgical gown. My legs were shaking so, I could hardly stand as I got in the elevator, and my morale was not eased by the sight of a woman crying softly and hopelessly as she leaned against the side of the cage.

Miss MacFarlane greeted me brightly as I passed the desk, "It isn't so bad is it?—he's out of surgery and everything's under control. Why don't you go over on the Avenue and have a cup of coffee?"

I bought some Talisman roses—the flowers Jim had always sent to me—some cigarettes and books. The sight of some new Hanson plugs in the sporting goods store caused the tears to pour down my face.

When I got back to the hospital, Jim was talking in a rapid thick voice to Miss Wayne. "I don't give a good Goddamn whether I'm suppose to or not—I don't want it and I won't take it. Hello—

Mary—you're kind of green around the gills—better order her a coffee, Miss Wayne—I don't want it—I don't want it."

Miss Wayne's R.N. expression was determined. "Dr Marsh ordered this hypo, Doctor. It is on the chart!" She sniffed and her cap jiggled menacingly.

"Lemme see the chart. Won't take it—not enough pain to justify anything now—"

"I'm sorry, Doctor. I can't give you the chart, you know that." She sponged off an area on Jim's arm and picked up the hypo syringe. "Won't take it—won't take it—" I tiptoed out. Miss Wayne followed in a moment, carrying the flowers I had brought for Jim. She walked down the hall with me, got a lumpy vase out of the service cupboard, rammed the roses down in it until only their glowing heads peered wistfully over the edge and said, "Would you like to have me order you a sandwich and some coffee, Mrs Jay? I'd be glad to."

"No thank you. What am I supposed to do? This is all so unfamiliar to me—hospitals and operations. I would really like to do the most intelligent and helpful thing—only—I don't seem to know what it is."

She looked pityingly at me and smiled. "I'll tell you what I think you ought to do. Go to a good movie, have a sandwich and a cup of coffee when you come out, you probably don't feel like eating now, and then come back at six. Doctor is still groggy from the anaesthetic. He'll be feeling fine about six o'clock and will want to see you."

I called Mother and told her Jim was all right and followed Miss Wayne's orders. I arrived at the hospital at five o'clock. Miss Wayne went out in the hall so I could talk to Jim. The minute she closed the door, he said, "Hello, where have you been? I called your office twenty times this morning to tell you Marsh was going to operate, but I couldn't get you."

"I've been to a movie", seemed a little callous so I smoothed his forehead, told him I'd been awfully rushed at the office and didn't get the calls from the hospital and asked him if he felt all right.

"I'd feel a lot better if Miss Wayne would stop fussing at me. I'd like to get out of this hell-hole as soon as possible. It's all damned nonsense—a normal appendix. Surgical patients would get well a lot quicker if they were allowed to walk around the second day. I'm sh to get rid of all these specials. I won't have them 'lace. Whisk, whisk, rustle, rustle, 'yes Doctor', 'no ced slightly and moaned. Miss Wayne promptly . 'We'd better get some rest now—we're just out of etic you know." She put a thermometer in Jim's mouth a cork, smiled at me and motioned toward the door.

He removed the thermometer and smiled his wonderful shining smile. "I hate to have you go home without me. Good night, snicklefritz. Go to bed early."

I walked dolefully down the hall toward the nurses' hidey-hole to ask about the visiting hours. Two young, white-capped nurses were sitting at the chart desk conferring over a chart. "Wayne's in 603 with the Doctor. I don't envy her that job. Boy! Are they stinkers when they're sick! Five gets you ten she'll be fired by tomorrow night."

"Brother! Were you on six when Burton got fired? And yet Wayne says 603 has refused every medication this afternoon. I'd rather special a mental than a doctor."

I left, feeling that it would be more politic to get the visiting hours from Miss MacFarlane at the desk. If you were a doctor's wife, it apparently made no difference anyway—you could wander in and out at will, it was permissible that is— if you didn't care what you heard or saw.

When I got home, Yuri had a fire in the fireplace, the table was set and everything looked normal and serene. It suddenly occurred to me that she didn't even know about the tragedy which had struck our home. She took my coat, brought me a cigarette and handed me two or three telephone calls. "Dr Marsh—he call—Doctor sick. Miss Jean—she call—Doctor sick. Mrs Bard—she call—Doctor sick." The news had filtered through to Yuri while I was at the movie. "The Doctor—he is sick?"

"Yes, he had an operation this morning. Appendix."

"My brother die of that—and my friend—will The Doctor die?" There was very real concern in her little black eyes.

"No, Yuri, he's getting along fine." The same fear had been haunting me, however. It was so difficult to sort out the hearty 'Don't you worry for a minute' technique from the 'Procedure normal, everything under control' which was due to skill and long practice. I found that I could only remember conversations which ended, 'He died. And you know it was the damnedest thing—that embolus was a sleeper. There was absolutely no indication of anything abnormal.'

Yuri's unusual words caught my attention again. "I could leave the school and help you. Myfather would let me—I call him." This was definitely the most charming and courtly gesture Yuri and her family could make. To leave school for any reason was simply unheard of. Unpleasant emotion displayed by facial expression is considered the height of discourtesy by a Japanese, so the two large tears which rolled out of Yuri's unblinking eyes were ignored by both of us.

Endeavouring to rise to the occasion, I said, "Thank you, Yuri. It is very kind of you and your father to offer to help us. I will not go back to the office until the doctor is well, so you will not have to leave school. Please thank your father and tell him the doctor and I appreciate this courtesy very much."

I called Dr Marsh. "Jim is fine, Mary. Intractable but then all doctors are hell when they're sick." His voice was warm with pride. "He's no worse than the rest of us. A week or so will see him back and hard at it. Better drop in twice a day, stay a few minutes and go out. Don't bring him anything to eat, pay no attention if he fusses at you. He'll be fit as a fiddle in a week. It was a little tougher than we thought, but he'll be fine."

Norman was next on the list. I told him Jim was out of surgery and that, if he didn't mind, I thought I'd come down to the office between hospital visits. "Suit yourself, chum, although it's nice and quiet around here without you."

The next day I found Miss Witherspoon on duty. As I opened the door, I heard Jim say, "I won't touch it and that's that." His voice was pleasant and lazily teasing. Hers was high with suppressed emotion. "You know the diet as well as I do, Doctor, and you know that the glucose will no longer be necessary as soon as you start to eat."

"Bring something edible, and I'll eat it", Jim snapped.

I stood quietly waiting. The intravenous contraption was still dripping fluid into Jim's arm through a needle which was strapped to the inside bend of his left elbow. I promptly decided that he'd had a relapse and they were feeding glucose to maintain life.

He turned and saw me, smiled like a sunny child and said, "Look at this library paste poured over various quivering substances. You wouldn't eat that would you?" He glared at Miss Witherspoon. "And you can take the glucose away, too—I don't need any more of that damned stuff. It makes the gas pains worse if anything. How'd you get along last night, Mary?" I told him that the millennium had arrived, that both Yuri and her family had decided to be kind to me, although I realized that it was only because The Doctor was sick, and that the house was a hell-hole without him.

Miss Witherspoon removed the untouched tray, her lips tight with strain, gave me the sad look a field dog gives its trainer when it has failed to retrieve, and flounced out in the hall. Jim thumbed his nose at her retreating back and snorted. "She's a good nurse. None better. It's just that I do not enjoy being in the hospital as a patient." I answered that from what I had observed I was sure the feeling was mutual and asked if he wanted anything. He motioned me closer to the bed and whispered, "Go over to the district and get me something to eat, a hamburger or something." His voice rose to its normal, perfectly cheerful, complaining tone again. "*Creamed* chicken, *creamed* rice and *creamed* potatoes, then junket. Did you know that when you put junket in your mouth, you can't even swallow the stuff—it sneaks down? Take this pap away and substitute some food, and I'd be out of here tomorrow. Hand me a cigarette."

Miss Witherspoon obviously heard that one from her vantage point just outside the door. "We're not going to smoke to-day—we'll wait until tomorrow morning. We'd better get some sleep now." She put two tablets in Jim's mouth, at the risk of having her fingers bitten off, handed him a glass of water and turned to me. "We're getting along just fine, better wait until tomorrow noon to come up. We'll feel much better by then." She put the thermometer in 'our' mouth so she wouldn't have to hear the bad words and I crept out, to be met by a delegation preparing to enter. Two internists and two surgeons, headed by Dr Marsh and behind them, a respectful queue consisting of house resident, two interns, head nurse, floor nurse and a couple of lesser nurses. Miss Witherspoon pressed herself against the wall and looked determinedly bright. They filed into the room and I brought up the rear to see what this new development in 'Doctor's Disease' was.

There were several loud laughs followed by, "How're you feeling, boy?" and, "Well, I see the surgeons got you!"—this by the internists. Then a stream of 'pulmonary infarct', 'retrocecal involvement' and other medical smart cracks. "I'm going to get up", Jim said through thin lips. There was a prompt and very disturbing argument as to whether it was advisable for a surgical patient to become ambulatory as soon as possible or whether he should remain at bed-rest. "And I don't want any more hypos." Jim's voice was pleasant but his eyes glittered.

Instantly, they all began to argue as to whether hypos added to the patient's comfort and therefore assisted the healing process. Everyone seemed perfectly cheerful and amicable. To me they sounded as if Jim were their first surgical case, and darned if they weren't going to try everything as long as he was limp. At each diametrically opposite medical opinion, the resident and the interns nodded their heads in unison and the nurses looked straight ahead into the distance. Finally, after much heavy humour and thousands of eight-syllable words, they all turned and filed out. The consultation was over and. Doctor was getting well. They had succeeded in giving me the impression that he was getting well by a happy combination of the Grace of God, Mother Nature and a strong physique rather than any chance surgical ability one of them might have possessed. I left and went down to the dear, familiar radio station.

Norman and I spent a peaceful afternoon planning a programme of good will for my nice untrammelled advertising dentist. Phrases like 'Plates unconditionally guaranteed to look absolutely natural', 'Never a moment of pain or your money back', 'Why be self-conscious you too can have beautiful dentures' poured from my typewriter and my mind was at rest.

About three o'clock Betty called me. "And how do you like being married to a doctor?" she asked. "Do you know any good divorce lawyers?" I retorted. Betty said, "I wonder what happened to that old musician we were both engaged to? I have a present for Jim. I'll go up to the hospital with you tomorrow."

"Oh Betty, I wish you would. Maybe you can make him eat and behave himself." Betty laughed. "Nobody can make him behave himself. He's a sick man and he wants you to realize it."

The next day when Betty and I went in, Miss O'Connel, the charge nurse, was sitting by Jim's bed. She rose. "Better just say hello—he's resting." I patted Jim's unresisting hand and introduced Betty. Miss O'Connel wiped off her 'Now, now, we can't have visitors' expression and substituted a reluctant "How do you do?"

"Jim, here's Betty with some dandy presents for you." As I kissed his forehead it seemed unnaturally hot to me. He tossed restlessly, said, "Hello Bets, you're looking mighty fancy", and closed his eyes. This time he really looked and acted sick.

We went out in the hall and met Dr Marsh heading toward Jim's room. He bridled as Betty was introduced to him, said, "You're not a doctor's wife are you?—too bad!" Betty smiled winningly at him, said, "No, thank God, but I've had other troubles", and I asked if Jim were really getting well or what all hospitals called 'as well as could be expected'.

"We've had a little trouble, Mary. He got a slight reaction from the intravenous—but his temperature is down now. I'll call you tonight at home. Everything will be fine—don't worry." His face was intent as he went into Jim's room.

"He looks nice—do we like him?" Betty sniffed. "Hospitals always smell so mournful. Come on, Mary—let's go try on some clothes we can't afford. Jim can't lose with two hundred doctors and two or three thousand nurses all panting for him to produce a symptom, so they can rush to alleviate it."

"That's what you think. Two nurses have quit already, and the doctors all sound like they were practising on Jim."

"Maybe they are." Betty sniffed again and shuddered. "Why don't you have a big fat tantrum? Wait until he gets over this, of course, but when he is convalescing and being 'like all men', as Gammy says, why don't you boss him worse than he is bossing them?—I'll bet that would work."

The prospect was so enchanting that I cheered up immediately and we spent the afternoon trying on hats so we could see who could look the most horrible. Then we went home to Mother's to dinner. It was heavenly to be home with the family. They boiled around, cooking, telling what stinkers their various bosses were, sympathizing with me for having a doctor for a husband and generally being warm and comforting. Anne and Joan, Betty's small children, stuck to me, greedily asking for more stories about the 'knives and the bleed' and, in the telling, my self-dramatization dwindled rapidly.

Dr Marsh met me the next night as I was going into the hospital. At my nervous question, he smiled and patted me. "I'd say he was practically well. He fired Miss Wayne and Miss Witherspoon, and Brown is leaving as soon as she can escape." He laughed proudly. "Wayne made him nervous—too fussy. Witherspoon talked too much. They're my best surgical nurses, but they don't have to stay on a case where the patient won't co-operate. As soon as he got past the actual need of them, they decided to leave. If he had been sick, of course, they would still be on the case."

"What do we do now?"

He smiled wickedly as he got in his car. "I got Bunny for him. He'll come around. He's all right now, actually."

When I went in Jim's room, he was morosely picking at his dinner. Standing by the bed, tapping her foot impatiently, was an extremely pretty nurse in a short white silk uniform, obviously covering brief panties and a brassiere. She wore high-heeled white shoes, and an unfamiliar hospital cap set most jauntily on fluffy blonde hair. She smelled strongly of 'Nuit de Noel'.

"Eat it up, honey, there's a good boy. Here's your sugar-pie to watch you. I can't wait all day for you to monkey with your tray—eat it up or I'll feed you." She fluffed her hair a little at one side and hummed a few bars from 'The Very Thought of You'. Jim took one fleck of creamed chicken and choked. "Mary, I can't eat this crud—it makes me sick just to look at it." He raised large blue eyes begging for pity.

"If you weren't sick, you wouldn't have to look at it." Bunny glanced at her wrist-watch. Jim sullenly took the last bite and lit a cigarette. "Boy, I'll be glad to get home and see some edible food once again; I didn't appreciate what a good cook I'd married." He gave me a winning look and sighed.

Bunny picked up the tray, held it casually on her hip while she opened the door, and said, "Pan him for me while I'm out, will you, honey? I'll just see if my call has come in." She switched her silk-clad fanny out the door, to the throaty strains of 'Just Plain Bill'.

"Is Bunny here for diversion or assistance? —do you know her well?" I enquired.

"Not well in the sense your voice implies, but I've seen her around. Marsh likes her and uses her a lot to go home with patients. Personally I think there are other professions that would suit her basic personality better. Takes special calls for Marsh. She's not so bad."

Bunny came back carrying a movie magazine. She was sleek with self-satisfaction. Apparently Just Plain Bill had called and all was well. Undulating over to the rocker she sat down, put a stick of gum in her mouth and began to squeak rhythmically back and forth, humming as she read.

I waited breathlessly for the explosion. Chewing gum, squeaking in a rocking chair and humming—in front of a doctor! Whoops! Jim glared and swallowed but he said nothing more venomous than "Mary, would you mind going over on the Avenue and getting me a hamburger and a good cup of coffee? Strained street scrapings and bilge is the hospital's basic coffee recipe, I think."

"Just have to dump it down the johnny if she gets it for you." Squeak-squeak. Bunny flipped over another page. "He's still on a restricted diet. Honestly—why they let Bette Davis wear bangs beats me. Bangs look plain corny after twenty and if she isn't plenty after twenty, I'm Shirley Temple. Speaking of the johnny—you'd better have your enema now."

Jim's nostrils swelled and white lines appeared on either side of his mouth. "I'M NOT GOING TO HAVE AN ENEMA", he snarled. "AND YOU CAN'T GIVE ME ONE!"

"Either I give it to you or your babykins does—it's nothing to me. Your chart says an enema before bedtime and an enema you get. *Who* gives it to you, it does *not* say. I go off duty at eight." She hummed a few bars of 'Yes Sir, She's My Baby!' and walked over to the bedside stand. "Roll over, Doctor."

I said hastily, "I'm going, darling, I'll see you tomorrow", and rushed down the hall to the charge nurse in her lair. "Miss O'Connel, could we possibly bring Bunny home with us? Does she ever do specialling at the patient's home?"

Miss O'Connel smiled knowingly at me. "Sure. She'll never be there at night, she won't take night duty—too many boy friends—but she doesn't care where she nurses—if you could call it nursing. Brown's on tonight." I decided to go back and say a particularly tender good night to Jim. Bunny was just going off duty and giving instructions to a meek-looking mouse named Miss Brown. "He's had his enema, his supper and his sedatives. Rub his back if you want to, I haven't got time. Toodle-oo." She flipped a hand in farewell and rushed down the hall to change her uniform.

It was Miss Brown's first case and it *would* be specialling a doctor. She tucked in the blankets nervously and looked like she wished she'd taken her teacher's advice and studied shorthand and typing. As she started to put the thermometer in Jim's mouth, he snapped, "Don't take my temperature—it's been normal for three days at least."

He put the thermometer on the bedside stand and smiled at me. "Did you bring me something to read? I wish you'd remember to bring my *Journals*—I've got a lot of studying to do." He kicked viciously at Miss Brown's carefully tucked-in covers. "*Don't* fix the bed so I can't move my feet, it stops my circulation—stop fussing—you drive me crazy."

Miss Brown burst into tears and rushed out of the room. I handed him the hamburger, which Dr Marsh had given me permission to bring him, and started the preliminaries of Betty's suggested treatment—a good, fat tantrum. It began with 'Listen you bullying, advantage-taking stinker', progressed through the fact that I might be deficient in my knowledge of medicine and surgery but knew a spoiled brat when I saw one, cited my various bosses who, previous to his illness, I had thought to be the champion bastards in existence and ended with the fact that the Bards were made of sterner stuff than the Browns of this world.

His eyes gazed speculatively over the huge bite of hamburger he was chewing. "Um-m-m, good. You know", he took the other half in one bite, "when you get mad your face turns red and your hair stands up on end. You look like a stuffed tomato. More frustrated than forbidding. You should try a quiet, modulated voice and use a few, well-spaced words. Much better. Try it now." I spluttered and glared. "Sh-sh-there are sick patients on this floor." He lay back triumphantly. It was my turn. I grabbed the edge of the bedside stand to keep from slapping him—but I did lower my voice to an impassioned bellow.

Dr Marsh came in, followed by a red-eyed Miss Brown and a stern Miss O'Connel. Jim promptly said, "Why can't I go home the day after tomorrow, Marsh?"

"That's entirely up to you. If you'll stay in bed, behave yourself, and not talk to patients on the phone you may go home; but Bunny won't go with you if you continue to behave like a mule."

"I'm not behaving like a mule—am I, Miss Brown?"

Miss Brown obviously thought the description a masterpiece of understatement—she sniffed and shook her head. "I do everything I'm told—don't I?" He grinned winningly.

Miss Brown said non-committally, "I haven't had any experience specialling before Doctor. This is my first case", and looked like she wouldn't *ever* have any experience if this was a sample of specialling.

Dr Marsh finished reading the chart and looked up. "Remember now, if Mary calls and says you are disobeying, back you come to the hospital and stay right here until you are well." He winked at me. "You'll go home in an ambulance of course." Jim spluttered. Friday afternoon we took Jim home in the car—the ambulance was another feeble medical joke. Yuri hovered and beamed and presented him with a beautiful flower arrangement for his bedside table. The house gleamed from every corner, and Jim was sweet and tractable. He grunted appreciatively, like a puppy in a familiar place, as he got into bed. "Now I can get some rest and some decent food. Boy, this bed feels good. What'll we have to eat?"

Bunny proved to be the nurse you read about but never see. She was silently and disinterestedly efficient, spent long hours at the telephone trying to arrange her love life so she could conveniently squeeze in a few hours of nursing, and did all the physical things beautifully. She checked the tray for dinner, took it upstairs or persuaded a very willing Yuri to carry it for her, ate her dinner with me in dreamy silence, whisked upstairs, out of her uniform and into a black dress that clung to her body like nail polish, and took herself off.

The moment the front door banged behind her, Jim sneaked downstairs and the icebox door beat like a tom-tom as he hunted for forbidden food. On the third day when Jim said, as he did every day, "May I get up and come downstairs?" Bunny answered, "Get up if you want to—it would be a lot easier for me if I didn't have to wait on you. Depends on what Dr Marsh says." She turned to me and smiled. "Aren't doctors terrors though, Mrs Jay? Prescribe like crazy for everybody else—but when it comes to themselves—try to see how many things they can do wrong."

She leaned forward toward the mirror and inspected her orchid-coloured lips critically. "That picture at the Paramount is a honey—you really ought to see it. All about psychology—gives me the creeps."

# 4

## The Little Death

DIABETES MELLITUS: *Diabetes mellitus is an inheritable, constitutional disease of unknown cause, characterized by continuing hyperglycemia and glycosuria and, in the more advanced stages, by acidosis . . .*

CECIL: *Textbook of Medicine*

"I'M SO SORRY TO DISTURB YOU—but Mama Fia will not let me give Mama the insulin." Guido Di Julio's nine-year-old voice was sharp with exasperation. "Mama Fia says in Fiorno no one has the needle."

"Let me speak to Mama Fia, Guido." I hooked the phone under my ear as I swiped at the bath water which was dripping on the bed, and tried to huddle into the bath towel. I could hear urgent Italian from Guido, interspersed with crackling, violent Italian from Mama Fia.

"She says she cannot speak English into the little black box."

"Tell her, Guido, that if the Doctor has to come over and give Mama the shot—it will cost five dollars."

There was a scream of rage and a cascade of protest from Mama Fia. Then: "She says"—Guido obviously eliminated several paragraphs of *what* Mama Fia had said—"I can give Mama the shot."

I got back into the bathtub and resumed my brooding about Morris's loathsome holocaust known as the Annual Picnic. For two weeks Norman and I had planned organized races, organized broadcasts, beauty contests, pie-eating contests, legs-tied-together-while-you-hopped-across-the-floor contests. Norman was convinced that if Mr Morris ever succeeded in palming off one of his overstuffed daughters—we'd have to make a contest out of that. Jealousy raged through the entire store—among the young and toothsome clerks when the participants in the bathing beauty pageant were chosen, among the older clerks principally because they weren't young and toothsome but also because each of them had some small relative who had *ten times* as much talent as that smart assistant manager's brat. The customers were unaware of this internecine warfare and continued to peer behind the counters hunting for the clerks who were upstairs in the auditorium practising.

"Rehearsal! Rehearsal! Christ—that guy Morris would rehearse his sex life!"

"If I have to go to the picnic tomorrow, you can damned well go to the rehearsal", I said finally.

Norman squinted his eyes at me. "Flip you, double or nothing." He flipped—and lost. I hastily left the studio to avoid laughing at his impassioned, low-voiced swearing. As a result, I was languishing, between telephone calls, in a nice hot bath and Norman was at the rehearsal. I magnanimously decided to attend the picnic if only for a few moments.

When Jim came home he said, "Tomorrow is the Italian Club Picnic. I promised Guido Di Julio we'd go and watch him pitch the baseball." At my low moan of horror, he said, "Good food—I've been to them. Mama Fia will be there."

"Where is it?" I asked guardedly.

"Appropriately enough—at Maloney's Grove. It's next to that Crescent Beach where your picnic is being held."

It was about two o'clock when we arrived at Crescent Beach. The Beauty Contest was in full swing. Hot and sweaty, shirt-sleeved husbands slapped and whistled and were glared at by their indignant wives. Bored children hung around whining for a nickel. Bewildered contestants hopped across the grass, their faces red with embarrassment while howling sycophants in the manager's office urged them on. The dining-room waitresses from the store muttered while they piled grey potato salad and cold wienies and buns on long bare tables. The store orchestra played languidly, hating the manager for making them work on Sunday. The assistant manager's brat, clad in a too short, electric-blue satin skirt, sequin-studded jacket and a glittering blue shako (reluctantly produced for her by the Alteration Department), kept up a St. Vitus' dance of tapping, while she shrieked into the microphone that she was 'Nobody's Baby Now'.

Norman sat under a tree with the control men. He said, "Cut that spidery bitch before I kill her with my bare hands", and continued to drink out of a pint of Old Crow. The control men cut the assistant manager's brat to an agitated mouse's squeak, and Jim and I left. The Morris's Department Store's Annual Family Picnic was everything that could be expected.

Although the two picnic areas were exactly the same—straggly fir trees, with littered and trampled grass underneath them, picnic tables and benches on a long grassy area which led down to the beach—the contrast in the quality of the picnics themselves was startling.

The Italian Club was having fun. An endless fountain of laughter bubbled up from every direction accompanied by liquid Italian and soft-voiced American. Guido rushed over to greet Jim.

"Doctor, I have waited for you. They have the ball-throwing game—come and watch me." His face was alight with joy and his huge black eyes glittered with excitement. "They have the Bingo too, I won a ham." It was the first time I had ever seen Guido when his intelligent little face was not wrinkled by the burden of rapid translation.

When Jim and I make house calls on any first generation family, whether they be Italian, Russian, German, Japanese or French, the bilingual children always fascinate me. They may be shrieking and riding their bikes, or playing kick-the-can and screaming, 'Awshut up' in impeccable American when we drive up, but the moment we start up the steps of the house, they say, 'I've gotta go now, the Doctor's here', dart in the door ahead of us—and a complete change comes over them. Their shoulders droop, they sigh with responsibility and look like worried little old people. They are interpreters—the children of neither country, but a bridge between the two. Not only of the language, but of customs.

It lies with them to explain the Doctor—this representative from their English-speaking American life of school—to the family. In turn, they must explain the mores and traditions of their home life to the doctor.

Guido pulled Jim along talking and laughing. Brilliant colours made this picnic a thing of gay excitement. A ring of adolescent girls, dressed in bright pink, green, yellow, blue and purple were outlined against the green grass and blue water as they sang to the lilting accompaniment of an expert team of accordion players. Behind the girls was a ring of adolescent boys, their white shirts setting off their enormous black eyes and gleaming white teeth in dark, vivid faces. Each boy had his hand possessively on the shoulder of the girl in front of him. Shirt-sleeved, laughing fathers, their hands streaming long red ribands of tickets, surrounded by laughing delighted children, stood in front of the stalls waiting to throw darts or play Bingo.

Tony, the balloon man who has always stood at the entrance to the Public Market, was having a heyday. "Free balloon to-day—havva da free balloon." The three-to five-year-old children stood in an enchanted ring around Tony and followed the ascent of many coloured balloons with wide, amazed eyes.

"Look at this, Mary!" Jim chuckled.

Guido picked up three balls, threw each one surely and expertly, hit a series of Donald Ducks on a moving band, and reached for another prize. He placed it carefully on a growing pile of kewpies, canes, pitchers and ashtrays, and looked up at Jim. "Doctor, I am going to try for the Grand Prize, a professional catcher's mitt."

Jim squinted his eyes, said, "I think you can make it. Don't forget to lead", and looked tenderly down at Guido's earnest little face.

Guido wound up, threw the ball, hit the white duck squarely as it moved past and was grudgingly handed the catcher's mitt by the whining stall-holder. Jim proudly patted Guido on the back, threw five dollars down on the counter and we moved on.

Mama Fia was ensconced in the place of honour—a large rocking chair near the covered, cooking area. She stopped waving her arms and snapping directions in agitated Italian long enough to greet us ceremoniously. Pointing to stove after stove covered with huge pots, all giving off utterly delicious smells, she said, "Plenty for the Doctor—Fiesta", and beamed.

Jim and Guido went on, and I settled down to be surrounded by gossiping, gesticulating mothers. At Mama Fia's imperious wave and sharp 'Rosa', a mother, with a full-blown red rose sticking jauntily in the neck of her tight black silk dress, lifted up the cover of a pot for my benefit. "*Tortino di pomodori*—tomato with eggs." She laughed gaily. "You make for the Doctor?" I shook my head. "I'm afraid not, I don't know how."

A little fifteen-year-old girl, who was stirring a tomato sauce, looked up and said, "I'll write it down for you. My mother makes it."

I thanked her and moved on to the next kettle. A mother in

crackling dark blue silk, wearing a brilliant pink scarf pinned at the breast with an exquisite intaglio, said, "*Asparagi alla fiorentina*." The eager little girl questioned her in Italian and wrote it down. *Pollo alladiavola*—great gold earrings and a pink rose over one ear. *Risotto con funghi*—a sheer white blouse covering warm, brown breasts. *Polpettone alla fiorentina*—an embroidered blouse over a full, red skirt. *Spaghetti con aglioe olio*—ash blonde hair, grey eyes, black lashes and a beautifully cut, gold linen suit.

Each smell and taste was more tempting than the last, as I was handed spoonfuls out of the kettles. They represented various sections of Italy, the beautiful blonde woman said, and each mother was straining herself to outdo everyone else.

The long tables were covered with red and white checked tablecloths. At intervals there were bowls of field flowers, bottles of wine and baskets of breadsticks. The little girl hesitantly touched my arm. "I take typing at school—I will type these recipes for you and mail them to you. For the Doctor he is kind to my father."

I didn't know about the Doctor, but by this time I was so hungry I was weak. I asked Mama Fia if she'd seen in which direction Jim and Guido had gone.

"Da babies—Guido show him da babies." She pointed to a golden circle of late afternoon sunlight surrounded by a ring of dark fir trees. Fat, wonderful, black-eyed babies, dozens of them, sitting or crawling or lying on a huge quilt made up of wrapping blankets. Jim sat in the middle of the ring, throwing a crowing, gurgling baby high in the air. The guarding mothers laughed contentedly and nodded their heads in approval. They were showing Jim the courtesy of asking his advice. He gravely examined a fat baby, admired it extravagantly and put it aside to take up the next one. The little bump, the slight rash, the birthmark—each was shown to Jim; and as he returned the baby, a beaming mother hugged her fat one to her and laughed at it.

He looked up and saw me. "Come on over, this is more fun!" He handed me a fat, dimpled baby and continued to play, absorbedly, with the rest of them. It was the first time I had ever seen Jim with babies, and I wondered why he hadn't become a paediatrician.

Guido came running back to Jim. "The dinner is ready. Mama Fia wants you to sit at her right hand." He turned to me. "My Uncle Giovarmi wished you to sit at his right hand as his honour guest."

We left the mothers to change and feed the sleepy babies and went to dinner.

Dinner was indescribably delicious. Such spaghetti. Such sauces! Mama Fia's raviolis were justly famous. The crisp Italian lettuce salad was swimming in olive oil and anchovies. The devilled chicken, which is eaten at the fair of the Impruneta in Florence, was almost better than the sauteed chicken Aretina made by Maria Di Julio—Guido's mother.

This was no slap-dash picnic supper, it was a ceremonial dinner accompanied by many toasts to the Doctor, to the various sections of Italy whence the food had come, and to the blushing, black-eyed cooks. When the desserts were served, Jim leaned over and murmured something to Maria—who merely tossed her head, laughed and said, "But this is a festival—it is not the time to weigh the food." Mama Fia cascaded a torrent of belligerent Italian on Jim's head and everybody chuckled. Uncle Giovanni, a wealthy and successful garbage contractor, promptly began to discuss 'the pain, right here' with Jim, a subtle flattery. He knew, and knew that Jim knew, that no Giovanni would consider going to any doctor but Dr Rinaldi—and that he was doing an excellent job of undermining every medical suggestion of Jim's for Maria—but he was an Italian and therefore a charming and considerate host. He was sitting next to Maria and laughingly daring her to eat as many of the forbidden foods as possible. "The Doc is right here, Maria—he will fix you up if you get sick. *Figliata* can't possibly hurt you."

From all sides pressure was being brought on Maria Di Julio to ignore diabetes, to pretend she was in the beloved Italy, where everything was beautiful and happy, and no one was ever ill. Against this pressure stood Guido—all alone. He was in the fifth grade—he took hygiene in school; he knew about sanitation and germs, vitamins and a balanced diet. And now he had the full responsibility of his mother's diabetic diet and must fend off this subtle, charming stream of disbelief by threatening the 'little death' if Maria ate sweets.

About eleven o'clock, after many songs and dances they piled the sleepy babies and children into the cars and the picnic was over.

"I think I'll stop at the Di Julios' on the way home", Jim said as we were driving along. "Maria ate far too much and I couldn't bear to dampen her spirits by being firm."

Then he told me about Frank and Maria Di Julio and Mama Fia—Maria's mother. Maria was in the eighth month of her first pregnancy when they left Italy. As Mama Fia had ably delivered most of the babies in the country around Fiorno, it never occurred to her that she would not be allowed to deliver Maria just because they would be in America at the time of the baby's birth.

When they got to Ellis Island, during the problems attendant upon entering the country, Maria went into labour and was snatched off to the hospital. Due to complications—previously uncared for diabetes and an abnormally small pelvis—the doctors felt it necessary to do a Caesarian. One of the interns who spoke Italian, in order to get permission for the operation, explained the necessity and the process to Mama Fia, the mother, and to Frank, the husband. Frank was too bewildered to do anything but acquiesce. Mama Fia regarded the whole thing as God's Will and began the long and almost successful campaign against American doctors, American nurses and America in general.

Mama Fia had not wanted to leave Italy. She had told Maria and Frank that they would be unhappy in America. Neither God nor the Virgin Mary would approve of going so far away. The Caesarian was the first sign of His Disapproval.

Now, neither Maria nor Frank Di Julio had much heart left with which to disagree with Mama Fia. After all, America had not proved to be the golden land of smiling idiots as represented to them by Luigi, Maria's brother in New York. Life had been hard and difficult. In all the years they had been in America, Frank had succeeded only in buying a small house, in the basement of which he had his barber shop, Maria had ceased to be red cheeked and shining eyed and had become thin and morose. And now, as a final insult, the American doctor was insisting that Maria weigh every mouthful of food or she would 'become like the dead again', in the dreaded diabetic coma. The 'little death', Mama Fia said, was God's way of showing his disapproval of the needle.

In the house, Mama Fia, her stout small body as neat on the edges and round in the centre as one of her delicious raviolis, was talking and gesticulating. Frank was sitting in a chair, his arms hanging limply between his knees. Maria was lying on the couch, murmuring little Italian prayers as she fingered her rosary. Her colour was bad and her breath short—she was flickering on the edge of diabetic coma. Jim had given her the shot of insulin and was sitting watchfully by her.

"You *did* eat the sweets, Mama, you know you did. You did not weigh your food, and you did not even think." Guido turned to Jim. "It is no use, Doctor. Mama Fia gives Mama the sweets all the time. She hides the needle so I can't give Mama the shot—her and her old Italy. Mama is sick and Mama Fia won't believe it." He slapped his fist despairingly into his catcher's mitt and looked old.

Mama Fia waddled out of the room and returned with a tray on which was a bottle of wine and four glasses. She handed Jim and me a glass of wine, murmuring extravagant courtesies as she did so. There was a plate of *figliata* on the tray. As Jim and I each took some, Mama Fia threw back her head and laughed at something Guido murmured to her. She answered him rapidly and chortled again. Guido grinned. "She says you seem to like the *figliata* although you say it makes Mama sick. In Italy they have a saying, 'Nature doth the cure and the doctor takes the fee'." Mama Fia nodded and smiled. Jim said, "Please tell Mama Fia that the system isn't confined to Italy. Nature makes most of the cures in every country. Nature, however, did not intend to have her children eat too many sweets. Therefore we give Maria the insulin—to help nature."

Guido carefully translated, and Mama Fia shook with laughter and raised her wine glass to Jim. Then she leaned over Maria and lifted her head to give her a sip of wine. Guido moved like lightning and intercepted the glass. "She can't have vino, it has sugar in it", he said, first in Italian and then in English. "I weigh her food and Mama Fia gives her more. Mama sneaks the chocolate bar—it is as though she were trying to die. Papa does not understand either, he thinks if Mama wants it she should have it."

Jim rose. "You're doing a fine job, Guido. Mama won't die, but you must watch her diet and weigh her food." The expression in his eyes was a gentle mingling of compassion and understanding as he put his arm around Guido's thin little shoulders. "Let me know if you need me to help you. You'll make a good doctor some day."

Suddenly the picture of Jim's absorbed, tender expression as he was playing with the babies came into my mind. The hell with advertising and fixing the furniture in Jim's office—what we needed was a handful of babies!

# 5

# It's Nature—You're Pregnant—So What!

PREGNANCY: *Condition of being with child; gestation*

FOR YEARS I'D WATCHED Myrna Loy hold out a sock she was knitting, smile mysteriously and reduce William Powell to a debonair father potential. Bette Davis, Katharine Hepburn, Mary Pickford, Marguerite Clark—all promptly began to be cherished the moment they got the news across.

I did detect a gleam of natural masculine pride in Jim's eyes as he handed me the Friedman pregnancy report—impersonally marked 'positive'. Actually I didn't expect the technician to write under it: 'And I think it's so wonderful—he's the luckiest man in the world', but I did expect some reaction from Jim other than "Yep—you're pregnant—your haemoglobin's a little down. Now don't get all worked up—these things are only about eighty per cent accurate. The doe might not have been sterile." He dived into his bag and handed me a heterogeneous group of samples, "Here's some iron and calcium—several kinds. Better start taking them." He hung up his coat, turned and grinned at me. "Pete wants you to come down this week so he can give you a preliminary—Wassermann and a pelvic."

"Wassermann! So he can give me a health card?" My voice was distinctly bitter. "Do doctors require them for their wives?"

"Of course not—so I'll know you can safely carry a baby to term." I was enveloped in large protective arms and kissed fondly, "What'll we name her?"

"Her? I thought we'd name him Jim."

For some time I had been whiling away the long evenings when Jim was at medical meetings by reading from his medical library. It was such a relief to find that I didn't have cancer of the uterus or some other horror that I added nonchalantly, "Of course we'll have lots of babies, so the order in which they arrive doesn't really matter." Suddenly it dawned on me that Pete, Maggie's husband and our bosom companion, was going to give me a pelvic examination.

"Jim! I can't go to Pete—I know him too well." Jim's expression was blank as he looked up from foraging in his bag for further samples.

"Why not?"

"Well—I'd be embarrassed and he would, too."

"I never heard such arrant nonsense in my life. To a doctor, examining a patient is about as personal and embarrassing as checking an engine is to a Ford mechanic. You may go to someone else if you want to, I'll naturally give you the usual list of five to choose from"—the medical ethics note was cool in his voice—"but knowing you, I know you would prefer Pete. Let's eat—I have to go to a staff meeting."

Myrna Loy died hard. "Jim are you glad we're going to have a baby?"

"Of course I'm glad, why shouldn't I be? Most natural thing in the world—that's what marriage is for."

I remembered Maggie's comment on the doctor's wife who had six children and was large with her seventh. 'And she'll go right on having 'em too, honey—all the doctors at home had millions of children. And why not, honey—why not? He gets them practically free and after he has 'em he's absolutely never home to count 'em — so they don't bother *him* any.'

During dinner we spent a pleasant and normal time planning when I'd cancel my advertising contract, about how long it would be tactful to my various male customers to work, and if I should tell Norman immediately so he'd have a chance to train another saleswoman. Of course I'd have my baby in Maternity, Jim was on the staff, and of course I'd have Pete as my obstetrician. Jim was grinning with a pleasantly fatuous expression and looking off into space quite a lot—so I was comforted.

Most of my friends were married and had babies and without exception, according to them at least, they had had days and nights of gruelling labour. 'The doctors all said they had never seen such a tiny pelvis!' *Ergo* there must have been a minimum of three doctors in attendance, and everything was definitely dramatic. Mother was inclined to say, 'I suppose so! I had Betty in two hours and Cleve in three, but then I was out in the country.' Betty said she was so thankful for a chance to lie down she didn't care what was happening.

I was sick at my stomach and apprehensive, and torn between the desire to be a Spartan like the Bards, and a modern medical miracle like my chums.

The day I had my appointment with Pete I went into his office in the late afternoon, pale green and very edgy. The office was full of patient-buds in various stages of swelling, all self-consciously holding magazines over their stomachs and trying, by means of flowered hats, to detract from their imminent issue.

Miss Barnes greeted me warmly, told me to sit down and turned back to a woman who was leaning on the reception desk arguing about her prescription*:*

"The calcium makes me even more nauseated. Do I have to take it?"

"Yes, it's very important and Dr Roberts prefers to have his patients take calcium in liquid form. You'd better have this refilled."

Pete came out, gave me a brief smile and greeted Mrs Jones. As they went toward the examining rooms, I heard him say, "Feeling all right today, Mrs Jones? The last months are hard I know—but you've been a good sport. Mrs Jones' back waddled with appreciation as she disappeared. I determined to be a better sport if it killed me. Mrs Jones came out with a last "I'll take a little walk every day then", and went out the door.

Miss Barnes said, "Mrs Raymond", and Pete appeared to take in another patient. The minute that Pete spoke to Mrs Raymond, she dropped the magazine, she had been attentively reading, assumed a martyred look and began to whine. "Even the smell of food makes me sick, Doctor. If I'd known what this was like—" Pete's warm voice replied, "Still nauseated in the morning? —that's too bad—try eating a soda cracker before you get out of bed—right in here—"

Mrs Brown's complaint was "Honestly, Dr Roberts, I can't even look in a mirror—I'm just revolting!"

"That isn't what your husband thinks—" Pete's laugh was comforting. "You do seem to have gained a little extra weight. Been getting your exercise lately? We don't want to lose that figure permanently you know. Mrs Brown's retreating fanny bridled as she waddled after Pete.

Here was a new Pete to me. Gentle, teasing, tactful and above all—watchful. It was very pleasant to be a doctor's wife. If Pete took this much care of perfect strangers, just think what he would do for Jim's wife. It was a heart-warming thought. Miss Barnes said, "Mrs Jay—this patient will take a little while—why don't you read this article? It will interest you in your condition." She winked and handed me a heavily underscored article entitled 'You Are Building a New Life'. It suggested listening to music, reading uplifting books, and appreciating the responsibilities of your condition. There was a strong and consolatory accent on 'the sacred and mystical prenatal condition' and an equally strong warning against listening to gruesome hearsay. It didn't *say* you were the only woman who had 'ever gone through this', but it inferred that you were a brave little kid and even if nobody cared—the article did. I clutched my sample and felt noble.

Pete came out again. "O.K., Mary, come on in. Did you bring your sample? Atta girl."

And from that moment, the campaign began. 'It's nature—you're pregnant—so what!' This slogan is pounded into a doctor's wife from the time she conceives until she delivers. Even if she does feel that she's the only woman who has ever been pregnant—and if she breathes, she does—each manifestation of self-dramatization is promptly and thoroughly squashed.

Pete is enormous. He has large strong hands with thick square fingers which, the nurses all stoutly maintain, are more delicately perceptive than radar when he is doing obstetrical surgery. He has deep dimples, shrewd, dancing, dark blue eyes, an acid tongue and a remarkable technique. Were he to stoop to a cooing bedside manner, he would have even more patients than he has now, which would be a physical impossibility. Most of Pete's sleep is caught in snatches in the Doctors' Room at the hospital while a patient is on the nest, and even obstetricians require a night's rest in their own beds now and then.

"Go on in there and get undressed, Little Mother, and Miss Barnes will give you a benny." I braced myself for the ordeal of the examination. From the time Pete entered the room where I was lying on the examining table, my feet in those horrible obstetrical stirrups, and the rest of my body as rigid as a cataleptic, he succeeded in creating a completely impersonal atmosphere. I had ceased to be a friend and had become another pregnant woman. The examination was not only not in the least embarrassing, but was actually very interesting. Pete explained the growth of the foetus and the process of birth with such pride, so many technical details and such enthusiasm that I felt like a Wright Brother about to produce my first little aeroplane. He stood up. "O.K., keed, get your clothes on and come into the office." He began to question me exactly as if he had never seen me before. At each 'Why Pete, you know perfectly well that we've been married one and a half years!' he didn't even look up—merely wrote on my chart. When the record of every breath I had ever drawn was at last complete, Pete yawned. "Well, chum, approximately six and a half months from now, you can lie down in the nearest field and deliver yourself."

Now for my special prescription. I leaned forward expectantly. Pete reached into the drawer of his desk and began to forage. He handed me a bunch of samples. "Here is some iron and calcium—and—oh, yes—one of the drug supply men gave me some new stuff—don't know anything about it but you might try it and let me know how it works and what it's for. Vitamins in some form combined with iron. Probably no damned good, but take a lot of it."

"Should I take walks, and have a special diet or something?"

"Unless you plan to resemble a blimp—you should take walks. Lots of housework and less resting is what you need. Plenty of exercise—especially pushing yourself away from the table. Is Jim playing golf Thursday?"

My preliminary examination was over.

As my girth increased, I made a host of morbid new friends. Not only was I pregnant but I was a doctor's wife—the perfect receptacle in which to pour stories of abnormalities of birth and delivery. Complete strangers leaned over me on buses and breathed that they 'knew someone who had died of that'. This odd personal magnetism grew in direct proportion to the growth of the foetus—sort of like the increased tactile sense the blind develop.

Jim and Pete over-compensated by telling me that any red-blooded woman could lie down and drop a perfectly healthy baby anywhere. Look at the Chinese. Look at the Mexicans. Look, in fact, at a great percentage of Americans. I looked in the mirror and felt sorry for myself.

Every night when Jim came home, I had a new story for him. The switchboard operator's aunt had a dry birth. What was a dry birth? It used to be fairly serious before the advent of modern obstetrics—but today it was non-existent, at least as a menace. "But they had to whittle out her aunt's baby in little pieces."

Jim sighed. "Just folklore and she might be referring to another medical problem—which has no reference to you. The next time you cook sturgeon try soaking it in soy sauce first, will you?"

The announcer knew a lady who bled to death in three minutes. The grocer's wife knew a woman who fell down the basement stairs and practically exploded. They all had droves of 'the best doctors in town'—who apparently did nothing but wring their hands and moan. Pete said obstetrics was a living but it was hardly a necessity. Jim said, "Look at the babies who are born in taxis—and delivered by a fireman or a policeman or a garage mechanic. You are a perfectly normal woman and you're lucky you have a doctor for a husband."

One night Jim said bitterly, "I wish you weren't so damned friendly. People wouldn't tell you those old wives' tales if you'd take that eager, empty-bowl expression off your face." He put his arms around me and patted me. "Come on, I've got to make a house call. I'll take you to a movie afterward, we can sit in the loges so you'll have some place to rest your stomach."

It was one of those dark, foggy March nights in which every street looks like one of Hitchcock's most scary movie sets. We drove way out north of the city to one of the residential sections in which the houses were good and far apart, most of them barely visible in groves of fir and spruce trees. Jim entertained me with the story of why he did not go into obstetrics when he was choosing his speciality.

He was taking a three months' residence in obstetrics and seriously considering it as a future career. The first night on duty he was scrubbed, sterile and medical as hell, waiting for a call. The call came from the Italian section of Chicago: "Doctor come quick! Mama is ready." He and another young thing—this one had been practising obstetrics for a year and was, in his own mind at least, a hoary veteran at the business rushed to the address. The water was boiling, clean sheets were on the bed and Mama was waiting patiently for the advent of her tenth child. It was a simple delivery and, after many superior obstetric observations, the hoary veteran went out to smoke a cigarette while Jim accomplished the more menial tasks. While he was gone, Mama casually told Jim she thought she had another baby inside of her. She had two more, both of which Jim delivered in the space of fifteen minutes.

"You see, honey, nature actually delivers the baby. Hell, we didn't know she had twins in her uterus—let alone triplets—and yet she got along fine and so did the babies. By the time we've had seven, you'll know what I mean."

Jim drove down a long winding street and stopped the car in front of a Colonial house. The fog wove mistily in and out of the black trees which met in a tunnel overhead. The wind howled and the windows of the car rattled.

Jim reached for his bag. "There are some magazines in the back of the car. I'll be right back—then we'll go to a good bawler so you can enjoy yourself."

The nearest street light, a good block away, blew back and forth in the wind, casting strange and unexpected shadows through the trees. Pretty lonely and pretty dark. I locked the car doors on the inside, turned on that whimsical Tinkerbell referred to as an overhead reading light and reached in the back seat to see what I could find to read.

Two *Journals of the American Medical Association*, one *Annals of Internal Medicine* and a large, thick volume called *The Anomalies and Curiosities of Medicine*. I leafed through the medical *Journals*—they didn't have any pictures and were full of long words. *The Annals of Internal Medicine* had pictures, but they were all of round purple and blue circles covered with little worms—abnormal cell structures. I opened *The Anomalies and Curiosities of Medicine*. Practically solid pictures and drawings. My apprehensive attention was riveted on visual proof of the stories people had been telling me! Two-headed babies! Women with six breasts! A man with an inflated balloon rising out of the top of his head, which was called meningocele.

I gulped and turned over a page. There was a photograph of one Hopkin Hopkins shown cuddled on the corner of a Victorian velvet couch, his bearded face resting on a Nottingham lace curtain. He was the size of a three-month-old baby, wizened so that he resembled a particularly revolting old man doll!

'In March, 1751, there died in Glamorganshire, of mere old age and gradual decay, a little Welshman, Hopkin Hopkins . . . He had been recently exhibited in London as a natural curiosity; he had never weighed over 17 pounds, and for the last three years of his life, never more than 12 pounds.'

I shuddered and looked wildly at my watch. Jim had been gone an hour. The wind had lessened and was now soughing through the trees, moaning in a hopeless way. Gusts of rain splattered against the windshield. I hastily turned another page. 'Cutaneous horns. Showing beginning epitheliomatous degeneration of the base (after Pancoast).' Accompanying this cheery title was an old gentleman who had two reindeer horns growing casually out of either cheek. I felt my face to see if it was beginning to get lumpy—and then felt my stomach to see if our monster was still alive.

Under 'the perverted appetites and peculiar longings of pregnant women', there was this contribution by Fournier:

'Fournier knew a woman with an appetite for the blood of her husband. She gently cut him while he lay asleep by her side and sucked blood from the wounds—a modern Succubus!' The picture showed Succubus lying quietly asleep in a gipsy costume, probably resting between cravings.

'Macro-Glossia in a girl eleven years old', achieved the nth degree in sticking out your tongue at mother. Her tongue was grossly fat, hung almost to her waist and looked like a puffy hot water bottle! I licked my lips gingerly. My tongue felt kind of coated but it wasn't swollen—or was it? A dog howled and then came yipping down the road pursued by nothing.

Where in God's name was Jim? He had been in that house for for almost three hours.

Then I came to Brother Paré:

'Paré describes and pictures a monster at Rome on 3 November 1520, with the upper portion of a child apparently about five or six years old, and the lower part and ears of a fishlike animal.' The picture accompanying this statement really reached the ridiculous, or else I was too terrified to absorb any more and was becoming hysterical. The budding Roman had a horn, two spread wings, mermaid legs and duck feet. Even in 1520 you would be slightly surprised, to say the least, if whatever passed as a nurse in those days handed you Junior and said, "We don't know exactly what he is—but he's yours."

Paré, having successfully gained the centre of attention by telling the biggest lie, proceeded to go completely mad—he produced whole chapters of bicephalic and hermaphroditic monsters. A little boy with an extra girl's head peering evilly over his shoulder. Two sisters, joined together like Siamese twins, clapping their hands in a macabre little dance. Three-headed sheep, four-headed monsters.

Millie Christine-Rosa Josepha Blazek, Siamese twins under the medical name of ischiopagi, added to their physical problems by wearing high button shoes, white ribbed stockings on which eyelet garters showed quite plainly and flowery poke bonnets. Their dresses had two tops but a mutual, voluminously ruffled skirt.

Louis and Louise, more Siamese twins, wouldn't cooperate. One sulked and cried all the time and the other was deliriously happy. Mama tried to curb this little personality discrepancy in what was, after all, one kid—by letting them dress up in Bohemian costumes, with diamond tiaras like the one the Statue of Liberty wears, peacock feather fans and yards and yards of pearls tied around their mutual middle. I was busily concentrating on whether Louis and Louise had one or two fannies under the slinky Bohemian costumes and the problems attendant thereon, when there was the wail of an ambulance right behind me.

I jumped six feet and yelped!

The ambulance parked in front of our car and two men got out, took a stretcher from the rear of the ambulance and disappeared into the house. I'd lost Louis and Louise when the ambulance wailed, so I still don't know about the fannies, but there were plenty of other items.

Matibelle McIntyre had a fibrocyst of the uterus weighing 135 pounds. A direct result of pregnancy. It looked like a gunny sack of potatoes, only smoother. For convenience she slept with it resting on a sewing machine. My stomach was a little lumpy—

At this point there followed a long dissertation on the dangers of prenatal impressions. Mothers who had been scared by a rhinoceros, by a strawberry or by a beetle, had the unmistakable marks of those frights engraved on their offspring. I slammed the book shut and prepared to cherish a little one with 'Anomalies' embossed on one head and 'Curiosities' engraved on the other.

The door of the house opened again and the ambulance attendants appeared carrying a patient. Jim walked beside the stretcher and supervised the loading. "I'll meet you at the hospital."

I unlocked the car door and as Jim slid into the seat he looked at his watch. "Good Lord, Mary, it's twelve thirty. I'm sorry. We were having trouble in there and I didn't realize what time it was. I'll take you home and then go over to the hospital." I moved over as close beside him as I could get, so that his warm strength and sanity could pour through me.

"What's the matter, are you cold?"

I shuddered even more convulsively and pointed a shaking finger at *The Anomalies and Curiosities of Medicine*. "Have you been reading that? Damned interesting, isn't it?"

"To speak mildly—yes. Do many people have glups instead of babies?" My voice broke as I asked him this all-important question, and the word 'babies' was almost a wail.

"I don't know what you mean by the word 'glup', but if you mean abnormal children—the percentage is very low. Your irrationality is what I can't understand. You'd rather be influenced by folk tales and horror stories than the figures indicating the remarkable strides medicine has made in the last fifty years." Jim's voice was grim with patient control. I subsided. Of course I should have asked him to stop the car, showed him the illustrations which had frightened me and asked about the exact tables on abnormalities in birth. Jim had a sick patient and he was in a hurry and it actually never occurred to me to suggest it. Also, I knew that I was acting like a neurotic fool and was slightly ashamed.

While he went over to the hospital, I went to bed and had nightmares.

During breakfast Jim said, "You seemed more restless than usual last night—did you have any pain?" His voice was casual but his eyes were intent. "Nope—I feel all right. It was just that disgusting book—it scared the wits out of me."

"I shouldn't have left that book around. *The Anomalies* is a collector's item, and I had an awful time finding it. Better take a nap to-day—you have blue circles under your eyes."

I could hardly wait until he left so I could confer with a retired nurse who lived in the building. I'd take a nap—yes—but after I'd seen Mrs Tripp.

Tucking *The Anomalies* under my arm, I went downstairs to Mrs Tripp's apartment. We had had coffee together many mornings while she told me stories of her hospital experiences, and I was very fond of her. She greeted me warmly.

"Come in, my dear. I see you've gained a lot more weight. Your ankles aren't swollen so much though, are they?—good thing—kidneys are bad—why I've seen—now just sit down and I'll make us a cup of coffee." She returned with the coffee, turned on her favourite radio serial as a pleasant undertone to our gossip and resumed her knitting.

"Mrs Tripp, may I show you this book, and ask you some questions?" With trembling hands I picked out the gems. Mrs Tripp lowered her glasses, held the book as far away as possible, and began to turn the pages.

"Mercy on us—I haven't seen this before. Where did you get it?"

"Oh, it's one of Jim's collection of old medical books. Mrs Tripp, do people really have babies with four legs, and six heads and—what on earth do they do?"

She began to stiffen up and pull down her caul of R.N.

"Well! I really wouldn't know. But one thing I do know—expectant mothers shouldn't be reading books like this. That I do know. Dr Roberts wouldn't like this a-tall, not a-tall." She rocked quickly, set her lips and looked over at her cactus collection.

"But you've had years and years of nursing, you certainly must know something about obstetrics. Are all these doctors just great big liars then?"

With a registered nurse, you can't call any doctor a great big liar and not get results. "Certainly not. Why I remember a case in a hospital, before I came out here—I won't tell you which hospital of course—that was the most awful thing!" She stopped knitting and gazed out the window. "Just dreadful! My, that poor little girl!"

"Tell me about it."

"Certainly not. You ought to be thinking beautiful thoughts. It's better for you—and for your baby."

I could literally have screamed. The hell with beautiful thoughts. Facts were what I wanted. I tried pushing another mental button. "Weren't you on the case, Mrs Tripp?" "Well certainly I was. I wasn't charge nurse or I never would have allowed it to happen."

I wound my fingers together and prepared to go through the familiar chaff of hospital prejudice for the kernel of information.

"Nope—that smart Mrs Hallett was. Well, it's no worse than

what you've been reading, and you might as well know what *does* happen."

As she thumbed through *The Anomalies*, Mrs Tripp was reminded of case after case of puerperal convulsions—"I'll never forget that girl, hair just like spun gold—of course they had to choose between the mother and the baby—she'd have been better off if she had died, poor thing—it was before the days when they gave them transfusions all the time."

My baby kicked convulsively and I couldn't breathe.

"Placenta praevia—Lorna her name was, kind of a pretty name—big strapping girl like you—didn't make a mite of difference—she died just as quick as the next one."

'Oh, why did I ever get engaged!' I thought wildly as I twisted my aching fingers. 'Why don't Pete and Jim tell me the truth instead of talking like delivering a baby is on the same par with taking out a splinter!'

Mrs Tripp pushed her glasses down on her nose and held the book further off. "Septicaemic peritonitis—used to be the dread of the delivery room."

Had she looked up and seen my white face and staring eyes and the obvious personal application that I made to what she had been saying, she would have snapped permanently back into her R.N. attitude and I would have retained my original impression of a couple of cases here and there of normal delivery.

Fortunately or unfortunately, she ran across a particularly terrifying photograph of an anencephalus. She began to read the revolting description aloud and then sniffed. "Six weeks. Mighty long time—in my experience they don't last more than a day or so. Looks like a toad!" She handed me the book and at my quavering: "Ye-e-s doesn't it?" —she pushed her glasses back up on her nose, peered at me and froze promptly into an R.N. "Now don't you worry. That won't happen to you. You have one of the best obstetricians on this Coast and don't think you haven't—and a wonderful hospital. There isn't a thing for you to worry about. *The Anomalies of Medicine* indeed! The idea of letting you read a thing like that—just trash that's what that book is!"

I met Pete coming home for lunch as I was creeping upstairs. He greeted me cheerfully with "Hi, sylph, what are you sneaking around for?"

I held up *The Anomalies of Medicine* and began to bawl. He sighed a gusty sigh and put his arm around me. "Come on, let's go up to your apartment and you can fix me some lunch. Maggie is down town somewhere and I have an hour or so between patients." He didn't even have half an hour and that I well knew, but I was too far gone to be considerate.

As I cooked and snuffled, I told him all. My fears and apprehensions as a result of the things I had read and heard. Maybe I did gravitate toward the bizarre, after all I'd spent years in promotional advertising and it had become almost instinctive with me to seek out the unusual. I wanted a baby, had always wanted one, but I wanted to just plain have it.

"You will." Pete smiled tenderly at me as I finally wailed— "and you and Jim never tell me the truth. You always talk to me about lying down in fields—"

"Well, you want the bizarre—"

"But when you are discussing patients—you never even mention a single normal birth!"

"When Jim and I are discussing patients—we are giving one another the benefit of the special knowledge gained in our particular fields. After you have been married for five or ten years, you will know that, and it will cease to have any personal application to your life at all. Right now, you are hypersensitive and all the half-heard things come swarming back to torment you. Instead of sneaking around trying to gather all the proof you can that we are fooling you—why don't you come and discuss these things with me? That is the major thing I can do for you, Mary. The normal delivery of a normal baby is only made easier by modern obstetrical methods—easier for both the mother and for the baby. Physically, you can have a baby—all by yourself. Mentally, I'd a little rather be around to help you."

My feeling for Pete almost became worship as I watched him calmly eating his lunch. How fortunate I was to have both Pete and Jim, watching and guarding me and at the same time pretending, for my benefit entirely, that they were callous.

"People", he continued, "have a peculiar inverted sympathy which they show to a pregnant woman. Actually they want you to know that they realize it isn't all beer and skittles to be pregnant. Their intentions are good but their methods are at fault. Also, their sense of drama is involved. You wouldn't even listen if a sympathetic acquaintance said, 'I have a friend who had a seven-and-a-half-pound boy yesterday.' It almost has to be a fifteen-pound boy after several days of racking labour—particularly when she is talking to you, dearie."

I resurrected my last remaining fear. "Pete, have you delivered any—glups?"

"Nope, and I deliver fifteen to twenty babies a month. I keep telling you, Saddo—obstetrics is a living—but it's hardly dramatic." He grinned, showing both dimples, and held out his hand. "Give Uncle Pete that book, please—I'll just keep it until after we produce. If you feel an uncontrollable urge to read, better stick to Joseph Conrad. There are no women in his tales. Thanks for the lunch—shall I call you Abbie—short for abdomen?"

"No. Call me Pandy—short for Pandora."

# 6

# Labour Relations

FALSE LABOUR: *One in which no progress toward delivery is made.*

ON MAY TWENTY-SECOND, with the brooding intensity of a prisoner watching the free flight of birds from his cell window, I looked longingly across the street at Maternity Hospital. The blue lights of the delivery room were as illusive as a will-o'-the-wisp and the curtains blowing in the O.B. patients' wards beckoned ceaselessly.

I turned from the window and looked with complete loathing at our apartment. The dark rooms followed one another like Pullman cars—dining-room, kitchen, bedroom, bathroom and bedroom. The windows of each room were pressed as closely as possible to a towering apartment house next door. In order to clean we had to have every light blazing like a—delivery room. Everything reminded me of my one avenue of escape.

Jim and I had moved into the apartment primarily because the grateful patient had come back from Alaska, decided on the spur of the moment to sell her house and had given us our choice of buying it or moving in two weeks. We didn't have enough money for the down payment. Jim's new basal metabolism machine and electrocardiograph had taken care of that.

Two days before our eviction, early in my pregnancy and at the onset of Maggie's, we were sitting at the dining-room table drinking coffee and waiting for Pete and Jim to come home and take us out to dinner. Maggie walked over and turned on the gas under the coffee. "Might as well have another cup, it makes me sick but so does everything else." She lit a cigarette, stubbed it out and shuddered. "You'll never find anything as comfortable as this place. Wouldn't you know that fool Yankee would sell it? I sweah people out here change their houses as often as they do their body clothes—back home people live in houses for generations."

"She's going to move to New York and has to sell. I hate to leave here too, but maybe by the time the baby comes we'll have enough money saved for a down payment on a house."

"Provided you haven't saved enough to put a down payment on some more medical equipment." Maggie sighed. "If we don't get out of that Incubatah we're livin' in, I'm going to kill myself. It's hottah than a fiah-crackah, day and night, and Pete's so big that every time he moves I have to crouch in the bathroom to keep from bein' hit. I hate apartments and always have."

The front door opened and Jim and Pete came bursting in. They hadn't played golf but had spent the whole afternoon hunting apartments, and they'd found two in the same building. Weren't they the good little providers though? They'd stop and show us our new nests and then take us out to dinner.

Jim stopped the car across the street from Maternity Hospital. Maggie wailed, "Now, Pete, don't go in there and start havin' another baby—I'm hungry and it makes me sicker to wait for hours." Jim opened the car door. "Come on, girls."

They had not chosen the apartments because they were light and sunny and had two bedrooms. They had chosen them because they were across the street from Maternity Hospital and would be so convenient for night calls. Along with being as dark as a tunnel, each apartment had a sign tacked over the doorbell. 'Children and dogs—NOT ALLOWED!'

"What will we do when we have the babies?" Maggie asked.

Pete and Jim waved that one away with "We'll find houses in the same block so you girls won't have to be separated for more than a few hours at night."

"Probably have little twin beds set up for us in the Doctors' Room so we won't have to be separated even at night—and the children can be reared in the hospital nursery", Maggie grumbled as we got back in the car. "I feel just like a cat who's huntin' a bureau drawer to have her kittens in and is thrown an old gunny sack out in the shed."

"You're just like a couple of broody hens. We got apartments for you, didn't we? Well, we'll get you houses too when the time comes." Pete started talking to Jim about diabetes in pregnancy.

Maggie and I both hated the apartment house on sight. But, as we were accustomed to living in houses, we felt that we would probably loathe any apartment house. Then we met Marilyn, a broker's wife, who lived on the floor below. She was coifed, perfumed, had a full-time maid and was also pregnant. Her husband had been brought up in the 'What women go through to bring us into this world' school of thought. The contrast to our husbands' airy medical attitude was odious.

Maggie came down to our apartment every morning for coffee and we did my housework while we complained about our pregnancy symptoms. Then we went to Maggie's, had coffee, did her housework and complained about being married to doctors who insisted in pretending that pregnancy was normal. After that, we called on Marilyn so we could envy the broker's latest offering on the altar of her bravery, and suggest quite a few symptoms to her in case she felt she was slipping. The husbands won the result of this merger each night at dinner.

Jim rebelled first. "Hell, I'm not perfect, but I do object to being given credit for other husbands' foibles. You get up in the morning as cheerful as a cricket, then you see Maggie and Marilyn and compare husbands, and by six o'clock we're a bunch of ogres. Take your choice, either cheer up or I'll lock you up when I leave in the morning."

Brutality as well as indifference—it was too much to bear alone. The next day we didn't do any housework but gathered in Marilyn's apartment right after breakfast and stayed there all day, comparing symptoms and the difficulty of the woman's lot in this life. Marilyn lay on the couch in a gold *lamé* peignoir and ordered sandwiches and tea for us at intervals to keep up our strength. At five o'clock her husband came in, gave her a worshipful look, three dozen long-stemmed roses and said he hoped that she hadn't been doing too much. His arrival reminded us that we too had husbands of a sort, and we rushed upstairs to make the beds before Pete and Jim came home. We stopped at Maggie's first.

Pete was sitting in the messy living-room. He glanced at his wristwatch. "It's after five o'clock—the beds aren't made and the breakfast dishes aren't done—where in hell have you little martyrs been?"

Maggie gasped. "Pete Roberts, I'm goin' right home—my father warned me not to marry a rude old Yankee!"

Pete's eyes narrowed and his voice was carefully controlled as he said, "Magnolia, if I'd known your petals would brown at the first touch of pregnancy, I wouldn't have brought you Nawth."

"My name is Margaret Mason Randolph Roberts and I sure wish the Roberts wasn't the-e-re." Maggie burst into tears and I sneaked out the door. By the time Jim came home, the beds were made, the dishes done and I was all ready to start complaining.

Due to the No Children and Dogs rule, we were all hunting houses. Marilyn's husband was looking for a house with plenty of room. She'd need a nurse and a maid, naturally no decent man could expect his wife to run a house and take care of a baby, it would ruin her health. Maggie and I were just looking for a shelter from the rain—our health was as good as gone.

For three months Jim and I had hunted houses, in a desultory fashion, when we made house calls. Jim's house requirements, in the order of their importance, were a study—within fifteen minutes of the hospitals;—a bathroom with enough light so he could see to shave and an all-in price of not more than $7,000.

Mine were friendly neighbours (the thought of leaving Maggie made me feel as lost as though I were eleven years old and entering dancing school for the first time); a sweeping view of the lake and the mountains; a fireplace, and a yard so I could take the baby outdoors.

Night after night we drove past blocks of comfortable, unimaginative, American houses with yards full of children and dogs, neighbours chatting back and forth over the hedges; all within fifteen minutes of the hospitals and all with a sweeping view of the lake and/or the mountains.

"Get hold of some real estate people, decide on one of these houses and let's get moved", Jim said. "We don't want to face the double hazard of your first baby and your first house at the same time."

Each day after lunch I had an appointment with a real estate man. As I trundled down the hall the landlady met me, shook an admonishing finger, and said, "Going to look at houses? Looks like you've got two things on your mind—another place to live and a little stranger." "And a bitch makes three", I muttered and went down to get in another Company Car, to be driven around and driven crazy by real estate salesmen.

Each night at dinner I'd complain about the horrible houses I'd seen. Real estate men were unimaginative imbeciles. All I wanted was something unusual, with a view, for a reasonable price. And yet, if I refused to be enchanted by a 'Spanish type house, kind of Monterey', ten miles beyond the city limits, plumped down in the middle of an alder thicket with a patio teetering on the edge of a Spongy swamp and costing $25,000 the salesman was hurt and insisted that I didn't know a good buy when I saw it. Then I was driven with the speed of light to the bowels of the wholesale district and shown a rabbit hutch with a partial view of Mount Rainier peering over the fertilizer factory. "They just write down our requirements so they can have an accurate record of things to avoid when choosing listings", I grumbled.

Jim thought perhaps if I avoided the words 'interesting, original and attractive', and substituted 'near a bus route, family type house', I might be more successful.

With great difficulty I swallowed 'Marilyn's husband doesn't think she's strong enough even to look for a house', and finished my dinner.

On May twentieth when Jim came home, I was crouched up in a corner of the living-room waxing my ski boots with fanatic fervour. He stooped over and kissed the top of my head.

"I'm glad you've got those ready. Certainly one of the prime perquisites for hospitalization."

"I was packing the things in the storeroom and my boots looked sort of dry—" He helped me with the awkward struggle to stand. "Jim—do you think tonight maybe?"

"Maybe. Did you find a house?"

"No. I saw an enormous Frigidaire for $13,000 with a view of Hamilton High School."

"Let's have dinner."

On May twenty-first, I finished packing all the china and books and was at last driven by my restlessness to vacuuming the fleckless living-room rug for the third time that day. Jim stood in the doorway and grinned at me.

"I know what you remind me of—the orange smock adds to the illusion—a road scraper." He joined me as I looked wistfully out of the living-room window at Maternity Hospital. "Had you thought of pitching a tent by the reservoir in the park—view of the water—"

I shook off his arm. "I'd like it a lot better if you pitched a tent for me on the lawn at Maternity and let me go in and get this over—do you think maybe—" "Maybe. What kind of a house did you see to-day?"

"No house. I've looked at them all. A duplex for a hundred and fifty dollars per month—no children and dogs allowed. What do people do who have children and dogs, drown them?"

On May twenty-second, I again looked back toward Maternity. The additional torture of seeing Pete running up the steps of the hospital reminded me to take my calcium, and I started toward the kitchen. The apartment was not only dark and hideous, it was as bare as an autumn tree, with packing boxes scattered here and there like the last sere leaves. If I ever did succeed in finding a house, they'd take me out of it in my coffin, nothing and no one would ever make me move again.

I took the hated calcium back to the window, and resumed my wistful vigil.

The soprano in the apartment across the hall was practising Carmen's 'Habanera'. She started on the E above middle C. 'La-la-lala-la-la-la-lala.' She slid down the scale with jerky bumps and landed on a hesitant B flat. Striking an admonishing B on the piano, she began again, 'Love is only a wood bird wi-ild'. She landed on C minus and struck B several times. This time she started on E slightly plus.

I bellowed,

> 'Love no longer seems so damned wi-uld,
> When you are homeless, and big with chi-uld,'

slammed the door into the hall, and went back to gaze at the Maternity delivery-room windows.

Jim opened the hall door just as the soprano landed on A.

I turned and snapped, "I've got to escape from this place or I'll go crazy."

"Take it easy", Jim said automatically and went out in the kitchen. The icebox door slammed and the breadbox squeaked.

Escape had become my mania.

Escape from the apartment lay in finding a house. I didn't give a damn what the house looked like or where it was—all I wanted was to get out of this apartment.

Escape from my stomach lay across the street and only my

obstinate lack of timed contractions prevented my release.

Jim offered me a bite of sandwich dripping pickles, anchovies, mustard and raw onion. I said 'no thanks' through gritted teeth and watched the muscles in his cheek flip back and forth as he chewed.

Escape from watching Jim unconcernedly chew while I suffered.

"*Don't* chew that way. Is induction dangerous?"

"No, but it isn't necessary. I'll bet you can't find a house because you're too hard to please—pregnancy makes women unreasonable."

"Unreasonable!" I screamed.

"Don't shout." He put his arm around me and patted my shoulder with little soothing pats.

"The real estate salesmen are so afraid I'll have the baby in the Company Car—they show me anything to get me home. That squalling soprano sings all the time off key, my stomach's so big I can't see my feet, and there's no escape."

Jim wiped my eyes with his handkerchief and said, "Come on—I'll take you for a house-hunting ride before dinner."

Everything I saw looked fat. Ferries squatted on the Sound, on their busy runs between the Islands. Heavily loaded buses lumbered awkwardly by. Plump housewives stood on the porches of their own houses and called their children in to dinner. Even automobiles looked stubby when viewed head on.

"I wish I could watch a greyhound race." My voice was still petulant. "Will I be as thin as a needle right after the baby is born? Not that I can have the baby until we find a house."

"Probably." Jim swerved around a rotund oil truck. "Carrying the first baby is difficult, Mary. You have all the discomforts and distortions of pregnancy without the actual realization of what your condition means."

The wave of relief which flowed over me was almost overwhelming. Combined with the ever-present fear of the unknown, which had been obsessing me, was a definite guilt complex because I wasn't dewy-eyed over my condition. I wanted a baby with all my heart and soul, but I didn't enjoy the nine months' period, gaily known as gestation, one iota. In fact I hated every moment of it. I hated being fat. I loathed being awkward and having various peculiar aches and pains. Most of all I hated being such a determined Saddo. So far this much-touted motherhood had been one great big bore.

I had finished telling Jim all this in great detail and was well launched into a belated paean of gratitude to him for his charming qualities of prescient understanding and forbearance when a crunching pain gripped the base of my spine. I grabbed his arm. The car swerved and almost hit a truck.

"I've got a labour pain!"

"That's the first enthusiastic note I've heard in your voice in weeks. We'll time the pains and see if they're regular."

He looked at his watch and calmly announced that he'd found a house. It was one of those masculine feats of legerdemain which makes a wife wonder why she bothers to do anything. A patient had come into the office to pay his bill, had said he was being transferred to Los Angeles and casually asked Jim if he knew someone who would like to buy his house. He had to leave next week and hoped to take his family with him.

Jim watched me out of the corner of his eye as he talked. "We might as well go by and see it—give you something to think about. Reeves says it has a view and three bedrooms. It's in the lake district."

We parked the car on a steep sidehill and walked down a little path. Clinging staunchly to a ledge were five small, nondescript Dutch Colonial houses, each with a neatly fenced or hedged yard and each gazing serenely at a breathtaking view. Mount Rainier was swathed in pink veiling, the Cascade Mountains were brilliant purple etched with shadows of snow, and each wave on the deep blue lake was tipped with gold or pink.

"It's the third from the end, the yellow one. Those overhanging eaves make it look like a toadstool", Jim said.

"I don't care what it looks like—just look at this view!"

# 7

## Special Delivery

OBSTETRICS: *That branch of medicine which deals with the management of pregnancy, labour and the puerperium.*

ON MAY TWENTY-SEVENTH, I was again gazing out the window towards Mecca—the delivery room. All day long I had been having pains in my back, in my stomach, and in my ankles—but none of them had the desired clocklike regularity. I had devoted the intervening five days to picking out wallpaper, mentally arranging the furniture and answering the telephone so I could say 'not yet' to the various well-meant but none-the-less infuriating inquiries.

Everything in the apartment was packed except my hospital clothes, a frying pan, two kettles, two knives and forks and spoons, two plates, two cups and Jim's clothes. I had also cooked enough food to gorge a regiment. Maggie and Pete were delighted with the stream of excess rolls, pies and salads I gamely prepared on my Boy Scout camping equipment, and then trundled down the hall to their apartment.

"Don't be depressed, honey—remember it takes an elephant three years. At least you know you're going to have yours pretty soon—I've got to wait clear till fall. And you've got a house—" Maggie said.

The pain that interrupted my longing gaze at the hospital was different. It was sharp and prolonged. I looked at my watch. Ten minutes later the same pain was repeated. When Jim came in I had produced six regular pains, ten minutes apart, and was standing in the hall by my suitcase. "If I'm not in labour now, I'm going to be induced. Come on—let's go over to the hospital."

Jim said, "Go lie down", and went down the hall to get Pete. While he was gone I had two more pains, ten minutes apart. I rubbed my hands with glee over each one—after they'd subsided. Pete came in and placed a large hand on my stomach. Jim's face was white and his fingers shook as he handed me a cigarette.

It never occurred to me that it might be difficult for Jim to watch his wife go into labour; that the dread potentialities of the unusual involvement haunt any doctor constantly and make him go through the tortures of the damned when a member of his family is sick. Nor did it occur to me that it could be other than unalloyed pleasure for Pete to deliver me—I was Maggie's best friend and Jim's wife—what could be chummier? I was delighted to note the slight crack in Jim's determined facade of 'it's nature—you're pregnant—so what!", and Pete's corresponding concentration on my condition.

Pete stood up. "We might as well go over to the hospital. Get your suitcase, blimp, and follow Uncle Pete. You'll be the centre of attention there—and that you will love."

Miss MacFarlane greeted me joyfully. "Go right up, Mrs Jay. Your room is all ready for you."

The elevator boy said, "I see you've decided to reduce, ha-ha."

Jim was patting my shoulder with little absentminded pats and asking me how I felt, a pleasantly unnecessary number of times.

A whole delegation of nurses was waiting in my room, the bed was turned back and there was a delightful air of expectancy about everything. Miss Ward took off my clothes and hung them up in the closet. "What are you going to name him, Mrs Jay?"

"Mari." Jim's voice from the doorway was firm. "I want a girl."

Pete came in and examined me. The bantering note was entirely lacking in his voice as he said, "Two fingers dilatation—" He smiled a warm, sympathetic smile. "Here we go, chum. I'll be right beside you."

By the time I was prepped, probed and monkeyed with, the pains were beginning to be quite sharp. The strange effect of severe pain for a moment or so, then complete alleviation of pain, was interesting rather than frightening.

The nurse gave me a hypodermic. Pete sat down beside the bed and opened a detective story. He rested his hand and the book on my stomach and began to read.

Twilight sleep is a strange anaesthetic—you feel the pain, considerably dulled, but you have no resentment toward it. I was aware of the nurses bustling in and out—I could hear what they said, but had no memory of my own reactions. Objects were blown up and distorted in size, and time had no meaning. My last clear-cut memory was Jim's firm hand holding mine, his strength and serenity flowing all through me, Pete's strong face on the other side of the bed, watching me with intent observant eyes, and the soft, competent voices of the nurses.

When I awakened the next morning, Jim was sitting beside my bed holding my hand. "Mary—it's a girl! A big fat one!" His face was vulnerable with love, pride in his first child and relief that all was well. Miss Ward was standing behind him holding—our baby! Mari screwed up her face, squeaked protestingly and snuffled. She was red, fat, and—completely remarkable! She was OURS! The lovely golden knowledge flowed all through me like warm sunshine.

Jim started fumbling in the neat square of the wrapping blanket. "Doctor—your mask!" Miss Ward's voice was shocked as she slipped a mask over Jim's face; then seeing his absorbed, tender expression, she smiled fondly, put my mask on and walked out of the room—breaking two hospital rules as she did so. One, she left the room so we could undress the baby, and two, she left Jim in the room, unsterile though he undoubtedly was.

Mari unfolded her face long enough to allow two blue slits of eyes to appear. Then she hiccupped, crossed her eyes and rolled them back so only the whites showed and resumed her snuffling. I was enchanted and asked Jim if, frankly, she wasn't the most beautiful baby he'd ever seen.

"No, but she's healthy." His smile was compassionate as he put his finger in her tiny, clawing hand. He ran his other hand gently over her head. "That subcutaneous hematoma will disappear in a few days—won't it, Mari?" His voice held the doting note of baby talk, but I heard only the long words. I jerked forward, the warning of *The Anomalies of Medicine* rushing through my mind.

"What's that—where?"

He pointed to two deep indentations ringed with purple on the left side of her skull. I started to snatch off the rest of her clothes in order to count her arms and legs. Jim picked her up, removed her diaper and shirt, leaving only a tiny square bandage over her umbilicus. I hastily counted each curled-petal toe and finger. One head, one body, ten toes and ten fingers.

I lay back with a sigh. "Thank God, she isn't a glup."

Miss Ward came in and looked stern. We guiltily tried to restore

Mari to her cocoon. It was like trying to put a diaper on a wriggling squid. Miss Ward, with three deft movements, dressed her, wrapped her up like a surgical bandage and whisked her out of the room.

A girl! I was a mother! I patted my stomach surreptitiously. Flat! Gone were the tiresome memories of the nine unpleasant months, the labour pains and the fretful resentment toward my body for being a constant source of irritation rather than a useful, unthought of instrument.

Jim rose. "Go to sleep now, snicklefritz. You'll get very little sleep from now on. I'll see you at lunch."

There were two large packages on the bedside table and a huge bunch of Talisman roses. The doctors' bell rang in the hall—three notes—that meant Pete—the elevator door clanged—and the whisper of the surgery cart was followed by the pat of nurses' feet. Pete was delivering another baby. I went to sleep—for practically the last time during the ten days I was in the hospital.

When Jim was in the hospital, I had been a lay wife—resentful, frightened, and bewildered by the impersonal efficiency and what I thought was a definite lack of sympathy and consideration. Now I was an old veteran of two years. I knew every nurse, almost every doctor on the staff, and was more than anxious to help run the hospital twenty-four hours a day.

Miss Ward brought in my lunch tray and grinned companionably at me. "I didn't think we were going to pull the Doctor through last night." She raised the head of my bed and put the bed tray across my legs. "They're the worst of course, can't keep them out of the labour room, can't keep them out of the delivery room, driving everybody crazy thinking up things that might happen. You'd think it was the first time anybody had ever had a baby to hear him rant around. Dr Roberts finally had Miss Grant take him down and feed him to get him out of the way—but he was back in about three minutes looking haunted. He didn't even care what kind of a baby it was—all he wanted to know about was you."

She checked the tray. "Doctor says you're kind of fussy about food—you can have anything you want. Just order it." She whisked out.

Just wanted to know about me, did he?—that was delightful. And I was fussy about my food. Hm-m-m. Now that I was a mother I would no longer be teased about my cheerful boa constrictor attitude toward anything edible. And he looked haunted. I was savouring that one to its fullest extent when Jim came in, loaded with books, magazines, cigarettes and another large present.

"Open it." He grinned happily at me. Pickled pigs' feet—two large jars; a box of assorted nuts; two boxes of candy—chocolates and assorted chews; a bottle of Three Star Hennessey and a bottle of champagne. I was exclaiming over this ideal post-natal diet, when the door opened and Pete and two other obstetricians came in.

"Food! Good!" They ranged themselves comfortably on my bed, began happily rooting in the contents of the boxes and discussing their patients. Pickled pigs' feet dripped on my new bed jacket, while they made vague obstetrical gestures. Miss Ward came in, stuck a thermometer in my mouth, carefully chose a chocolate cream, and went out. This bus station prevailed all afternoon.

Following Miss Ward's suggestion, I had ordered two thick lamb chops and an avocado with French dressing for dinner. When she brought my dinner tray in and put it on the bed, the two doctors leaning against the wall each reached for a chop and chewed it thoughtfully, while they discussed the reaction of the kidneys to sulfanilamide. Jim ate my avocado and complained about the French dressing. Miss Ward brought in a large pot of coffee and six cups. Beside the coffee pot was a chicken sandwich. "They don't like chicken sandwiches", she murmured as she handed it to me. "Eat it quickly before a resident comes in who hasn't learned to hate 'em yet. I'll bring you something later from the diet kitchen."

Pete was sitting on the foot of the bed eating the rest of the nuts in large gulping handfuls. His patient was coming in from out of town. "She's a doctor and a doctor's wife", Pete said mournfully. "She'll either be within three or four days of term, or the head will be presented. Apprehensive as the devil and knows it all. What's in that box over there?" He stretched a long arm across my stomach to hand the box to me.

"Candied fruit, and I hope you hate it."

"Don't actually like it—but it's better than nothing. See you later." He ambled out to induce a patient, bitterly humming 'Water Boy'.

The nursery nurse came to the door promptly at six. At the words 'the baby', the doctors obediently scattered. She dumped Mari unceremoniously on the end of the bed and began to sterilize me. She jerked off the fancy bed jacket and substituted a sterile benny, pinned my hair back and put on a sterile mask. Then she placed Mari in the curve of my arm. Mari loathed me and she didn't care who knew it. She wouldn't nurse—she slept.

"What's the matter with her—is she all right?"

Miss Burt disdainfully picked her up. "Certainly she's all right. They just get colostrum the first two days—milk isn't in yet. She's not hungry anyway—too fat."

When she got to the door, she said "You may remove your mask now and put on your bed jacket. She looks like the Doctor", and whisked out.

Jim came in carrying a tray on which reposed a cheese omelette, two crisp lettuce salads and a pot of delicious coffee. "Dinner", he beamed at me. "Cooked it for you in the diet kitchen." It was utterly delicious.

Flowers, presents, a beautiful healthy baby, lots of notes of congratulation and a stream of guests to entertain me. This was living!

About nine-thirty, Jim lettered a large sign, 'KEEP OUT—THAT MEANS YOU!' and pinned it firmly on the door. "Pete says you need rest and I'll see that you get it." He yawned widely. "Didn't get much sleep last night—didn't get any in fact. Think I'll go home now and go to bed. If any doctors come in here—kick 'em out. See you in the morning—good night—Mother."

He had been gone five minutes when the nurse came in with Mari. After she left, I settled down to read. I felt well, rested, and completely at peace. I was just dozing when I heard a sharp scream, followed by low moans. I punched the bell frantically. Miss Dean, the night nurse, came in. "Want your back rubbed?" She straightened the sheets, plumped the pillows and began rubbing my back with alcohol. Long, soothing strokes.

"Who is next door, Miss Dean?"

Stroke, stroke. "Poor little thing—it's the one I took some of your flowers in to." She turned me over on my back and began tucking me in like a chrysalis. Her face was set in the regular R.N. expression, a charming combination of bustling efficiency and determined pleasantness, although something was obviously very wrong.

"Is she in labour?" I thought I recognized those moans.

“Has been for forty-eight hours with no anaesthesia except nembutal. Her doctor isn’t on the staff—one of those brutes who feels that a woman doesn’t appreciate her baby unless she has labour pains.” I broke out in a cold sweat as the screams and sobs grew louder. Two days and nights of that tearing backache—those red flames of pain. Dear God, no.

“Why doesn’t somebody do something? Can’t Pete help her?”

She relaxed her guard a trifle. “Out-of-town doctor. He sent her in, and after the first day hasn’t even been in to see her. Of course, the house doctor is watching her, but her doctor left strict orders for no medication. I’d like to have him have one labour pain—that’s what I’d like.” She put the thermometer in my mouth and picked up my wrist. “We’ve doubled the nembutal—it would mean our caps of course, if he wanted to make something of it. Dr Williams is coming down—may do a Caesarian.”

“Where’s her husband? Can’t he do something?”

“Not married.” She turned on the night-light. “I’ll close your door so you can’t hear her.” She filled my water glass. “You can’t be a good nurse if you get all gummed up with sympathy, but some of these poor kids just about drive me crazy. She’ll be all right in the morning. You go to sleep now.”

She set her lips and went out the door, every inch of her crisp white self-radiating impersonal efficiency.

Suddenly Edith Stokes’ controlled, intelligent face rose up in my mind. Perhaps what I had thought was an unpleasant ice-maiden quality was a restraint built up through the years. As chief surgical nurse she had been required to stand by and watch an endless stream of human beings being subjected to surgery, most of the time skilfully done by well-trained men—occasionally carelessly handled by inept surgeons. At no time was she supposed to exhibit any reaction—she was there to produce competent surgical nurses and a sterile surgery, and no emotional response. I sighed and opened my book. Was there no end to this learning and adjusting?

By the evening of the fifth day I was sitting up in a wheelchair, feeling better than I’d ever felt in my life. I’d been down to the nursery and been shown how to bathe the slippery oyster that was Mari, and had found Faith Morgan and nine other mothers all learning the same absorbing process. The complex routine of the hospital had been patiently explained to me by the nurses. With a constant stream of doctors coming in and out of my room from six in the morning until ten at night, I found that an ordinary day in a hospital was more fascinating than any book I had ever read. Leaving the door open let me in on more things.

The elevator stopped—the door opened and I heard an abrupt female voice say, "Nonsense—I'm all prepped and medicated. I'll just get undressed and go to bed."

I heard Pete's lazy drawl, "Are you going to deliver yourself too, or shall I help?"

Miss Dean looked in. "You still up?—better get you in bed, *we're* going to be busy." I told her I didn't want to go to bed yet—would get in bed by myself when I wanted to go—and asked her what was up.

She laughed abruptly. "Worst combination in the world, doctor's wife from out of town, ex-doctor, first baby *and* Dr Roberts' patient. Don't worry if nobody answers your light for the next hour or so—we'll be hopping sidewise."

She hurried out. There were sounds of hasty preparation from the next room, broken by sharp protests in a feminine voice and occasional drawled answers from Pete. Nurses' feet scurried around like the sound of dry leaves. Miss Ward's clipped 'I've panned two and three, but five's light is still on', was thrown over her shoulder as she hurried into the diet kitchen.

The water was turned on and off and the icebox door slammed. The sounds were disturbed and annoyed rather than quietly routine. I got up and put on my bathrobe and slippers, so I could sneak out in the hall. I was dying to see a patient under twilight sleep. Suddenly there was a loud crash—in fact, a series of loud crashes. I peered around the door. Silhouetted against the street light was the patient, her benny flipping gaily back and forth as she danced up and down, crunching light globes and broken glass with gay abandon and skilfully avoiding the nurse's frantically clutching hands. Pete made a wild snatch at her. "Good God—she's drunk with power—find that light and get me some sutures, her feet are probably cut to ribbons." With that she made a wild leap, missed all the nurses and lunged past me down the hall. No mandrill monkey ever had a more gaily decorated fanny. She had been prepped with acriflavine and was shocking pink from her waist to her knees. She grabbed the telephone off the night desk and began to mutter rapidly into it. Two nurses and an intern darted out from the chart desk, captured her and returned her to the room. The labour nurse fitted the sideboards into the bed, replaced the broken bed light, pulled the refitted surgical cart beside the bed and sat down. Pete examined the patient's feet carefully. "Only a drunk could do that neat a job—not a scratch." He wiped his brow. I giggled and he looked up. "Get back into bed, Helpful. You are something I don't need right now." The patient lay quietly, long lashes resting peacefully on slightly flushed cheeks. A gentle, wistful smile played around her mouth.

Miss Dean followed me back into the room.

"My, I'm glad I didn't act like that when I was in labour. Have a cigarette, Miss Dean?"

Without a word she lifted up her uniform and petticoat and showed me a huge black-and-blue area on her leg. "Not like that, but you sure had the strength of ten. You put a half nelson on Miss Burns when you were on the delivery room table and pulled her over on top of you—and she weighs one hundred and eighty-five pounds. Not like that, dearie, but you were no rose, let me tell you."

"Did I say anything out of the way?"

She grinned at me. "Ask Burns what you called the ether mask." She tucked in the side of the bed. "You go to sleep now. I've got work to do."

I decided to observe professional ethics and not bother Miss Burns about the ether mask.

On the tenth day, Faith Morgan and I were sitting companionably side by side in our wheelchairs, comparing notes on our remarkable babies and discussing the fact that other mothers were allowed to go home right after the two o'clock feeding, whereas doctors' wives went home when and if it didn't interfere with their husbands' patients. In our case it was a whole day later. There was a medical dinner, which both Tod and Jim insisted they had to attend.

"Speaking of doctors' wives, it's too bad about Dr Calhoun's wife, isn't it? Lying in 608 all by herself and wondering whether they're going to remove everything and leave her empty like a paper sack—or decide she's well and let her go home. I think observation could be more accurately called slow torture."

We didn't particularly like Dr Calhoun's wife, nor know her very well, but the thought of anybody having a potential hysterectomy and never being able to have any babies was more than we could stand. “Has she actually got a malignant tumour?” I asked.

“They’re X-raying again to-day—will know tonight probably. Meanwhile she’s quietly going nuts.”

Jim’s bottle of Three Star Hennessey stood on the bureau, awaiting an appropriate dinner in celebration. We looked at the bottle and then at each other.

“Let’s cheer her up!”

“First, let’s toast each other for being such miracle kids and producing children, in case the nurses see us and snatch the bottle away”, Faith said practically. I went over and poured out a thimbleful of brandy for each of us. We drank it straight and ceremoniously shook one another’s hands. I put the bottle under my housecoat, Faith found three tooth brush glasses in the bathroom—we got ice from the diet kitchen, which we put under Faith’s housecoat, then we got in our wheelchairs and rolled down the hall to 608.

The charge nurse came bustling over to us. “Where are you girls going?” she said, trying not to look as though she wished to God all doctors’ wives were delivered in veterinary hospitals. Faith looked up and widened her large grey eyes. “We were just going down to my room—I want to show Mary my baby book.”

The nurse snapped, “You’re supposed to be resting”, and went into 609 and closed the door.

The ABSOLUTELY NO VISITORS sign was large on Mrs Calhoun’s door. We opened it a crack and looked in. The shades were down and the room was a murky gloom. She was lying absolutely flat and bawling. Faith went over and pulled up the shades, taking the screen away from the window where it had been carefully filtering out stray wisps of the lovely June fresh air.

“How are you, chum? I’m Faith Morgan who’s been writing you notes. You remember Mary.”

Mrs Calhoun looked even more bleak. “I had to sneak to read the notes even. I’m being observed for surgery—have been observed for three days.” She began to root under her pillow for her handkerchief, while Faith turned on the lights, rolled up the head of the bed and plumped up the pillows.

“The way they observe me is to make this room as much like a death cell as possible and then leave me in solitary confinement.

Also I'm absolutely starving, and the only thing they'll cough up to eat is this junk." She looked at the tall glass of chocolate barium on the bedside stand and shuddered. "I throw it up every time they give it to me. I'm supposed to start drinking this now so they can X-ray me again at one-thirty and watch it go down. I felt fine until they decided to observe me and see if I needed surgery. I wish my husband were a plasterer—or an aviator, so he wouldn't be so damned curious about my insides. I'm scared to death too—what if they find cancer?" She began to bawl again.

This condition called for more than a thimbleful of Three Star Hennessey—it called for action. I fixed her a good dark brown drink and made Faith and me a slightly lighter dose. "Here's to your early dismissal without surgery. They practically never find cancer in doctors' wives—bad for their reputations." We clinked glasses and drank. "Here's to your future heirs and heiresses. May they live long and contentedly." Mrs Calhoun took a deep swallow. "And may none of them marry doctors." Faith said, "To the medical profession, God bless 'em. May they all be operated on by one of their members, so they will know the tortures they inflict on their wives."

Mrs Calhoun began to have a light in her eye and quite pink cheeks. "Would you like a little sip of barium as an appetizer?" Faith asked, handing it to her. She drank half of it and shuddered again. I asked, "Why chocolate? I should think it would be even more revolting that way."

"I don't know. I've had gallons of it—so they could X-ray all my little organs while they were functioning. I haven't any symptoms you know—just suspicions."

She alternated barium with brandy. "It doesn't taste nearly as bad as a chaser as it does straight." Faith laughed. "You'd better take it easy. Dr West doesn't believe in eating, let alone drinking—"

The door opened and Dr West stalked in followed by his usual impressive queue of a resident, an intern, the charge nurse and two lesser nurses.

"What are you drinking?" He rushed to Mrs Calhoun's side, snatched the glass out of her hand and smelled it as if he expected the bitter almond smell of cyanide. "Spirits!" He turned furiously toward Faith and me. "You know better than to disturb a patient who is in for observation. You are both doctors' wives."

The combination of the fact that he looked so much like a pouter pigeon in his grey suit over a round fat stomach, with the first alcohol that we'd had in several months—was too much for us. We both burst out laughing. Then we scrambled into our wheelchairs and tried to tear out of the room. Faith ran over the feet of the last two nurses and made it, but I stuck in the door. "Miss Dean!" Dr West's voice shook with justifiable rage. "This patient was supposed to have complete rest and quiet."

Miss Dean swallowed twice—the resident, the intern and all the other nurses swallowed twice. Then they dispersed to let down the head of the bed, pull the blinds, restore the screen and generally depress Mrs Calhoun to her original limp state where surgery or anything else would be a welcome change. I tried again to sneak out the door, but unless I took an intern and a nurse or two on my lap—it couldn't be done. Then they formed a dense cordon around the bed, and I managed to get the wheelchair through the door.

The last words I heard Mrs Calhoun say were, 'Barium, hell—it was Three Star Hennessey. If you put brandy in your damned old barium instead of chocolate—I wouldn't raise such a stink about taking it. Go ahead and operate—see if I care—take everything out—but the next time I get married I'm going to marry a member of the liquor control board—that's what I'm going to marry—see if I care.' The door closed.

Faith was waiting outside, her face purple with suppressed laughter. She grabbed my arm and whispered, "Spirits—I can't bear it." She leaned her ear against the door for a moment. "Oh—oh—this is serious. He's Chief of Staff, even if he is a fat little teetotaller, and he could get Tod and Jim into some real trouble. Let's get out of here."

We wheeled down the hall to my room thinking up excuses. "Let's rush down and litter my room with baby presents so we'll look awfully maternal."

"After we brush our teeth—we probably smell like an old bar." We left our wheelchairs in the hall and tore into the room, to find Jim and Pete sitting on the bed. At our hang-dog looks and a glance at the bottle I was still clutching, they said simultaneously, "*What* have you been doing?" We told them about Mrs Calhoun, *poor* little *thing*! At Faith's description of Dr West they both burst out laughing. Jim said, "It's a good thing for these warm-hearted Florence Nightingales that her X-rays are negative. Just saw them—she's O.K."

Pete reached in the closet and brought out my suitcase. "You were going home tomorrow—you are now going home today. Start packing your things and I'll call Tod. Damn it—now we'll be late for the dinner meeting."

# 8

## High Pressure

CORONARY THROMBOSIS: *The formation, development or presence of a thrombus.*
ADVICE: *Advancing knowledge has made it desirable to revise our nomenclature by adopting the term 'myocardial infarction' instead of the older and commoner ones of coronary thrombosis or occlusion.*

CECIL: *Textbook of Medicine*

WITH THE HANDFUL OF BABIES still in mind, Sally was born sixteen harassed months after Mari. I was so busy that I didn't have time to notice the fact that I was pregnant—let alone do any medical research. The hospitalization, far from being the fascinating adventure it had been the first time, was more like a short nap in the afternoon—when what I really wanted was a good night's sleep.

I felt as if I were handling all the positions on an assembly line at once. Feed Sally, feed Mari, feed Jim—dress Sally, dress Mari—bathe Sally, bathe Mari, put Sally down for her nap, put Mari down for her nap—do breakfast dishes, make formula, wash diddies—and it was only ten o'clock in the morning. Mrs Dunny's advice wound through this maze of activity as regularly as a radio time signal and although well meant, it had become just as irritating. If I was weeding, she dropped to her knees and with the speed and precision of a woodpecker pulled everything out of the bed—including the seedlings I was saving. If I was cleaning, she grabbed the rag out of my hand and scrubbed the paint until bare patches of wood showed. She snatched the babies and jounced them until they spit up—she was my neighbour but I certainly missed Maggie.

During this period I had various mothers' helpers—high school girls, college girls and business college girls—who very obviously felt that a doctor should know better than to have his children so close together—were sorry for me for a month or so—and left for jobs that were not quite so confused. Doris, a business college girl this time, had just left for a job where 'they have the same amount of kids, but older. Gee, these are just like twins!' I was jumping from job to job on the assembly line again, trying to get the things done first which would draw Mrs Dunny's eagle eye. She was awfully thorough but so is a bulldozer.

It was about ten-fifteen in the morning—I had just fished my new hat out of the toilet. Mari had accomplished this during the brief moment I had my back turned and was bathing Sally. The doorbell rang. I wrapped Sally up in a big bath towel and put her in her crib and picked Mari up under one arm to answer the door. On the way downstairs Mari pointed proudly to the lipstick which was smeared all over the hall rug and down the stairs. She had accomplished this during the brief moment when I had rushed downstairs to get Sally's bottle. Mother's helper wasn't the only one who wanted a job where things were not so confused. I opened the door.

A tall man stood there, hat in hand. He had deep blue eyes, iron-grey hair and a remote, stern expression. Without speaking he handed me an oval, painted photograph on a metal background. It was a picture of a three-month-old baby lying on a rug and smiling into the camera. It was a picture of Sally! Then he smiled, Jim's slow luminous smile, said, "Good morning, daughter!" and Grandpa, Jim's father, had entered our lives.

"You go on with whatever you're doing, and I'll make the coffee", he said, walking in and dropping his hat on the hall bench. He followed me out into the kitchen and I handed him the coffee pot and the coffee and went upstairs to put the children to bed. I stopped long enough to telephone Jim and tell him that Pa had arrived. Jim said, "Good. Make him some coffee. I'll be home as soon as I can get there."

I couldn't believe that this tall, strong-looking man was Pa. Jim had told me that Pa had come over from Denmark when he was twenty years old, had worked very hard all his life—as do most immigrants to this country—and that since Ma had died, Pa had spent most of his time travelling.

None of Jim's stories about Pa were recent. They hadn't seen one another since the time Jim was so ill. Pa had spent three weeks in Chicago waiting for visiting hours at the hospital. He had put in the entire lonely dreary time riding streetcars, buses and elevated trains and, at the end of the three weeks knew much more about the city than Jim did. He had been a sewer contractor in the Middle West; he had built the viaduct over the river at home; he had lived in Texas at the time when to argue was to shoot; he had built the telephone company building in Houston. He had had great gangs working for him and never had any trouble with his men for two reasons: one, he could and did do any form of work better and faster than they could; and, two, he could swear in any known language. Yes, Grandpa had been active—but now he was very old, eighty-three or four, Jim couldn't remember which.

Grandpa looked not a day over sixty—and active was not the word for it.

When I got downstairs Grandpa was sitting at the kitchen table examining the electric mixer. He smiled at me as I came in the kitchen and pointed to two cups of coffee––thick and black. Jim's coffee, too.

"You know, daughter, electric gadgets contribute to divorce in this country. They take away the homey things—the smell of fresh bread, cider being pressed, soap making—all of those things which make a man feel Mama is working too." He put a lump of sugar between his teeth and sipped his coffee through it. "Yes sir, time on your hands always makes trouble—whether it's a man or a woman—is Jim busy?" I launched into a long prejudiced version of Jim's activities.

"Does he still like kippered herring and stuffed olives—and gjedost?" Grandpa asked. His voice, when he spoke about Jim, had the same warm pride that Jim's voice held when he spoke about Pa.

'Jim is going to look exactly like this when he is old', I thought as I listened to Grandpa talk, and watched his clear far-seeing blue eyes. His heavy blond hair was only slightly grey at the temples and the lines of his face were the fine wind lines of a life out of doors rather than the loose wrinkles of old age. It was not a particularly cheering idea to know that long before we were sixty, people would inevitably mistake me for Jim's mother.

Grandpa felt that in this country no one really knew how to play. People worked for the sheer joy of working, rather than to earn the money to enjoy their leisure hours. In Copenhagen, any civilized house party lasted from Thursday noon until Tuesday afternoon. They drank *aquavit*—only went home to change their clothes—

danced, went to plays, went to Norway to ski, took a little jaunt over to Germany to hear music. Yes sir—he'd certainly like to take me to Copenhagen with him when he went—there was a city. He thought he'd go to Denmark in a couple of years, if the war held off long enough.

Grandpa didn't believe that in-laws of any variety should live with their children. It caused friction. When you got to be eighty-three years old, you'd seen and done practically everything and you liked to be able to choose your amusement—not have a lot of inexperienced children fussing over you and telling you what to do. He laughed shortly. "Jim, now, wants to doctor me. He doesn't realize that I have got along pretty well without his medical care so far."

Grandpa felt that grandparents should confine themselves to playing with their grandchildren. Parents should discipline, but grandparents should charm and delight children.

Take this coffee now—the doctor back home said that with Grandpa's heart, he was supposed to stop drinking strong coffee. Well, coffee was only drinkable if it was black as road tar, and twenty cups a day was what Grandpa had always had—and he was always going to drink twenty cups a day. He was alive and that doctor was dead. Jim had that fool notion about drinking coffee too—but he'd probably outgrown it by now, just as he had outgrown driving cars too fast.

After lunch Grandpa went out to find himself a house—near enough to us so he could come over every day and play with the children, but far enough away so he could do what he pleased. I told him that houses were as scarce as hen's teeth and that he'd better wait until Jim came home so he could drive him around. Grandpa said, "I'll find one—see you at dinner" and went out the back door.

At dinner Grandpa and Jim sat across the table from each other and smiled. They talked very little, but exuded that warm, masculine serenity in the joy of one another's company that always seems so much more intense to me than the little kisses and shrieks of joy that women give. Grandpa said, "I found a cottage, Jim. Ten blocks down this street—in a lot with big madrona trees—I like it." Jim said, "Good" and continued to beam.

After that, Grandpa came over every morning. He watched Mari while I bathed Sally, he held Sally while I bathed Mari. He answered the telephone in such a curt, business-like fashion that I found I had many extra hours per day as a result of that service alone. He mended everything in the house that was broken, said, "Jim never was handy with tools—it is a good thing he didn't choose surgery", and while he worked he talked.

There was going to be another war and fairly soon, too. He remembered when Bismarck invaded Denmark (this little historical titbit gave me as much of a start as though Grandpa had told me he remembered floating down the Nile with Cleopatra.) The Germans killed his pony, killed the cows—all but the two his father hid in the woods—and then quartered six soldiers at his house. It was a hard time for Denmark but they had weathered it, as they would always weather a German invasion, by a sense of humour and a subtle lack of obedience—two things no German could ever understand. All the time the soldiers were living in his house, his mother was feeding the children late at night from stores hidden under the kitchen floor. The soldiers never could understand how the ten little boys kept their rosy cheeks. Grandpa had always been prejudiced against the Germans since that time. He could forgive their militarist attitude, but not a national lack of humour.

Mrs Dunny and Grandpa clashed the second day. I was making cookies and Grandpa was chopping the nuts for me when Mrs Dunny came in.

"Oh—I see you're making cookies—I always use gluten flour—the recipe calls for white flour but it goes further. How do you do?—you must be Dr Jay's father—mercy don't cut them so fine—they'll disappear in the gluten flour—"

Grandpa said, "How do you do? You must be German", cut the nuts a lot finer—and looked through and past Mrs Dunny as neatly as though she were a big blue spirit.

Right in the middle of her instructions on how to open the oven door—what heat to use—mercy, that dough looks lumpy—here, let me feel it—why don't you add some raisins?—they add bulk—Grandpa lit his pipe.

Grandpa didn't believe in smoking his pipe in the house—Ma had never liked it and he didn't believe any woman did.

Mrs Dunny promptly began to cough, pat her chest, give a series of little horrified shrieks—she was allergic to tobacco—soiled the curtains—she didn't know how many times she'd said to Mr Dunny that she didn't care where he smoked as long as it wasn't in her house. She batted at the smoke and held her handkerchief to her nose.

Grandpa said, "Kind words, and few, are a woman's ornament", and continued to envelop Mrs Dunny in such clouds of smoke that she ran out in the back yard and howled her advice from the bottom of the steps.

Grandpa's treatment of Mrs Dunny made me have a sneaking sympathy for the German soldiers. Every time she came in the house, he brought a piece of steel pipe up from the basement and banged on it with a wrench so she had to scream every word of advice. He held his hand behind his ear and said "How?" at intervals. If she still persisted, he smoked his pipe in continuous puffs like a steam engine, and caused her to cough until the tears streamed down her face. As a last resort he walked out on the porch, poked Mari and Sally until he woke them, and then came in and told me the babies were crying and I'd better go and tend to them. Germans, Grandpa said, were slow to take a hint.

Fidele was Grandpa's second local prejudice. He was the Filipino gardener who came once a week and presented me with tender poems about the Doctor, and occasionally about me. After the presentation of the poem, he would carefully select a flower, preferably a lily, stick it behind his ear and walk languidly around behind the lawn mower singing folk songs from the island of Luzon. Fidele was a patient of Jim's and so great was his courtesy, and such a god was Jim in the poems, that I had a tendency to ignore the fact that he always left stripes of eight-inch grass on the lawn, merely patted the surface of the flower beds with his finger tips, and chose only the largest and most sweetly scented flowers to wear behind his ear.

Not so Grandpa. "I've hired those Eyetalians for years on the sewer gang—there isn't one of them that can do a lick of work."

"Fidele isn't an Italian, Grandpa. He is a Filipino and one of Jim's patients."

"Well, he works like an Eyetalian, and Jim's patient or not I fired him. I'll cut the grass." Which he proceeded to do rapidly and perfectly. He dug the garden fork deep into the beds and loosened the soil. He removed every weed and then turned his attention to the planting.

Grandpa didn't care much for flowers unless they were red. He stood in front of my bed of stock, nicotiana and sweet peas, their delicate perfumes and pastel colours blending like potpourri, and snorted, "Sickly looking things. Never did like pale flowers. Like useless women, try to get attention by perfume and vapoury actions. A row of red Swiss chard now would look nice in here—make the bed look healthy and useful." The flowers, astonished at being able to move their feet for the first time in two years, but even more astonished by having as bedfellows great purple cabbages, dark green curly kale, carrots and radishes, bloomed violently in desperation. Even they could see that if they didn't outdo themselves, their days were numbered.

When Grandpa decided a rock garden would be nice, Jim produced one Mr Swensen, a grateful patient who was very anxious to do something for the Doctor. Just what he had in mind I never knew because he charged twice as much as anyone else would have done for the rocks, and seemed to have only one sentence in his vocabulary—"Naw—ve do not do it dot vay!" He worked so slowly that I was forced to take a bead on a tree in the back yard to know he'd progressed at all. He charged $2.50 an hour for this inertia.

Grandpa watched him work for a day or so, then said, "He never wrought a good day's work who went grumbling about it", and began to work with Mr Swensen. The rocks were enormous natural stone from up in the mountains, and moving any of them, even with a pulley arrangement, looked like a two-man job to me. Grandpa, however, leaned over, got both of his strong experienced arms around the rocks and lifted them into place. Mr Swensen said, "Ve do not do it dot vay", and didn't move a muscle to help Grandpa.

I had two choices, one, and definitely the more tempting one, was to kick Mr Swensen's rear and say, "Well, we do, so get moving", which would crush a grateful patient and accomplish nothing. The other was to tell Grandpa that he wasn't supposed to lift heavy weights because he'd had a coronary, and plan to have Mr Swensen creeping around the back yard as long as his gratitude (and our money) held out.

Jim had said, "Don't treat Grandpa as though he were old. Be tactful. He is a proud Dane and he wants to help you. Just remember that he has had a coronary—a blood pressure of about two hundred fifty—and mustn't strain himself. Let him potter around the house and the garden but no heavy lifting nor strenuous work of any kind." I noticed, however, that Jim did not say this to Grandpa. Instead he gave me a little phial to break and hold under Grandpa's nose if he had a heart attack, and added that he might even help Grandpa in the garden in the evenings from now on. I couldn't decide which threat made me more apprehensive.

Grandpa continued to lift the rocks, talking gaily in Swedish meanwhile to cheer Mr Swensen on. I went out to be tactful, took Grandpa to one side and told him Mr Swensen was doing Jim a favour, and his feelings would be hurt if Grandpa did all the work. Grandpa gave a loud 'ha' of disdain. "He who has money to throw away, let him employ workmen and not stand by. Two dollars and a half an hour is quite a price to pay for favours. I'll help", and went back to work. I had to admit that Mr Swensen's movements became perceptible to the naked eye while Grandpa worked with him, so I brought both babies out in the back yard, put them in the pen, and we all sat and watched while Grandpa heaved the big rocks and Mr Swensen crept back and forth with the smallest ones.

Grandpa had lifted about ten of the hundred-pound rocks as though they were beach pebbles and put them in position—when he leaned over, staggered slightly and came and sat down beside me on the back steps. His lips turned blue and he began to breathe stertorously.

I rushed in the house, got the little phial, broke it and held it under Grandpa's nose. He waved it away and said, between gasps, "Put half a cup of whisky in half a cup of coffee and bring it to me."

"But Jim said—"

He fixed me with a firm blue eye. "Do as I say, daughter."

I brought it out to him. He drank it, his colour promptly returned, and he went back to work on the rock garden. "Ye do not do it dot vay", was Mr Swensen's sole comment, and for once I agreed with him.

In the middle of the afternoon, Mr Swensen, worn out by Grandpa's example, decided that even as a favour to the Doctor he couldn't watch anybody work that hard without being exhausted, so he quit.

Grandpa continued to work at the rock garden. He said he'd had lots of heart attacks and that Eyetalian doctor in Kansas had given him some pills—said to take one after every meal. That was such a time-wasting piece of advice that Grandpa ate the pills all at once. They didn't do him any good that he could see, so he continued to drink whisky and coffee—he knew that cured his heart attacks. "An Eyetalian", Grandpa said, "would do or say anything to get money."

The next day Grandpa rolled an enormous rock down a sloping board at the base of the wall and in some way struck his forearm. He came into the kitchen with a deep six-inch gash bleeding profusely, washed it off and asked for a clean handkerchief. I offered to drive him to the hospital for an X-ray and some stitches. His arm made an unpleasant crunching noise when he moved it. I got the merthiolate solution, some sterile pads and bandage, and prepared to dress the cut. Grandpa waved me away. "Get me some whisky and a half a cup of coffee, daughter."

He poured some whisky over the cut, and some into the cup of coffee. "You know, Jim used to be quite a sensible kid except when he got a notion."

I watched Grandpa wrap his handkerchief around the cut and muttered, "I wonder where he got that tendency." He pulled the knot tight by biting each end and giving it a jerk. "Jim wanted to work the steam shovel once when he was a kid. He pestered me and pestered me to show him how. He was too young and neither the driver nor I would explain the mechanism to him. Do you know that kid worked all night on that steam shovel and in the morning he knew how to work it?"

The handkerchief got red and little drops of blood dropped on the sink. Grandpa sipped his whisky and coffee and ignored it. Then he went back to work on the rocks.

When Jim came home I told him about Grandpa's arm. After dinner we drove over to his little cottage to see how he was getting along. We looked in the window as we went to the door. Grandpa was sitting in a rocking chair in front of the fire, reading. His injured left arm rested in a sling made with a plaid scarf. At the sound of the knocker, he took the sling off, put it on the bureau and rose to open the door.

Jim said, "Pa, I hear you hurt your arm. Let me see it."

"No", Grandpa said. Firm Danish blue eye met firm Danish blue eye and there was a complete impasse. Jim reached for Grandpa's arm and Grandpa backed off. "I came to take you down to have that arm X-rayed", Jim said.

"Ha", Grandpa retorted—and that was that.

The next morning Jim said, "I'll stop on the way to the hospital and pick Pa up. I'm going to have his arm X-rayed."

Grandpa came over about noon with his arm in a cast. He was quiet, played with the children, but said very little to me. I tried some more tact. "You know, Grandpa, modern medicine is a wonderful thing and Jim is very proud of being a doctor—" my voice trailed off. It was hard to be tactful when Grandpa insisted on turning on the water faucet, filling the coffee pot, measuring the coffee and putting the coffee can back in the cupboard—all with his back to me.

"Jim always was proud—always did have notions. Why, I remember one time in Texas—we were using dynamite—" Grandpa told a long fascinating story involving Jim's experiments with dynamite which were very nearly fatal to Jim.

"Like the time I had that cold sore", Grandpa continued. "Jim was an intern then, studying all about a thing called cancer. He promptly got a notion that this sore on my lip was cancer. It wasn't a regular cold sore—it lasted a long time. I'd been to a doctor in Houston, Eyetalian, I think, although he didn't look it. He wanted to take a piece of my lip and look at it under the microscope—he thought it was cancer too but I said it was my lip and I'd keep it, if he didn't mind. Well, Jim had the same idea. He kept after me all the time he was home to give him a piece of my lip."

Grandpa laughed. "I gave him a piece of my mind instead. Told him that he could treat all those patients in the hospital if he wanted to—I had no control over that—but that I'd used Mecca Compound for sores and whisky for my heart for more years than he was old and I was going to keep on doing it."

He sipped his coffee reflectively.

"Did you cure the cancer, Grandpa?" I asked.

He smiled, Jim's shining smile. "God healeth and the physician hath the thanks", he said. "When whisky won't cure a disease, I figure you might as well be dead."

While Grandpa's arm was in the cast, he dug in the garden. By this time the flowers had the same defeatist attitude that an occupied country has—they grew and bloomed but their hearts weren't in it. They knew that next year they would inevitably be Chinese lettuce, Danish cabbage or Italian tomatoes—and there was no further use in struggling. Also due to the cast, Grandpa spoke very little to Jim—he was willing to let Jim have his way up to a point, but he was damned if he was going to be enthusiastic about it. That was when Jim got the notion to help Grandpa in the garden.

Also, with the true scientific mind, Jim began to read. *The Garden Encyclopaedia* made him dig up all my delphinium seedlings because the withering tulip leaves behind them obviously needed more sun. "The leaves looked yellow, Mary, and I presumed they needed sunlight—plants breathe carbon dioxide just as humans breathe oxygen—they absorb it with the help of the sun's rays." I told him to absorb the section in the encyclopaedia about delphinium seedlings and the section pertaining to bulbs which were drying off in the summer, before he dug up my plants. Grandpa said the Germans always were thorough—that I sounded like Mrs Dunny. I apologized.

Then Jim read the rhododendron section about acid loving plants. He asked me casually one night, as we were walking in the startled garden, if I had many acid-loving plants.

"Certainly. Most plants native to this country prefer an acid soil. Rhododendron, camellia, magnolia, most of the shrubs in the garden are acid loving." My voice was loud with a mixture of condescension and unsureness, as it always is when I offer Jim any scientific information. "With the exception of the rhododendron, and we haven't any, the shrubs you mention are not native to this area", Jim said with infuriating accuracy. "What about the perennials?"

I watched two pink lupins gamely waving good-bye through a sturdy hedge of red Swiss chard. "They used to prefer a light loam. Now all the plants are concentrating so hard on peace at any price that they no longer have any soil preference", I grumbled.

"Good. I'll get some coffee grounds from the hospital. They'll serve to break up this clay and will furnish acid to the soil." Jim cast his research eye over the garden. I should have remembered the night he made sixteen bowls of mayonnaise in order to have an accurate measure of the correct consistency, but the night was soft, the babies were finally in bed, and I was coasting. I patted him fondly, told him that was a marvellous idea and smelled my one remaining sweet pea. I should also have remembered Grandpa's cast and the fact that Jim was vainly trying to get back in his good graces.

Since Grandpa had come, Jim and I had taken to going to a movie occasionally while Grandpa sat with the children and I had resumed my practice of going over to Maggie's or to Faith's when the men were at meetings. Therefore it was almost a week later that Jim and Grandpa and I were taking a walk in the garden after dinner. The stock bed was now one row of beets, one row of stock. Where the nicotiana had been, there was a row of red cabbage, then one row of kale; then, where the sweet peas had been, a row of scarlet runner beans. I loved Grandpa, but I had also loved my sweet scented flower bed which filled the living-room and the porch with a haunting perfume, night and day. I sighed. "Do you suppose we could have a farm some day, Jim?"

"Nope. Not practical for doctors. Wait until you see the camellia bed!" he said proudly.

I almost screamed when I saw the camellia bed. Every plant was buried up to the hilt in coffee grounds. There was a filmy grey mould—like the moss which hangs from trees in the Florida swamps—creeping along the ground and waving among the plants.

"What on earth have you done, Jim?" I moaned, feeling the wet steaming surface.

"Control groups", Jim said. "Coffee grounds. I asked the cook at County Hospital to save all the coffee grounds for me. There are only three hundred pounds there now, but by next week there will be a ton or so. Now this bed has lots of acid—" He picked at the mould and pinched it experimentally between his fingers. "Well, what do you know? Penicillin I'll bet, or darned near the same thing. Look at this, Mary." He beamed. I was looking at the rest of the beds. Everyone had an accurate measure of coffee grounds, some of them ten pounds, some twenty pounds—and this one was about to have a ton. Test tubes containing progress charts hung from sticks at the end of each bed. Control groups. My God!

Jim walked ahead of me with Grandpa. "By the way, Pa, your cast comes off tomorrow. The callus is quite firm." He bent down to feel the surface of the ten-pound coffee ground bed, drew the chart out of the test tube and wrote something on it.

Grandpa reached down and pulled up two or three delphinium seedlings that could just barely keep their heads above water. "Roots look sickly to me. More notions I expect." He pulled up the rest of the seedlings, reaching around in the coffee grounds to find the few that weren't showing. "Beets would do all right here I think—they aren't fussy—or Eyetalian lettuce—it doesn't care where it grows."

He picked up a handful of coffee grounds and let it fall through his fingers. “You seem to have a lot of slugs here, don’t you? In Denmark we used barley chaff in a ring around each field on the farms. The slugs wouldn’t cross it—too scratchy.”

Jim’s eyes lit up. “I wonder if one of the flour mills wouldn’t have barley chaff.”

They moved on, arm in arm. I picked the two pink lupins and followed them.

# 9

## Dancing With Tears

KERATOCONJUNCTIVITIS: '*If the cornea becomes involved and fibrosis follows, there may be varying degrees of blindness.*'

JIM

THE FIRST FALL ROUND-UP, or branding of new wives, in medical circles, is usually in the form of a dinner dance. Every doctor's wife has every intention of going to the dance—and no doctor has any intention of putting his foot inside the door. Therefore, the Wives Committee has long since discovered that it is as idiotic to mail an invitation to the doctor's office as it would be to mail a four-colour ad. for Lydia Pinkham's Compound. It is equally foolish to mail the invitation to his home. Who knows?—that might be the month HE decides to open HIS mail instead of throwing it away. So the wives, from long and bitter experience, have discovered that the only way to have this round-up well attended is to begin early the secret telephone communication known as 'getting HIM to go'.

The first few calls are crafty. If the news goes up-wind and one doctor happens to overhear his wife's telephone conversation and to interpret it correctly there is an immediate stampede followed by a series of epidemics which require twenty-four-hour, unremitting medical care.

My telephone call was an early feeler, in the morning of course, but late enough to be sure HE'D gone. "Mary, HE'S gone so I can talk. Is YOURS? Fine." Faith's voice was urgent. "Listen, the Medical Auxiliary Dance is going to be at the College Club this year. Yes—the ninth—Uncle John's coming up from San Francisco I'm giving a cocktail party first. Can you come?"

My automatic reflex was perfect. "I'll have to ask Jim. There might be a meeting."

“Don’t be a complete mental deficient! I’m on the committee and we’ve checked—there isn’t any medical meeting nor any convention of any kind that weekend. They’re trapped. Now listen.”

She hastily went on with plans. Formal clothes, cocktails at her house Uncle John always brought the most marvellous drinks with him, and, anyway she had a terrific new dress, which, of course, HE’D hate.

“So even if you’ve got to hog-tie him, you’ve got to make him come, and besides—wait till you see what Bill Logan found under a board somewhere and married, she’s—” Faith’s voice suddenly changed from a rapid conspiratorial contralto to a lyric soprano. “Coming, dear, just a minute.” Then a hoarse whisper, “HE’S come back for a *Journal*—I’ll call you later.”

MINE had already gone to the hospital so I went unenthusiastically upstairs and opened the closet door. I had my choice of two long dresses, the black which hadn’t had a chance to cool in five years—it stretched so easily over early pregnancy—and the white which made my freckles stand out and was tight across the stomach and hips where I wasn’t. It seemed to me that I’d been pregnant ever since I could remember. I slammed the closet door and began to throw on some clothes to go down town.

I walked slowly up Fifth Avenue. It was the first of December and each window was alluring with winter clothes, not that style made any difference to me—anything that didn’t wrap around was hauntingly beautiful. Mari was three, Sally was two and Heidi was one month old and I’d been ballooning around in what were revoltingly known as ‘Storky Time Prints’ for practically five years. I warily approached Fritzi’s window prepared to drool with longing and move on.

Fritzi is one of those devils who have exquisite taste, astronomical prices and a fiendish talent for displaying in their windows the one garment which makes anything else look as if it had been resurrected from a missionary bundle. This time I stood rooted to the spot. Her window held a copper bowl of pinkish brown chrysanthemums on a soft green rug. A dull gold evening bag hung from a disembodied hand and the red-haired, faceless model displayed the most beautiful dress I have even seen. The hell with the budget that dress was mine and I had to have it!

With steel in my heart I opened the plastic door of the grey velvet box which was Fritzi's *salon* and walked over, in a trance of desire, to touch the dress. It was deep flame colour at the hem and shaded gradually, through all the colours of a beach fire at night, into a pale lemon yellow at the neck. The wind from the door made it billow slightly, giving the effect of dancing flames. Just as I raised a reverent hand to stroke it, two scented saleswomen dressed in good basic blacks stalked toward me like a Royal Guard.

"May we s-a-a-rve you—modom?" they intoned in unison. "Plea-a-ase be sea-a-ted." They pointed to a shocking pink pouffe, the only place to sit down, and fingered their pearl earrings. The heart-shaped pouffe proved to be one of those down-filled foolers which lower you into a crouching position and lower your morale proportionately. I struggled to my feet again and pointed haughtily. "The dress on the model—I want it." I glared and they stared. Finally they glanced at each other out of the corners of their eyes, turned on too-high heels and rocked to the back of the room to disappear in folds of grey velvet. There was a twenty minute silence while everybody, including me, hoped I'd go away.

Fritzi decided to give me the treatment. She manifested herself through a grey fold, glanced at me, shuddered, and turned her back to gaze long and lovingly in a heart-shaped mirror. She smoothed her black satin bust and bolster stomach, patted a lavender curl with a puffy white hand and said, "Ya-a-a-s?" without turning around. *Her* basic black had awfully high style black chicken wire around the neck. Seething, I snapped, "That yellow dress in the window—I want it."

She smoothed her black satin fanny with an irritable motion and breathed, "The original?" At this signal the basic blacks appeared and stood on tiptoe-their mouths open. "Mo-o-dom wishes to see the original." She turned toward me again. "I'm afraid it's qua-a-te expensive."

This time I was genuinely stunned to hear coming out of my mouth, "Pra-a-ce is no object. Naturally."

Naturally was a masterpiece of under-statement. The night before Jim and I had had our semi-annual budget conference and I was so mortally wounded by Jim's merciless logic that I'd promised—nay, tearfully insisted—to cut everything to the bare bone. I presumed that he would allow me sufficient food to maintain an adequate vitamin intake. (After all people would think it a little odd if a doctor's children had rickets from malnutrition—although that was obviously what Jim was striving for, wasn't it?) *I* did not want any clothes allowance at all, just enough clothing to prevent chilblains or pneumonia. Naturally, as a heat conservation measure, I would turn off all the radiators in the house but one—in the little baby's room!

Jim had said, "My God! All this because I mildly ask you to keep your cheque stubs. 'Man with coal?' What does the question mark stand for?"

At my "Do you mind if I light one used candle while I pore over my cheque stubs?" Jim had stamped off to bed.

"Will you step in here—modom?" The basic blacks, one on either side, guided me into a chartreuse velvet dressing-room and averted their eyes from a safety pin holding my shoulder strap and another, larger safety pin forcing my suit together at the waist. They put the dress on over my head and pulled it into place. I looked in the mirror and was lost. Fritzi parted the curtains and allowed a frosty smile to crack her lips.

"Yes, it is yours—the colours are wonderful with red hair." She adjusted a lemon yellow fold over the shoulder. "It needs no fitting."

After dinner Jim and I were sitting in front of the fire, reading. That is, Jim was studying and I was gazing into the fire—each flame becoming a part of my new dress. The doorbell rang.

"Now what misbegotten fool is that?" Jim started toward the door, his finger firmly held in the article in the *A.M.A. Journal*. I stiffened, ready for the fray. Jim is charming and courtly to guests in his house except when he is studying; then he has a tendency to treat drop-in trade of the too-hearty type as though it were a manifestation of ectoplasm—undoubtedly remarkable but medically unsound. He peers at them as he would through a microscope, allows ten-minute pauses to follow each nervous sally and wanders around picking things up and putting them down.

He opened the front door, waited just too long and then said, "Oh hello" in his most 'we don't need any' voice. I rushed to the front door to intercept the pass as I recognized Bill and Kate Miller's voices, but I was one awful moment too late.

"Oh, Jim—you know the Medical Auxiliary Dance—well, we think it would be fun to have a breakfast at our house afterward—

don't you, Mary? Ping-pong—stingers, just a general go-to-hell. Nobody will be worth a damn the next day anyway—so why not?" She beamed up at Jim's remote medical-article eye. "Aren't you thrilled about the dance? Bill can hardly wait."

It wasn't a strictly accurate description of Bill's attitude judging by his expression, but he was at least passive.

Jim turned his radar in my direction and said ominously, "What dance?" and immediately began planning a special meeting of the Board of any hospital for whatever night Kate might mention. She threw an arm around Jim's rigid body and snuggled up to him. "Honey—haven't you heard? The Medical Dance. It's going to be at the College Club this year—December ninth—Faith's giving a cocktail party first—her fabulous Uncle John—you know—the one who is filthy rich—is coming with his usual trailer of fancy drinks." She let go of Jim and threw herself down on a chair, beaming with plans. "I hope we can get something beside Old Arm Pit. Competing with Uncle John is going to be difficult from a liquor standpoint."

Bill broke in. "Might as well face it, .Jim, we have to go." His false laugh was wary, he had been Jim's resident and he was obviously torn between two loves. There were three minutes of dead silence which I devoted to prayer. Then I became babblingly cordial in exact ratio to the remoteness in Jim's eyes. Marvellous idea, might as well be completely comatose over the entire weekend—how did Kate think up anything so creamy as a breakfast? Faith had called me of course, but I hadn't one moment to tell Jim, what with three babies practically an hour apart—I had the fanciest dress in the world and could hardly wait to show it to hordes of people—of course we were going—I could hardly wait to see Uncle John again. Jim would adore it—he loved parties.

Jim's adoration took the form of picking up a vase on the mantel and putting it down, snapping his cigarette lighter twice and carefully blowing it out—and one venom-filled look. Then he walked out to the kitchen. By the time he returned with three anaemic drinks—he wouldn't touch alcohol on a study night and destroy the full effect of his frontal lobes—I was gushing as though I had been marooned at Point Barrow during the dark months and Kate and Bill represented the first boat through the ice. Jim said nothing. Naturally they stayed until twelve-thirty, I was so hysterically glad to see them.

When Jim finally shut the door behind them he had white lines down either side of his mouth and his words were measured. "Mary, you defeat me completely. I hate stingers and you know it. I hate breakfasts and you know it, and—"

I interrupted, "Honey, I know you do and we won't go to breakfast. But you will go to the dance, won't you? I have a new dress"—the white lines deepened—"and I've been pregnant ever since I can remember."

He picked up the *Journal* and turned toward the stairs. "I'll go, but you don't have to give the impression that I keep you chained down the cellar except when we have guests."

For two or three days before the dance I devoted every spare moment to little beauty aids I read in the paper. I put white of egg masks on my face, and then forgot they were there and that I am allergic to eggs. That was the first day and fortunately the swelling went down with the aid of Benadryl and soda packs. I tried doing my hair in various lumpy new ways to change my personality. My head was sore but my personality remained the same. I put all sorts of night creams, day creams and lotions on my face.

Therefore, when I woke up Saturday morning, the day of THE DANCE, I was not at all surprised to find tears streaming down my tortured face. My eyes felt funny and looked slightly puffy around the upper and lower lids. I ate two Benadryl tablets, three B complex, two ABDOL and two iron tablets for breakfast and bathed my eyes with two kinds of eye lotion—one medical and one guaranteed to make the eyes sparkle.

When Jim came home he was so completely psychopathic and introverted during the process known as 'dressing' that I hesitated to mention my symptomatic streaming eyes lest they produce a further hurdle. However, as no type of mascara would even stay on one eye while I applied it to the other, I finally weakened and went over to Jim. He was sitting on the bed jerking at his shoelaces hopefully.

"Honey, look at my eyes, will you? They're inflamed and I keep crying all the time."

He broke a shoelace and swore dolefully.

"A chalazion probably—I'll bet I haven't another pair of black shoelaces." He looked up and squinted his eyes balefully at me. I handed him a new pair of black shoelaces.

"That's a stye, isn't it? I don't think so—I've had styes and they feel differently. This is itchy and it makes me cry all the time. Tears just stream down my face."

"Tears of guilt for making me go to this damned dance." He sighed and started another thoroughly familiar delaying action. "The pants to my Tux are too tight—would it be all right if I wore a dark blue suit?"

"It would not. Faith said formal and you know it perfectly well. Besides you haven't even looked at my new dress." I turned in front of him so he could get the full effect. He held his head on one side, dangled a shoe from his left hand and looked me carefully up and down. "Um-hum-nice. Good colours for you—it looks kind of like a *negligée* though or one of those tea things."

He had hit with evil accuracy on the one small doubt in my mind when I had tried it on. It did look a little like a tea gown and Fritzi had never mentioned what it was—merely that it was mine. I counted to twenty-five and resisted pounding him on the head with a shoe.

"Stand naturally. You're still walking with pregnancy lordosis—that yellow's nice around your neck." He walked over to his bureau and began taking shirts out of the drawer and dropping them on the floor. "I'm not going to wear a stiff shirt." He set his mouth.

"I got you one of those soft pleated ones today—here." I counted to thirty. Jim peered suspiciously at the collar size and put it on, pinching it hopefully to see if it wouldn't scratch his neck. "Where are we going first? I have to make a call on the way. I always feel like such an ass making a house call in a Tux."

"I told you—don't you remember? Faith's Uncle John is here—"

"You haven't mentioned one damned thing about this dance if you could help it and you know it. Idiotic performance. A lot of morons wandering around to thump-thump-thump—beaten out by a lot of marijuana-smoking fanatics."

"Uncle John has brought all the ingredients for a marvellous drink called a Zombie. Faith has asked all the people at our table, about twelve I think. There are seven kinds of rum in it—in layers. In Oakland a gardenia floats on top of the bowl, but Faith says she isn't going to float gardenias at two dollars a float."

He tied his tie and turned toward me. "Let's get going. I have to stop at the hospital." As we started out the back door he reached in the icebox. I grabbed his arm. "Don't start to eat now, Jim. You know Faith will have tons of food."

"I'm not going to eat." He handed me a florist's box. "Thought you might like a corsage for your coming-out party." Lovely yellow and flame gerbera tied with a brown ribbon! I kissed him rapturously. "Jim! It's just the colours of my dress. How did you know?"

"Saw it in the closet. Come on, you can pin them on in the car."

When we arrived at Faith's and Tod's house, most of the guests were already there. Uncle John was bartending and handing out what looked like glass wastebaskets full of delicious-smelling liquid. The wives were shining like little girls at a birthday party. The doctors, tense with suspicion, were clustered around Uncle John. I tasted my drink and found it had a faint flavour of rosewater and coconut, exotic, even tropical, and obviously very strong.

"Take it easy, Mary", Jim said. "You haven't had anything to drink for some time, and unless I'm very much mistaken this will have exactly the effect of cyclopropane."

Uncle John laughed jovially and slapped Jim on the back. "Oh that won't hurt her—it's a Zombie. It will just make her eyes sparkle. Nothing in it but good old rum and a few secrets."

My eyes were filling with tears and leaking with the irritating drip, drip, drip of a broken gutter. I had to make several trips to Faith's room to apply new mascara. Both eyes were swollen almost shut, which gave me a squinty, suspicious look, but the Zombie had at least made them cease to itch so unmercifully.

It seemed that in Oakland no one flew on one wing, so Uncle John made us all another wee Zombie before we left for the Club. That is, he made the wives another Zombie. The doctors all refused except Warren. He's a skin specialist and as his patients never die and never get well his life is his own after six o'clock. Warren put a full hip-flask in his pocket. "Merely a form of preventive medicine."

We arrived at the Club, each doctor hopefully murmured his table number to the steward and was led by a glowing wife to the table. There was an exciting number of strangers, and a delightful number of unattached males. Apparently there was another dance going on simultaneously. Each wife gave a wriggle of joy. For once they wouldn't have the choice of dancing with each other, or sitting at the table with six other wives at a lonely female wake, waiting for the doctors to come back.

Before we were seated, the calls started coming in and the

doctors began to cheer up. The two or three who were left had to decide between dancing themselves into a coronary trying to be gallant, or looking up stray bachelors in another profession who could hold down the fort while they joyfully went out to make totally unnecessary house calls on undoubtedly startled patients. By the time the soup was served, there were six wives, two doctors, one bond salesman, one insurance broker and two lawyers at our table. Jim's contribution was Duke Tucker, a faded bond salesman. "Here's Duke, Mary. He'll take care of you while I make this call." There was much false laughter and "I'm leaving her in capable hands." Jim fairly ran from the room.

In spite of the obviousness of this ruse, it touched me almost as much as Jim's flowers. I had been quite unpleasant about Duke, and had quoted him long and often during our marriage. "Duke loves to dance—he says dancing is an important part of married morale." Jim felt that Duke should get married first and talk about morale afterward.

Duke swooped me away, told me my dress was a flame, my perfume was dangerous, and hoped I was unhappy in my marriage so he would have a chance. He leaned close to my ear. "Will Jim be jealous if I am selfish and dance with you all evening?" I rubbed my streaming eyes and mumbled, "Probably give you free medical care all the rest of your life if you do." Duke held me closer. "Cheer up, honey. You know I warned you not to marry a doctor."

He squashed me comfortingly. It occurred to me that he might be misunderstanding my streaming eyes, so I hastily excused myself and made another futile trip to the mascara box. By this time the anaesthesia of the Zombie had worn off and my eyes were burning like fury. When I came back to the table, I sat down next to Milt Hanson, who was moodily picking a bun to pieces. His speciality was eye surgery, and he hardly ever got any nice convenient night calls.

"Milt, look at my eyes, will you? Jim says I have a chalazion, but they don't usually make you cry all the time, do they? And my eyes hurt like the devil."

Instantly his face lit up and he turned tenderly toward me. "Here, let's see." He peered diagnostically deep into my eyes, causing Duke, who was waiting for me, to say, "Oh-oh, look who's beating my time." Milt rose and took my arm, ignoring Duke. "I'll dance you over to a bright light—I want to see this." His voice was deep with tenderness which I recognized bitterly as sheer joy in finding a symptom in a desert of pleasure. He smoothly and expertly danced me over under an enormous bright light and began pulling up my eyelids and behaving generally as though we were entirely alone in the ophthalmology room of his office.

"Brother, is this a honey!" he crooned. "Yes sir, wait until Dean sees this one." He turned and scanned the room eagerly. "Stay right here." He hailed Dean from across the room where he had been stalking mournfully around with his wife. He, too, was an eye man—the blessed release of the telephone was not for him either. At the exultant consultation note in Milt's voice, Dean dropped his wife's arm and rushed over. "Just look at this." Dean looked and nodded his head, almost licked his lips. Then they said simultaneously, "Get your coat. We'll meet you in the lobby."

I got my coat and left a message at the table for Jim, then I obediently followed the now happily hatted and coated eye doctors down the stairs of the Club. As I got in Milt's car he warned me not to touch ANYTHING! With a long flowing evening dress and a long evening coat, my bag and my gloves, following this medical advice was impossible. They assured me in unison that I had shipyard eye, otherwise known as Keratoconjunctivitis, that I was frightfully contagious, and they certainly didn't want the damned stuff all over the upholstery of the car. Then they ignored me completely and lapsed into a maze of ten-syllable words, case histories and dandy potentialities offering promise of virus infiltration of the cornea; if I was real lucky, scar tissue permanently affecting vision, and, as a grand prize, one patient whose temperature had reached 104. 'It actually proved to be what amounted to fever therapy—eventually destroyed the virus'. I mustn't get the idea into my head that I was going to be that fortunate. It was a very rare and interesting case—whereas I, well, they didn't know *what* I would do.

I wrapped my coat tighter around me, shivered, and made a furious mental note that I would start by finding something, somewhere, sometime, that would scare the hell out of doctors who scared the hell out of doctors' wives. 'Don't touch anything!' Medical advice that was as serenely impractical as the way they told a mother with three small children to 'go to bed and rest—just let everything go and don't worry!'

My right eye was swollen shut and my left burned hideously. Every time I tried, furtively, to wipe my eyes, both of them screamed, 'Don't touch anything, idiot.' Little blinding white dots jumped around in front of my line of vision and rage blotted out what little I could see. I was considering pressing both of my hands to my eyes and then suddenly wiping my fingers over each of their faces—preliminary virus warfare—when we arrived in front of the Medical Building. With the very tips of their fingers they gingerly helped my shoulder pads out of the car and led me over to the elevator.

'Don't touch anything, Mary', was repeated monotonously as they switched on the lights of the office, went into the ophthalmology room, wiped my sweaty hands off with Lysol and sat me down on the examining chair. Then they prepared to treat me like a doctor's wife.

I try to be resigned to this attitude on the part of Jim's confrères in the profession, but each time I have a medical examination of any kind, I get mad all over again.

One, it is presumed that I am not going to cooperate—this is the normal result of half-knowledge being a dangerous thing—so I am spoken to as though I were a particularly fractious child whose mother has always given him aspirin in a spoon of honey.

Two, nothing is going to be explained to me, or toned down for my nervous mental consumption. I have heard everything possible or medical in my home—so nothing is going to come as a shock to me.

Three, Jim will tell me all the dull details. Jim naturally assumes that I have had intelligence enough to question the doctor, which I have not had, because I am a non-paying patient—so nobody tells me anything.

Four, I should never have any disease of any kind. To do so is to join the herd of neurotic women who clutter up a doctor's office so sick patients haven't a chance to be examined.

Therefore, I did not wince when they put what felt like straight prussic acid in either eye, or complain when their glittering headlights blazed into my tortured eyes like klieg lights. I promised quietly that I would wash everything I touched and not rub my eyes fondly on the babies. I would explain to each and every person with whom it was absolutely necessary to come in contact that I was a twin sister to a dripping leper and not to be socially tolerated.

I would stop being obstinate and come down to the office every single day for treatment, no matter how many bridge parties I had planned to attend—I loathe bridge and never play it—and would not forget to put these drops in my eyes three times a day. If I felt the drops did not contact the cornea, then I was to put them in again. Better yet—have Jim do it, then they would know I had not cheated and thrown the medicine down the toilet. Seething with frustration, rage and pain, I gritted my teeth and promised anything and everything they asked me to. Then they put a pirate bandage over my right eye as a final decoration and told me to sit still.

"You should know that in spite of all the precautions I take, have a special room to put them in so they won't contaminate the other patients, never let them touch anything—do everything I can—one of the nurses got this infection. Man asked her to cash a cheque and she loaned him her pen—not thinking of course. It is the most virulent stuff." Milt remembered me again. "When you get home, go to bed and—"

"I know, go to bed and rest—just let everything go and don't worry." They beamed at my first glimmer of intelligence. With my hands hanging limp and sterile in mid-air, there followed another half-hour of joyful consultation on Keratoconjunctivitis, during which time they told me the rest of the stories they hadn't had an opportunity to scare me with on the way down. The impression I received from the maze of long words was that I'd better apply for a Seeing Eye dog, if I wasn't stoned out of town first for being a wanton infector.

On the way back to the Club, they gave me more instructions. Wash your hands constantly, always put Lysol in the water, remember your comb, your brush, everything you touch is potentially dangerous to everyone else. If the babies got this they would really be in trouble. And Jim would be livid if he got it. Yes, sir, they'd certainly like to know where in hell I picked it up. Although, they grudgingly admitted, it certainly was no respecter of persons.

The minute we got back to the table, they gleefully told everybody within earshot that I had Keratoconjunctivitis, more informally known as shipyard eye, and probably each and every one who had been at the table had it now. They pointed proudly to my pirate bandage as proof of the pudding. I confined myself to asking bitterly where Jim was.

There was an instant roar of laughter. “He’s dancing.” More screams of delighted laughter. “Mary, he’s the funniest thing I have ever seen. You should have been here. We’ve been absolutely rolling on the floor.” My seeing eye opened a quarter of an inch in astonishment. “Go on in and see him—he’s out of this world.”

Dean and Milt finger-tipped me into the room where there was dancing. Jim was leading one of those crack-the-whip dances. My mouth fell open and stayed open like a gasping salmon. He bowed, jumped, ran a few steps—the howling youths followed; he twirled twice, and folding his arms like a bullfighter, stamped six times—they stamped six times. I sucked in my breath and rushed over to him. His eyes were glazed with the pride of creation, his brow covered with beads of perspiration. He ignored me completely.

“Jim!”

“Stamp-stamp-uh-uh-uh.”

“What on earth are you doing—are you tight? And you tell me to go easy on the Zombies!”

He twitched his fanny from side to side, put his arms up over his head and roared, ‘Wo-he-lo’—they camp-fired behind him.

Suddenly the entranced creative look left his face as he noticed the bandage. “Stop shouting. What have you been doing?”

“What have you been doing?”

“Folk dancing, I like it—make it up as I go along. Haven’t had anything to drink.”

His comet tail was screaming for more original dance steps. He paused long enough to eye me balefully. “What are you wearing that bandage for?”

“I’ve been playing with your little chums here—Dean and Milt. I have Keratoconjunctivitis in case you’re interested. Making a spectacle of yourself. Perfectly revolting. I’m going home.”

“Look who’s talking. It certainly depends on whose ox is being gored”, carolled Milt and Dean delightedly.

There were cries of “Don’t go, Jim, you’re wonderful. Take her home and come back”, as we left the dance floor.

“Really, Jim, she’s got a honey. It’s contagious as the devil you know”, Dean said.

I put on my coat and stalked out to the car. Jim was hearing all the lovely lurid details of my potential stone blindness from Dean and Milt, who were very reluctant to let ‘little symptom’ go. They sang out a final 'Don't touch anything', as we drove off.

Jim turned toward me. "I hope you didn't touch anything on the table. That stuff is—"

"I know, hellishly contagious. Of course I didn't touch anything, I merely skidded to a landing, held my hands high in the air, dipped my lips down and sucked in my food. After all, I didn't know I had bubonic plague until after you'd disappeared."

"You don't have to be nasty—I'm just warning you. Don't touch the kids, let Catherine take care of them and you do the work. You know, this wasn't a bad party. I'm glad you made me go." He sang, 'I'll be down to get you in a taxi, honey', and tapped his foot on the gas pedal. "That La Conga, or whatever it is, is fun. Everybody on his own."

He patted my shoulder pad comfortingly. "Never mind, honey, there's a medical meeting in San Francisco next month. I'll take you and you can show your new dress to lots of people. Now don't cry—you'll irritate the cornea. Of course, if the cornea becomes involved and fibrosis follows, there may be varying degrees of blindness."

# 10

## Baby Talk

PAEDIATRICS: *'General Practice with an age limit'*
DR ARTHUR DEAN BEVAN

WE WATCHED THE NEW neighbours move into the house north of us with the usual curiosity and speculation—would they be nice? And more important still, would they have children, so ours would have someone to play with?

They looked interesting—a very pretty dark-haired woman in a soft blue coat with a big fox collar, an attractive young man and then a fat, comfortable looking coloured woman shepherding two little boys. Barrels, boxes and some wonderful old furniture followed next. Their name was Trimbull, the telephone company man said.

About three o'clock, the doorbell rang. I picked Mari and Sally up under either arm and went to answer it.

"I'm Fairfax Trimbull. I declare I hate to bother you, but I just can't find the coffee anywhere in that house." She followed me into the kitchen to get the coffee. "Webster can't do another lick of work without a cup of coffee—what darlin' babies—girls, aren't they?—I just adore girls. Three? My, aren't you fortunate! Webster says he's glad we have boys—but I'd sure like a honey-lamb to dress—wouldn't I, big eyes?" She reached for Mari who cuddled down on her lap. In an accent as Deep South as blackstrap molasses, she continued, "Have we just got a terrible old wreck in that house? I declare I didn't even look at it I was so glad to get some place to live. Web's just out here for six months—but with two little boys we just couldn't live in an apartment."

I reassured her about the house, told her the McNairs wouldn't have leased it had they not been moved to Chicago. She fastened her enormous blue eyes on me as I talked, said, "I declare you're so smart—how do you know those things?—Web and Winky would adore to baby-tend for you—they just love babies—any time you want to borrow Athlene let me know—she is a good cook—thanks for the coffee", and left.

One of the important things I had learned since I'd had the children, was the comfort of knowing my neighbours. Even Mrs Dunny, in her odd fashion, meant to be kind and she certainly was a blessing when I wanted to run up to the store and leave the children for a few moments. She and Grandpa had an armed truce—they each peered in the kitchen window to see if the other was there, and then, if the coast was clear, came in and took over. I decided to go and ask the new neighbours if they wouldn't like to have a cocktail before dinner.

Mrs Trimbull opened the door. "Hello, come on in and sit down. You know I was just wonderin' if it wouldn't be best just to burn this whole thing down and go back to Louisiana. I declare I never saw such a mess."

"Come on over and have a cocktail. Moving is always a nightmare", I said.

She beamed. "I declare that's sweet of you." She called Webster, who was in the living room. "Honey where are you?—this sweet Mary Jay has asked us over for cocktails. My grandmother's name was Mary—I'm Fairy—baby for Fairfax—and this is Webster."

Web shook my hand heartily. "It certainly is nice of you to be so friendly." As he spoke I realized that he had been making this moving day a little less ghastly by having a wee nip now and then. I smiled understandingly. Even if he were completely comatose which he was not—just weaving—it wouldn't mitigate the nightmare of boxes, bales and barrels in the hall, the living-room, on the front porch, and probably all over the upstairs.

"Come just as you are and bring the children. We can give them a cookie and a glass of milk—or some supper with mine if you like", I said.

"Oh thank you", Fairy said. "The children will probably be in bed—they're worn out. Athlene will take care of them."

The banging in the kitchen, which had punctuated our conversation, was obviously created by Athlene, who came in just at that moment to say, "Better get those chillun out from under my feet—one of 'em just poured salad oil in the clothes basket."

Fairy and Web arrived about six o'clock, clean and shining. She said, "Don't look at me, I'm pig dirty and Athlene couldn't find me a thing in all that mess but this horrible old rag." The horrible old rag was a very smart blue wool dress, the exact colour of her eyes. As she sat on a footstool in front of the fire, her delicate features and misty black hair outlined by the firelight, I found that I was glad that Jim wasn't home yet. My reciprocal neighbourliness hadn't included a neighbour with delphinium blue eyes as big as saucers, fringed with half-inch black lashes. I'd had in mind more of a dowdy woman who was worse at housekeeping than I was and who needed lots of advice.

"Web, honey, you help Mary make the drinks. You do make the most marvellous drinks. I declare if Web ever gets out of a job, he'd make the most marvellous bar-tender." She continued, in her soft, flattering, Southern voice, to tell me the house was lovely, the flowers perfectly wonderful, that I had the most beautiful children she'd ever seen and she could hardly wait to meet Jim. She wanted him to tell her just what doctors to go to for everything. She simply couldn't believe that she'd been lucky enough to find a house right next door to such charming people, and a doctor!

Web brought in the old-fashioneds, drank his in one gulp, murmured, "Mind if I have another?" and disappeared back into the kitchen.

When Jim came in I introduced him to the Trimbulls and said, "You'd better take a good look at him now. He's a doctor and this may be the last time you see him for some time. He's almost like an eclipse, I see him so seldom."

Jim said, "To be strictly accurate, I'm home most of the time", and smiled at Fairy. Her accent promptly deepened thirty degrees as she said, "I sure hope I get real sick with something you can take care of."

Web said, "May I make you a drink, Doctor? Mind if I have another?" and he and Jim went out in the kitchen.

When they came back, Fairy raised her drink to Jim and said, "To the only doctor I've ever seen who is both good-lookin' and smart." She continued in an accent that was almost a foreign tongue—my mother her name was Mary too—isn't that a co-incidence?—thought they were so brave to come out West—just full of Yankees—both she and Web had lived in Louisiana for four generations—but we were so friendly and all and imagine having a doctor right next door—wasn't that marvellous?—she was going right home and call her mother and tell her they were as safe as they would be down South.

Web rose unsteadily, said, "Mind if I have another?" and wove toward the kitchen. Jim followed him.

"I particularly want to know the name of a baby doctor, because we have nothin' but trouble with little Web. He has colds all year long—just fadin' away before our very eyes. The doctor back home was real sweet but he didn't know a thing about doctorin'. What's your baby doctor's name?"

Dick Martin was my paediatrician—the most marvellous and charming man she had ever seen—adored babies—had six of his own—would be able to make little Web like Charles Atlas in two weeks. The ethical red light flashed on in my mind, 'Never recommend a doctor—always give a list of at least five!' I brushed it aside. Jim meant strangers or patients on the telephone—not neighbours.

Fairy rose as Web and Jim came back into the room. "Honey pie, drink your drink and we must go. Athlene'll be black thunder if we're late for dinner."

Jim said, "If we can help you at any time, let us know. See you later", and closed the door.

I turned on him promptly. "Why weren't you more enthusiastic? They're darling, and so lonely. It's hard for Southerners to live up here with all these Yankees"

"I'm tired of Southerners who talk like they were marooned with head hunters in the Philippines whenever they get north of the Mason Dixon line. Also 'Mind if I have another?' was so lonely that he drank my last quart of bourbon. Is there anything to eat? I have to go to a dinner meeting."

The Neglected Ones were meeting at my house. The beds upstairs were lined with sleeping babies. We had finished our lunch and were about to get organized. We put the sewing machine up in one corner of the room to take care of the long rents and tears, divided all the mending according to each one's special ability, and prepared to dissect the doctors' wives who were not members of the group. It was sometimes difficult to hear all of the details over the whir of the sewing machine, so we took turns at that job. My contribution was

Fairy Trimbull. She was an absolute lamb—quite unnecessarily pretty—was so pathetically grateful to be living next door to a doctor—I'd just thrown caution to the winds and told her to go to Dick Martin. That list-of-five stuff was so coldly impersonal—her accent was wonderful. "You've met her, Maggie—isn't she darling?"

Maggie said, "Uh-uh. Southern like a crocodile. You look out for that one, honey."

Then I told them about 'Mind if I have another?' and that Fairy had said she wouldn't have a doctor in the house if she smelled liquor on his breath. Of all the unreasonable—ridiculous—insane things—here Webster absorbed liquor like a sponge—Fairy didn't seem to mind, said all Southern men drank like that—but had a mania about any doctor ever taking a drink.

Faith said, "Oh, Tod hears that all the time—particularly from the dypsos. They scream to high heaven every time they hear a doctor has a glass of beer. It's amazing, but it's true."

I went upstairs to see if the rows of babies were still sleeping, and came back to hear, 'I can't go to that meeting—they're older and have maids—getting a divorce so she can marry another doctor talk about out of the frying pan—nurse told him it was a normal uterus and she wouldn't stand there and let him operate, imagine old stinky taking that one on the chin made about seven hundred house calls on those devils, they've never paid him a cent, say the most awful things about him and, now, they're paying a chiropractor ten dollars cash a treatment.' Familiar and fairly harmless—no names—no hospitals—no doctors. It took the flavour out of the gossip—but it took most of the danger out too.

At three o'clock there was a cry from upstairs—then, like the descending notes on a xylophone, a series of cries. The babies were awake and the meeting was over.

For one who was so pitifully lonely, Fairy had an active social life. She had discovered a large number of other marooned Southerners, and spent all day, every day, 'visitin''. Web and Winky, the two little boys, got up in the morning, had breakfast and, like Mother, dedicated the rest of their day to social calls. Winky's birdlike appetite, about which we heard constantly, was obviously engendered by his consumption of cookies. 'Mind if I have another?' was an inherited trait.

Right after breakfast there would be a knock at the door. Web and Winky would flip off their caps, bow from the waist and say, "Good mornin', ma'am. We just came for a little visit. Now don't let us in if we're going to bother you." It was almost impossible not to be cordial to such Chesterfieldian manners, and I always let them in. They would be meticulously polite for a few moments, ask about our health, about the babies, about the Doctor, and then—as they were normal little boys—all hell would break loose and they would proceed to tear the house to pieces.

About nine o'clock, after they'd finished the contents of the cookie jar, and I had stood all I could bear they would prepare to leave. Their leave-taking was as formal as their arrival. They would hold their caps in their hands, bow from the waist, send their regards to the doctor, hope I had a pleasant day, hope the babies had a pleasant nap, and leave. Then they would go across to the house on the south side of us, where you could see them ringing the doorbell, caps in hand. Fairy wasn't sending them to school—she didn't want them to talk like Yankees.

Fairy's daily gossip over a cup of tea was almost as cheering as the good old days with Maggie. She'd rush in about five o'clock, tell me what Sue Ellen had said about her husband, what Mrs Turner's new house looked like, what the Smiths paid their maid, borrow some sugar or an egg for Athlene. "I declare I forgot to order the groceries this mornin'—you Yankees are so efficient—I do envy you." and dash home to get dressed for dinner.

One morning while Athlene was in the kitchen borrowing some vanilla—"I'm goin' to make those chillun some sugar cookies, so they'll stay home where they belong"—I had Mari and Sally in their highchairs, each chewing a raw carrot. Sally choked. I held her hands over her head and patted her on the back, but I couldn't dislodge the piece of carrot. Athlene jerked her out of the high-chair, held her by the ankles and began to shake her—with hard, stiff shakes. She said, "You go call the Doctor, Mrs Jay. This here's in her windpipe—I know—I've seen lots of 'em. Then you get Miss Fairy to hold her and you drive down to the Doctor as fast as you can. This baby's turning blue." Sally's eyes rolled back in her head; she was making a terrifying gurgling sound and the shaking was doing no good. I called Jim's office. He was making rounds which meant that he might be at any of six hospitals. I called Dick Martin's office. He was making rounds, but the nurse said he was supposed to be at County. I called County, found Jim there, and asked him what to do. Athlene continued to shake Sally, but she was moaning. "She can't get no breath—that's why she's blue—she can't get no breath." Jim said, "You've got the car, drive down here. Get someone to hold Sally. I'll meet you. Drive fast, honey, time is important." Athlene held Sally and I went over to get Fairy. Athlene called after me, "Take your time, honey. I'll mind the children while you're gone."

"Thank God for neighbours", I thought as we got in the car. Fairy held a limp and frightening blue Sally for me—and I drove to the hospital, just as fast as I could make the car go—through arterials, down hills, through red lights—my hand on the horn. Numb with terror, I was vaguely conscious of Fairy's 'She'll be all right, honey—I know she will—babies choke all the time at home—and they always get it down—she'll be all right, honey." I didn't look at Sally—I didn't dare.

As we pulled up in front of County Hospital, I glanced at her for the first time since I'd put her in Fairy's lap. She was pink and white and breathing normally. Then I looked at the result of my frantic telephone calls—lined up on the hospital steps. Jim—pale and intent; Pete, ready to stand by in case I collapsed; the throat specialist with the bronchoscope; Dick Martin the paediatrician; the anaesthetist; the head surgical nurse—and ten or so other nurses to take care of further emergencies.

Jim came down to the car, picked Sally up and said, "She seems to have swallowed whatever it was. You made a fast trip, didn't you? Good work." Then he turned to the mass of medical care on the steps. "False alarm—baby's all right." They turned, matter-of-factly, and walked back into the hospital.

"Well, you do get service, don't you?" Fairy said, utterly enchanted. "I never saw so many doctors and nurses in all my life."

"Probably the last time I'll see any of them", I said, as I turned the car around and started home.

That afternoon Fairy brought her sewing over. She'd taken Little Web down to Dick Martin. It wasn't that she didn't like Doctor Dick, but he was so cold and impersonal. You could tell by just lookin' at Little Web that he wasn't strong—but imagine glancin' at him and sayin' he looked perfectly normal. And another thing, I knew how she worked over that child to make him eat—he just wouldn't touch anything but steak and artichokes and maybe a little puddin'. Dr Martin said that from now on he was to have more vegetables and fruit, and otherwise—just what the family was eatin'. Oh he was probably a good doctor—she wouldn't say he wasn't—but he wasn't like home folks and he had so many babies in there she really didn't think he had time to give each one special attention. Didn't I know any other baby doctors?

She took a few thoughtful stitches on the quilted satin bed jacket she was making. "Web likes me to have breakfast in bed—it makes stars in my eyes."

I asked her how Web was getting along in this branch of the office.

"I declare, you just don't realize how lucky you are to be married to a doctor. Web's just no good when anything goes wrong. Drinkin' the way he does, he's just no good most of the time."

I recognized one of those traps that women so often set for one another, and I was determined to avoid it. If I said, 'It does seem a shame that Web drinks so much', then—when she made up with Web, which she would inevitably do—I would be the old devil who called him a dypsomaniac. If I said, 'Why Fairy, he does not', she would be crushed and think I was an unsympathetic prig.

"Being married to a doctor isn't all beer and skittles, believe me. Jim is just a half-wit when there is anything the matter with the children. You saw him this morning. He thinks the sniffles is the precursor of polio; the slightest cough is pneumonia, and a temperature of one degree is meningitis", I said.

Fairy laughed. "Oh Mary, the way you talk. I think he's just wonderful." I told her not to get me wrong—I thought Jim was brilliant—had practically no flaws that I could think of at the moment—but he was so crazy about the children he was extremely apprehensive when they were sick. It was difficult to be a doctor when your children were sick anyway—there were so many awful things that a common cold, for instance, might be the forerunner of—like polio, or scarlet fever, or diphtheria. I imagined that was one time when any doctor wished to God he couldn't tell a symptom from rigor mortis.

Fairy looked thoughtfully into the fire. "Jim doesn't seem to drink much. Does he ever get tiddley?"

"No, it isn't a moral complex or anything. It's just that alcohol doesn't agree with him particularly and then, too, being a doctor he never knows when he's going to have to make a call", I said.

"I'm certainly glad of that. You know what Web says, if a doctor ever comes in our house with liquor on his breath, he'll just show him the door."

I swallowed 'look who's talking' with great difficulty, and said that Jim limited himself to one cocktail before dinner, and that only occasionally, and I'd observed that most doctors stuck pretty close to that rule of necessity. Then added, "They see so much of the befuddling effects of alcoholism—and are aware of the fact that it eventually destroys the frontal lobes. I suppose that fact colours their attitude."

She nodded and looked pensive. "Well, I declare, Web just drinks all the time. It worries me to death. He never gets drunk—of course all Trimbulls can hold their liquor like gentlemen—but honestly the things he says to me when he's been drinkin'—they'd just tear your heart. Why last night—"

Determined to get out of this confessional, I interrupted her, "Well, he's certainly crazy about you, Fairy, for which I frankly can't blame him."

"He ought to be, I certainly kept him guessin' a long time. Oh, I always planned to marry him—ever since I was a little girl—but some of my beaux sure felt dreadful when I got married." She lowered her voice and widened her eyes. "Do you know—one boy drowned himself in the lake and another boy shot himself? I didn't dare tell a soul, but I'd refused both those boys." She rose and lit a cigarette. "Don't you get awful lonesome when Jim is out so much at night?"

I said something about of course I did, that I'd rather he didn't go to so many meetings—if I had my way I'd have him handcuffed to my wrist—but that was part of the profession—that and answering the telephone twenty-four hours a day.

Right on cue, the phone rang and I told an importunate female voice that if Jim wasn't at the office, he was probably making calls on his way home. Yes, I'd have him call—no, I wouldn't forget—yes, I'd reach him if I could. Fairy listened with wide contemplative eyes. I put down the phone and said I did wish that bore would fasten herself to some other doctor.

"What about Jim's women patients? They're all just crazy about him—I know they are—I should think you'd be worried half to death—I know I'd be."

"Well, the thought never occurs to me with Jim. In the first place, they'd have to be banging on bells to make him notice anything but the disease, and in the second place, if I were a doctor and heard women whine about themselves all day, I'd seek consolation if consolation were necessary—in some woman I'd never seen professionally. And then—there is also the little question of ethics in case all else fails", I added acidly.

"Of course everybody can see that he's just wild about you", Fairy said disinterestedly, "but there was a friend of mother's at home, a doctor's wife, and I tell you she just had the most tragic life. Her husband was in love with patients all the time and she sat home all by herself just bein' fooled like crazy."

I was going to get off this doctor-as-a-husband subject if I had to rave about what a bang-up job Abraham Lincoln did in the Civil War. "Are you going to the Parkers' tea, Fairy?" Whether to go or not to go, had been the theme of her conversation for a week—the Parkers were kinfolk and hadn't bothered to call.

"They still haven't called on us, but Web says bein' out here so long has made them forget their manners. He's fussin' at me to go." She wandered over toward the door. "I got a new dress—Web will probably beat me if he finds out, providin' he hasn't had so much to drink he doesn't even notice. Well, honey, I've got to fly, Athlene's gettin' grumpy again. She belongs to me just as much as I belong to her—I've had her ever since I was a little girl—but she hates it out here and wants to go home. I told her if I could stand bein' so far away she could, and to just stop talkin' about home."

She sounded homesick and looked forlorn as she said, "Don't you ever get mad at Jim, Mary?"

"Of course I do. I get so mad I wonder how I ever got engaged, let alone married—and spend hours figuring over my secret bills to see if I can work out enough to pay for a divorce."

She laughed. "Well, you're sure darlin'. 'Bye, sweetie, I must run."

The Neglected Ones were hemming diapers for Children's Hospital and doing a little private surgery on a new doctor's wife they'd met at the Parkers' tea. She was pretty, in a kind of a glossy way—but she was so old—must be thirty-five anyway—and her husband was in Tod's class at medical school. Rich, probably.

Faith looked up and said, "Say which one of the morons in our crowd is getting a divorce?"

"We all would if we could catch our husbands long enough and didn't have to take so darned many babies to court with us—why?" Maggie said. There was a bubble of contented laughter.

"No", Faith continued, "I'm deadly serious. I sat next to a pretty, dark woman yesterday at the Parkers and she was telling me all about some doctor and his wife who lived next door to her and the wife was getting a divorce for cruelty."

Maggie looked up. "I'll bet she had curly hair and a sort of a soft blue coat with a big fox collar, didn't she?"

"Yes—that was the one—did she tell you?" Faith asked.

My heart dropped with a thud.

"Uh-uh—she always gives me the triple brush-off. Professional Southerner—I know millions like her at home."

"I tell you, I was ready to slap her face." Faith reached for another diaper. Barbara Martin looked up. "Tell us the gore. I couldn't go—I had to wash."

"It seems that this poor little doctor's wife was alone all the time at night—" There were cries of 'Oh, the poor kid, how did she stand it?' and 'Good, she had enough money to pay her grocery bill then, what was she screaming about?'

"But just you listen", Faith persisted, "she said the whole neighbourhood knew that he was going out with his women patients. They called all day and all night. There were three little children, one of them was sick all the time, and the doctor either wasn't interested or didn't have the faintest idea what to do. The poor little wife had a burning desire to go to luncheons and have fun but he gave her so little money that it took every cent she could save and hoard to pay her bills and she was behind all the time."

There were shrieks of 'Who isn't? Who does she think she is?'

Barbara said, "So far, Faith, it sounds like a slightly garbled version of any of your Monday morning telephone calls after a gruelling Sunday with doctor and the little ones."

Faith laughed. "Remember, she wasn't a Neglected One—she was a lay wife. But wait until you hear the reason why she thinks the doctor's wife is getting the divorce—he can't eat his dinner without taking a cocktail and it's getting so his patients notice it."

Barbara said, "Oh-oh-that's bad. What addle-pated doctor's wife would unburden her soul to a sieve brain like that?"

Maggie walked over and put her arm around me. "I would, for one. Anybody might. Sweet talk—that old sweet talk—and from a plenty sour grapevine. I get my feet stuck in that old sweet talk almost every day and the first thing I know I'm up to my neck and tellin' everything I don't want anybody to know—let alone old sweet talker."

She hugged me and muttered, "That ole crocodile!"

"What do you think, Mary?" Barbara asked.

I put down the diaper I was clutching. "Personally, I think that doctor will be really lucky the day his wife gets her pitiful little savings collected and runs down to the divorce proctor. I think I hear the babies—I'll go."

# 11

## Sun Spots

ACTINIC DERMATITIS: *Inflammation of the skin produced by exposure to the sun's rays.*

EDITH STOKES leaned forward over the speaker's table, her voice was vibrant with emotion as she concluded, "You have no idea what it means to those diabetic children to get out on the beach. For the first time in their lives, they have exactly the same restrictions as the other children with whom they are living. They arrive at Camp, white and thin and apologetic—and go back to the city, brown and fat and confident. No amount of effort is too great to achieve that, I can tell you." She sat down and waited serenely for the onslaught of volunteers, all panting to throw themselves on the altar of her latest plan—a city-wide campaign to raise funds for the Diabetic Camp for Children.

Maggie muttered. "Wouldn't you know doctors' wives would be killin' themselves raisin' money to get other people's children to the beach when their own poor little tykes never set foot outside the city." She picked up her purse. "Let's get out of here before Edith remembers I was a technician and grabs me."

The Stokes have no children of their own and Edith employs her sublimated maternal instinct in doing really wonderful work for unfortunate children. The Diabetic Camp, for instance, ran almost solely because Edith saw to it that the appropriations were large enough, the grants had no strings attached to them, and that the staff was well paid and well housed. Most important, she went up to her cabin in the summer and kept an eagle eye on the Camp. I was still a little afraid of her uncompromising efficiency—but my admiration for her as an executive was rapidly overcoming my original, childish dislike of her as a person.

Edith remembered that I had done publicity before I was

married. She dropped in that afternoon to notify me that I was to be publicity chairman for her campaign. She took out her little black book. "You'll have to go up there, of course, to get material for feature stories."

"I can't get away, Edith. I haven't anyone to leave the children with."

"Take them with you." She checked my name on the list. "I am attending a diabetic conference in California for the month of August and our cabin will be unoccupied. You will get a rest—there's absolutely nothing to do but rest—and you have no idea what it will mean to the children. You won't recognize them after one week of sun, salt air and an opportunity to run free."

"But our children are so little, Edith."

"Have you any conception of the figures on incipient rickets from paediatric records? Avitaminosis—due to lack of sunshine principally." She noted my swelling nostrils at her inference that no ray of sunlight ever penetrated our children's slum conditions, and promptly switched to a masterful description of the beach. Long sweeps of white sand, great piles of driftwood, beautiful sunsets and no telephone. My eyes lit up. "There's a telephone at the Camp and at the village in case of an emergency. It's a strain to be a doctor's wife, as you well know, and in our cabin I refuse to have a telephone. It's primitive, but I know you'll enjoy it." She rose.

"I'll have to ask Jim."

Edith smiled. "Jim will appreciate an uninterrupted opportunity to write that paper for *North-west Medicine*." She patted me. "A separate vacation is good for a husband and wife. Ed and I found that out years ago. Jim can go up on week-ends, wonderful salmon fishing you know." She left.

I took the children out in the yard. It *was* an awfully small yard. Grandpa had made them a little canvas pool and I sat on the steps and watched them as they fought and splashed in the sun-warmed water. *Poor* little *things!* Just think how they would enjoy unlimited stretches of salt water. Did lack of sunshine make them seem whiter than most children, or was it just because they were so blonde? Heidi sat fatly in the pool and gasped as Sally poured water over her head. I rescued her and wondered if she was making no attempt to walk at ten months because she was so heavy or did she have weak legs from incipient rickets? Grandpa came around the corner of the house and I asked him if he didn't think the children would adore to spend the month of August at the beach.

"That depends", Grandpa said. "Most children prefer to do the same thing every day. Change makes them rambunctious."

Jim called and said he wouldn't be home for dinner—he was going to grab a bite and stay at the office so he could work on his article for *North-west Medicine*.

When he came home he went straight to the kitchen and I followed him around telling him what Edith Stokes had said. "Funny she'd ask you to handle the publicity—I should think she'd use a regular agency for a thing like that."

I told him icily that an agency knew absolutely nothing about diabetes and he seemed to forget that I'd been rather competent before I was married. He drank a glass of milk and looked thoughtfully at me. "Don't you think the children are a little young?" I told him in a throaty voice that the most cherished memories I retained of my father were those of the camping trips we had as children. Daddy and Mother took us on prospecting trips before we could walk. That was the only reason we were so healthy to-day. Jim pointed out that Daddy was with us and that, although there was nothing he would enjoy more than taking his family to the beach, he couldn't get away in August.

I retorted that after all Grandpa would be there. "What would you do about the washing, for instance?" Pioneer women had managed and so could I.

By the time Jim finally weakened, I was so hearty I could have crossed the Olympic Mountains alone with nothing but a knife in my teeth and the children strapped to my back.

The night before we left, as the pile of absolutely essential equipment grew in the front hall, I wondered how we would ever get that much stuff up to camp in anything less than a series of coal barges. Jim, grudgingly helping me, added two fur-lined parkas, four trolling rods, two casting rods and two large boxes of fishing tackle. Three cribs, high-chairs, a pen, a toidey-chair, six suitcases, four cases of canned baby food, two cases of canned milk—Jim didn't want the children to have fresh milk, too much danger of undulant fever from unpasteurized milk.

From the kitchen he brought six cans of salmon and twelve cans of shad roe, said, "Just in case we don't catch any fish", and surveyed the pile.

"Where's your medicine kit?"

I pointed to a small Red Cross First-Aid box, lying beside a mountain of diapers. He opened it and looked in. "Inadequate." He went upstairs again.

He came down carrying a large green tin box in which were gentian violet, novocain ampoules, three types of burn salve—adding that of course they were useless—surgical needles, gut and scissors, sterile pads—several sizes—bandages, adhesive tape, antiseptics—'no damned good of course'—several phials of amyl nitrite, Seconal, phenobarbital, Nembutal, a phial containing one-half grain codeine tablets, cough syrup and Mentholatum. I brightened at the last two items, told him I was relieved to note two things I'd dare use without a medical licence, and asked why we had to take enough medical equipment for three years at the North Pole when the Diabetic Camp was so near. He said, "Never can tell what will happen", and added a few tubes containing sterile sutures, out of his breast pocket.

By this time the front door was entirely blocked and to get upstairs we had to take a flying leap from the living-room door. He surveyed the equipment again and frowned. "You've all had booster shots—tetanus, etc haven't you?"

"Um-hum—the children had them about a month ago. I guess I've had them."

He rummaged around upstairs for a while, and then went out to the kitchen. I went on checking my list against the mounds of bare necessities. For the first time it occurred to me to wonder if other people enjoyed leaving a comfortable home and a pleasant familiar routine to torment themselves with all the trouble of a vacation. A whole month. I'd miss Jim like the devil.

He came back in the hall, grabbed my arm and gave me a shot. "Tetanus, just to be sure. Your arm may be sore for a couple of days, but it won't last."

By one o'clock in the morning I wasn't so sure I'd miss Jim. He had just added three large bound volumes of the *Archives of Internal Medicine*, saying that he'd have to have something to read on weekends, and added casually that now I'd better separate the pile into two heaps, one which had to be taken in the car with us, and one for the van to take.

Then he began to pick up each item and say, "Why are you taking this?"

By two-thirty we weren't speaking and the living room contained the pile that had to go in the van. If it had been possible to dehydrate and compress it, it would have filled a freight car. The hall and half the stairway were piled with what Jim considered had to go in the car. At my bitter remark that it was too bad we couldn't get a little old surgery cart in there—Jim said that we could always come back home if major surgery was necessary, that I must be getting tired, and how about a cheese omelette? He'd fix it while I got undressed and bring it up to me.

I'd miss Jim at two-thirty in the morning when I was hungry.

As we lugged the stuff out to the car, my heart bled for the wives of the various nomadic tribes, the Pilgrim mothers and all the other unsung heroines of history. They were probably just as confused as I was, but they had to go on treks. I was just doing it for fun, and because Edith Stokes had implied that my children were little, white, rickety grubs.

At that moment the sun was beaming down on the back yard. Grandpa was sitting in the lawn swing, surrounded by comfortable babies, the deodar spread its cool green arms over the lawn table and chairs, and frankly, I couldn't imagine a more delightful place to spend the month of August.

Jim said, "Edith's drinking water comes from a spring up there, doesn't it?" I nodded. "Don't let the children have any without boiling it. I'll bring some down and have it tested when I come home."

Grandpa and Jim got in the front seat of the car with Mari and Sally, and I wedged myself in between two heaps of luggage. Jim put Heidi on my lap, said, "Look out for that highchair, it might topple over and hit Heidi", and we were off.

As we drove along the shore, the melodic thread of shrouded white mountains, grey-blue water and the continuous accompaniment of green trees was soothing. Islands, in varying shapes and colours, broke the long line of the horizon. Great grey freighters, fat white ferry boats, long brown log booms and winged sailboats were dotted here and there on the water. Overhead wound the opalescent mist.

The road took a sharp turn and plunged down a steep hill. Here the lush growth of cedar and fir stopped abruptly, and scrub pines and madrona trees, the ground swept clean and sandy beneath them, twisted and leaned in an agony produced by the winter wind and blowing sand. As we came out on to the long white beach, there was a signpost which read, 'Hainesville' to the south, and 'Lighthouse' to the north. The salt sand beach was shaped like a long sickle. The southern, or pointed end, sheltered Hainesville, a group of small buildings which had once been barn-red but were now faded by the salt spray to a soft rose colour. Along the four-mile curve of beach were great piles of grey driftwood, a few summer cottages and an occasional pine or madrona tree. A huge greyed-blue sign, on a squat building to the north of us, said, 'Diabetic Camp'. On either side of it were about a dozen cottages in a stiff row like children's blocks.

The northern end of the sickle blade was an ominous pile of jagged black rocks on which perched the Coast Guard lighthouse, white and neat. Its red-roofed auxiliary buildings sat in prim little rows in an apple-green meadow, enclosed by a white picket fence. Behind the meadow rose the cliff, the sickle's handle, sheer and black, the fir trees bending dangerously near the edge to watch the lighthouse.

The angle of the lighthouse and cliff was so abrupt here that a big lumber freighter seemed to be taking a short cut, right across the meadow, to the sparkling blue channel in front of us.

We took the lighthouse turn and stopped before a log cabin nestled beneath the hill in a ragged half circle of scrub pine.

Grandpa said, "This reminds me of the coast of Norway. Each vista greatly enlarged of course." His eyes lit up at the piles of driftwood. "I wonder if they have a crosscut saw. It would be nice to leave the Stokeses some firewood." I tried to remember whether or not I had included the little phials of amyl nitrite for Grandpa's coronary and eyed the distance to the Diabetic Camp and the telephone.

Jim said, "I put the amyl nitrite in the medicine kit", and started up the long walk toward the cabin door. Across the dark blue channel, the long green arms of the islands leaned against purple foothills, which rose to the aloof white Olympic Mountains.

Jim took the flushed, sleeping babies, one by one, carried them into the cabin and put them in a row on the bed. I looked at the view and exulted in the thought of thirty days without a telephone, nothing to do but take the children down to the beach, and go fishing with Jim on weekends.

The cabin was log on the outside and panelled pine on the inside. There was a long living room with a huge stone fireplace. Windows to the floor, on either side of the fireplace, showed the full sweep of the mountains and the Sound. Draped over the windows were fish nets tied here and there with Japanese glass floats like aquamarine balloons. The furniture was made entirely of driftwood, with bright cushions. The only colours in the room were the soft blue of the water, the yellow of the pine, and driftwood grey.

Three small bedrooms and a kitchen were across the back of the house. The bathroom was about fifty feet from the back of the house in a grove of trees. It contained a modern toilet and large black spiders. I was glad I'd brought the toidey-chair.

Jim made a drink, said he hadn't noticed any laundry trays and was I planning to wash the diddies in the little soup bowl of a kitchen sink? I basked in the view and said it didn't make any difference where I washed them, the sun and wind would bleach them as white as snow.

Jim offered to help me unpack. I assured him that it wasn't necessary, we'd just have dinner in front of the fire, go to bed and listen to the wind through the trees—then he and Grandpa could get up early and go fishing.

Grandpa and Jim were up before dawn, their hurried preparations accompanied by loud bangs and bumps and, 'Sh-sh-sh, you'll wake the children.'

The tide went out almost half a mile over the beach, leaving small warm pools of water. The children, naked and delirious with joy, rolled in the pools and ran along the sand bars. They ate hugely, slept all afternoon and awakened to demand that they be taken to the beach to watch Grandpa and Jim in the boat. At dinner they grabbed at their food with the abandon of hungry puppies. I bathed them and put them to bed, where they lay, their flushed faces ringed with tendrils of damp hair, their arms thrown back and their fingers curled, in the complete sleep of happy exhaustion. Jim and Grandpa came in about seven o'clock proudly bearing six gleaming silver salmon.

Grilled salmon in front of a roaring fire. No patients, no telephone—it was wonderful.

Sunday afternoon, Mari was running up and down the heavy plank walk to the bathroom when she slipped and ran a two-inch splinter in her foot. It was a jagged splinter, of old wood, and my feeble attempts to remove it merely broke off little pieces of wood and made me sick at my stomach. I ran down to the edge of the beach and hailed Jim and Grandpa. Then I opened the medicine kit, put some water on to boil and blessed Jim's forethought in bringing novocain, a scalpel, needles and surgical gut. Grandpa held Mari while Jim removed the splinter and bandaged her foot.

"You're sure she's had her tetanus booster shots?" Jim asked again. I told him that Dick had given them all booster shots. I had not asked what the shots were for, but I assumed tetanus was included. Jim said he'd call me Tuesday night about eight o'clock, at the store in Hainesville, to see that Mari's foot was all right. He wasn't worried, but it would be easier for him to reach me than for me to try to locate him.

As Jim drove away to go back to town, I suddenly felt as forlorn as though he were going away to war. I turned and asked Grandpa if he didn't think Jim was a remarkable person. What if he hadn't been there when Mari ran that splinter in her foot? And what if he'd paid any attention to me when I was teasing him about the medicine kit?

Grandpa patted my back, said, "Good is a good doctor, but Bad is sometimes a better", and left me to think that one over while he went to saw wood.

Grandpa had remained neutral about the vacation except to say mildly that his footing wasn't as sure as it used to be and I'd have to carry the children on uneven ground. Now, Mari would have to be carried as well as Sally and Heidi. Jim had said the salt water wouldn't hurt her, but to see that she didn't bruise her foot.

Tuesday evening, I was rushing through the supper dishes, in order to get the children in bed and have time to walk to the village and get Jim's call. Mari came running in the kitchen with a box in her hand, said Sally had eaten some of it and it was nasty. I looked at the label on the box. It said, 'RAT POISON. KEEP AWAY FROM DOMESTIC ANIMALS AND CHILDREN!' Then the death's head. Then—'Emetic: Avoid all oils. Use emetic of mustard or copper sulphate—3 grains every five minutes until vomiting occurs. Chemical emetic: copper sulphate and potassium permanganate.' The rest of the label was torn off!

Sally was spitting and wiping her mouth and whimpering. I washed her mouth out with cold water. I didn't dare use soap because of the fat content, put her on the bed, called Grandpa and told him to watch the children and rushed down to the village—the box clutched in my hand.

I got to the general store just as Jim's call came in, told him Sally had eaten some rat poison and where in God's name could I get copper sulphate. He asked me to read all of the label to him—slowly and carefully. As I read each frightening statement, I became more terrified.

Jim said, "Listen, Mary, I doubt if she ate any of it. It probably burned her mouth and she spit it out. But just in case, get some dry mustard from the store, mix it with warm water, keep giving it to her until she throws up, and then put her to bed and call me back."

"Should I watch for any symptoms?" I asked.

"With serious poisoning, vomiting, abdominal pain and diarrhoea occur usually in less than an hour. If she shows any of these symptoms, call me back. I can get there in two hours. Call me back later anyway—I'm at home." I got the dry mustard and ran back up the beach. Sally was sleeping peacefully in Grandpa's arms, Mari dozed at his feet, and Heidi was lying on the couch asleep.

I awakened Sally, forced her to drink the burning mustard and warm water, and keep drinking it. She vomited after the first half-cup, and obediently finished the next half-cup. We continued this process until she had finished six half-cups of mustard and water. I probably would have continued until she'd thrown up her toe nails if Grandpa hadn't intervened. "Daughter," he said sternly, "put that baby to bed. She didn't swallow any of the rat poison. I asked Mari what happened and she said they both tasted it and spit it out." He handed me a cup of one-half whisky and one-half coffee. "Drink this, and then put the children to bed."

I drank the violent pick-me-up, which didn't seem to faze Grandpa although it made me feel like the top of my head was coming off, put the children to bed and walked back down the beach to call Jim. As I walked through the soft, starlit night, I mused on how much I had changed. In six years, which had moved as swiftly as the speed of light, I had come to depend so much on Jim and on medicine that I was terrified to be a driving distance of two hours away from home. I wondered how Mother had felt while she, in some remote mining village, handled any and all emergencies, without a telephone, without Daddy and without any doctor.

I remembered the time my brother Cleve and Betty and I had climbed on a wiggly camp stool to get some peanut brittle. Cleve had slipped and fallen, breaking his arm at the elbow; it must have been a comminuted fracture and yet Mother gave Cleve some brandy to alleviate the pain, left us with Gammy and drove sixty miles to Butte to have his arm set. Mother's stern New England blood was crossed with Southern clinging vine in me and I wanted Jim.

Just as I got to the crossroads a car stopped beside me and Jim's voice said, "Want a ride?" I've never heard such a heavenly sound.

I told him that Sally had been sleeping peacefully until I poured mustard and hot water down her, that she was again sleeping peacefully and he would never know how wonderful it was to see him.

He said, "I'll run in and look at her and then I have to go back. I have a patient in the hospital I don't dare leave." I moaned that I couldn't stand it without him. He laughed. "Do you good, then you'll appreciate me. I'll be down Saturday night."

He checked Sally, who seemed to thrive on rat poison, had a cup of coffee and went back to the car. "I'll call at eight o'clock again Friday night to see if you need anything. Jean can always locate me for you in case of an emergency." He drove off. I understood for the first time why Mother said she loathed to say good-bye to anyone.

Sally showed no ill effects from the poison, other than a tendency to stick out her pink tongue like a lizard and suspiciously taste everything before she put it in her mouth.

I didn't have time to put anything in my mouth. The children woke up at five, lively and roaring for food. They ate a huge breakfast and were ready to go to the beach. I locked the doors while I drank my coffee and fixed Grandpa's breakfast and they pounded on the full-length windows and banged on the beautiful blue glass floats, wanting to get out! Grandpa kept them from killing themselves while I washed the dishes and then washed the diddies. The water was hard and full of minerals so I hung a line of grey, stiff diddies on the porch. I made the beds (the sandman not only visited the children, he dumped a quart of sand in my bed every night), swept a ton of sand out of the house and by seven o'clock we were all ready to go to the beach.

It was a block from the cabin to the beach, piled high with great logs and masses of driftwood. On the first trip I left Heidi in the pen and lugged Mari and Sally, their limp relaxed bodies dragging me down, while I clambered over logs and under roots and finally achieved the beach. Like the man with the fox, the goose and the bag of grain, I had to decide which two would be damaged the least by leaving them together. With many warnings to Mari and Sally not to leave Grandpa's side, I went back to get Heidi. By the time I had lugged her down, the other two had disappeared, and I rushed around desperately trying to corral them, while Grandpa held Heidi. The moment I sat down on the sand, one of them had to go toidey. The first morning I had said, 'Go behind a log over there.' The children recoiled in horror and, in an exact imitation of my fatuous voice, said, "But, Mother. Don't you remember?. We have a place for every thing—a cup to drink out of—a bowl to eat out of—and a toidey to go toidey in. We *never* go toidey outdoors."

So I carried them in relays back to the cabin, then back to the beach, then back to the cabin, then back to the beach, then back to the cabin. Then they were hungry or sleepy or cold or hot. I couldn't let any of them out of my sight for one moment or they would drown, get lost in the driftwood or disappear in the woods. I began to dream of little cages with strong bars and as for visiting the Diabetic Camp, it might just as well have been on the Cape of Good Hope.

Friday evening by five o'clock, supper was over. I was bathing the children in a washtub on the kitchen floor preparatory to stuffing them in bed. Mari said, "But, Mother, the sun is still shining!" I replied, harassed, "I know it, but it shines practically all night up here. You need lots of rest so you can go to that—a—beach tomorrow."

Grandpa chuckled. "Daughter, you seem to have lost a little weight. I think you could do with some rest yourself."

I shrieked, "Wouldn't you be tired after carrying these lumps back and forth to the beach two hundred times a day, cooking over a smoky wood stove, washing diddies in a teacup and—"

Grandpa hastily interrupted, "Home will look pretty good to you I expect." Mari said, "And we can see Mrs Dunny and the pool and Maggie." I almost wept. Then Grandpa pointed out some pink spots on their round brown bodies. Heidi had spots on her face, Mari had spots all over her stomach, and Sally had a few spots on her right arm. Grandpa offered to get me the Mecca Compound but I said they were probably spider bites, the whole place was crawling with spiders, rubbed the children with baby oil, powdered them and put them to bed.

I threw myself down on the driftwood couch, gave a shriek of anguish, said Edith's darling driftwood furniture was just like trying to lounge on a pile of cordwood, dumped the cushions off the couch and lay down on the floor.

Grandpa said he didn't like the look of all those spots on the children. One time in Waco he'd had some spots like that and they turned out to be barbers' itch. He didn't even bother to go to a doctor—just put Mecca Compound on them and they went away. He thought I'd better get started if I was going to the store to get Jim's call.

As I walked down the beach I watched a fat seagull dive after a piece of orange peel, drop it and scream to his friends that he'd found a school of herring. A drift of sea gulls turned in mid-flight, swooped down and fought over the useless titbit.

That morning when I fished a broken clam out of Heidi's mouth, dropped by an inconsiderate seagull, and told Grandpa that I'd got so I loathed seagulls, dirty, messy birds, Grandpa had observed that seagulls were just like a lot of other things. Really much more charming when you watched their swift, free flight from afar, or read the amazing story of how they once saved Salt Lake City from the locusts, than when you got too close to them. Intimacy with seagulls made it difficult to disassociate their senseless quarrelling cries and brutal treatment of any injured member of their flock, when admiring them in flight.

The sun was setting over the Olympics, turning their peaks to pink and making the foothills a deep purple. There was a softness over everything—little pink and yellow ribbons of mist floated gently around the islands and the seagulls formed a silver arrow in the sky.

A loon stood on one leg at the edge of the water, his weird hopeless cry accentuating my wish that Jim were there to walk along the beach with me. I kicked irritably at a log and the loon rose and flew low over the water, the little pink-tipped waves reaching for him in his flight. And vacations at the beach with little children were loon-lonely, not to speak of actively dangerous, unless your husband could be there with you. I decided to give in and ask Jim if I could come home.

The Hainesville store was full of fishermen, comparing the size of the day's catch, adolescents giggling while they sat at the fountain drinking sodas, and other exhausted vacationing mothers buying lots of groceries after the children were safely in bed. The last time I had called Jim, I had been so frantic about Sally I had not noticed the breathless silence in the store which accompanied a Long Distance Call.

I said, "Jim, may I come home?"

"Is anything wrong?" he asked promptly.

"No—" I looked at the open-mouthed row of listeners, dismissed as impractical my original plan of telling Jim about the exquisite sunset and how much the beauty made my heart ache for him, and substituted a lurid description of the spots on the children's stomachs.

There was an immediate uneasy rustling among the vacationing mothers. Spots! Contagious! They ceased to rattle their paper bags and gave their undivided attention to my conversation. "You might bring some calamine lotion." I ended forlornly and hung up.

By the time Jim arrived the next night, the spots were angry red splotches well smeared with Mecca Compound and the children scratched them constantly.

We all ran out to the car to meet Jim. As he picked Mari up to kiss her, he looked carefully at her face. "Impetigo", he said. "Where on earth do you suppose they got that?"

I remembered Web's and Winky's spotted faces. 'Just heat rash—there's no sense in calling a doctor—every child at home has it all summer—that and summer complaint'. Grandpa caught my eye, shook his head, grinned and said, "Lots of children at that Diabetic Camp."

Jim examined Sally and Heidi. "Yes, it's impetigo all right. Where's the medicine kit?"

We went in the house and painted each baby from head to foot with gentian violet. My nice, round, brown babies were now spotty royal purple and looked like a group of beggar children on the Soochow Road. I walked out to the kitchen.

Jim followed me and handed me a crumpled letter. "This came for you a couple of days ago. It's from Edith."

'DEAR MARY:

Convention recommends paid agency handle publicity for city-wide campaign. How about chairman of telephone committee?

Hope you are enjoying the beach.

Regards, EDITH.'

I threw it on the table in front of Jim and began to bawl.

Jim put his arm around me. "You know, I find I study better when you're there to interrupt me all the time. How would you like to come home with me Sunday night?"

# 12

## Specific Reactions

ALLERGY: *We may define the allergic state as one of potential specific reactivity. . .*

CECIL: *Textbook of Medicine*

MOST PEOPLE, when remodelling becomes a necessity, call an architect, *he* calls a contractor, and he calls plumbers, electricians, painters, and whatever workmen are necessary to complete the alterations. The job is taken on a competitive bid basis, there are no personal issues involved, no recriminations tolerated, eventually the bill is paid, and the new kitchen, bathroom or whatever is presumably a thing of beauty and a joy for ever. At least that is what doctors' wives think as they peer wistfully over the medical fence at the workmen employed by the outside world.

The remodelling of *our* kitchen was necessitated by a basket of grapefruit a grateful patient sent us from his farm in Texas. Jim was in St. Louis at a medical meeting when the present arrived, and the children and I opened it. Huge grapefruit, as big as melons, with deep pink flesh. I sat down to read the note.

> 'DEAR DOCTOR:
>
> 'Just wanted you to see why I had ulcers from being homesick. Never felt better in my life, thanks to you—and Texas. If you and the family are ever down our way, drop in and spend some time with us, we'd sure love to have you.
>
> BILL and EMMY RANDALL.'

I was glowing with warmth and pride in Jim when Mari said, "Look, Mother, there are some Texas bugs in here, too!" Several little brown beetles were skittering over the floor at an amazing rate of speed. "Are they Texas earwigs, Mother?" I said um-hum I guessed so, told the children to put napkins around their necks and left them joyfully eating a whole grapefruit, an unheard of luxury, while I went upstairs to thank the Randalls before something distracted me.

By the time Jim got home from St. Louis, the grapefruit were gone but the little beetles weren't. We went out in the kitchen to get Jim's Wheaties before he went to bed, and, as he turned on the kitchen light, little brown Texas earwigs scattered into the cracks and drawers.

As I got the bowl out of one cupboard, the cereal out of another, and the cream out of the icebox, I commented on the size of the Randalls' grapefruit and the fact that anything from Texas seemed to be bigger, and able to multiply faster, than anywhere else on earth.

"Cockroaches", Jim said as he crunched his Wheaties.

I couldn't have been more horrified if he'd said they were bubonic plague-infested rats. Of course they were not cockroaches—*they* only lived in filthy places and my kitchen wasn't filthy.

"Neither are hospitals, and cockroaches are the worst problem they have. Almost impossible to get rid of. Better get roach powder and if that doesn't work get an exterminator. They get into everything."

I opened every cupboard door and, each time, COCKROACHES skittered out and disappeared behind pans or down cracks.

The next month was a living hell. Roach powder made the cockroaches wave their legs a little, but otherwise did no visible damage. The exterminator filled the house with nauseous gas, and warned us to stay out of the kitchen—better yet, the entire house for twenty-four hours. We took the children to Victoria for the weekend; and when we came home, we choked and gagged and swept tons of yellow dust out of every nook and cranny. The cockroaches lurched and waved their feelers wildly. Some of them even died—probably of old age—but their progeny instantly hatched and flourished.

We began to be furtive about the whole thing. Guests who wanted a drink of water, were told not to go into the kitchen—'we'd be glad to get one for you'.

The day I opened the clothes chute, preparatory to sorting the laundry, and cockroaches leapt out of the dirty clothes, I called Jim at the office. "You've got to think of something. And don't tell me to take an aspirin."

Jim's voice was unhurried. "I was talking to Dick Dayton this morning. He came in about his rash. Suppose I have him drop over and see about remodelling the kitchen. He says old wood makes cockroaches flourish."

Dick Dayton is a painter, paperhanger, baby sitter, gentleman and artist and no doctor's wife should ever be without him. We call him for advice about everything, so naturally he won the cockroach problem.

That afternoon I had every drawer, pot and pan, utensil and dish out of the cupboards, and was preparing to wash the entire kitchen with straight Clorox to see if by any chance cockroaches hated the smell of it as much as I do. I heard a roar of laughter and looked up to see Dick, his feet spread far apart, and his thumbs tucked in the straps of his paint-smeared overalls.

"The Doc says you've got grateful patients—and cockroaches; and the combination is too much for you. I see it makes you clean out them cupboards anyway." He walked around pounding doors and surfaces. Every time he pounded, a disgruntled cockroach would stalk out, wave his feelers indignantly and disappear down a crack.

"Yep, it's this here old wood. Well—we've been going to get at this kitchen ever since you moved in here. Suppose I round up a carpenter and a couple of electricians, and come over next week." He handed me a large can of powder. "Meanwhile, put this down the cracks and around the sink. It may not kill the little bas—pardon me—bugs, but they'll quit being so sassy anyways. They don't hurt nothing, but they make the womenfolk nervous. Put it everywhere where there is water."

He took a cookie out of the cookie jar and reached in the refrigerator for a milk bottle. "Let's open up this side of the kitchen, so you can see the Cascades and the lake while you're cooking. It'll make the stews more tasty." He finished the milk and the cookies and ambled toward the door. "See you later."

After dinner I put the powder over every available inch of the kitchen, down the clothes chute and around the laundry trays in the basement. Just as I was getting into bed, Mari gave a shriek from the bathroom. "Mother! One of those Texas earwigs is in our bathroom." I got up and got the can and poured the bright Prussian blue powder all over the bathroom floor and out in the hall for good measure.

Dick came the next week with his crew. "This here's Mississip—

he's a carpenter. This here's Worden, electrical contractor. This here's McNaughten, plumber." Dick beamed as Mississip said, "Pleased to meet you, ma'am. I'm powerful fond of the Doctor. You certainly have a lovely view here." He bowed and flourished a ten gallon hat.

'This here's Worden' flipped the light switch, said, "It's a wonder the whole house hasn't burned down long ago. All this here wiring's got to come out. Where are the fuse boxes?" and shifted his toothpick to the other side of his mouth.

'This here's McNaughten' walked over and peered suspiciously under the sink. "Lead pipe, I thought so—all got to come out."

'This here's Mary' looked at the leaden and dripping November day, watched Mississip as he walked around mentally removing windows, doors and walls, and asked Dick if he thought they would be finished by Christmas.

"Sure, easy", Dick said looking in the cookie jar and thoughtfully choosing a chocolate cookie. "Kids like these, huh? Personally I prefer ginger cookies. Chocolate makes this here rash worse. Allergy, the Doc says." He squinted his eyes and looked at the ceiling. "We'll lower this here ceiling two feet—makes it easier to keep clean—paint it a nice bright yellow, with delphinium blue cupboards—inside that is." He pounded on a cupboard door and two cockroaches fell on the counter. To my astonishment, they didn't skitter away, but were apparently dead.

"Might as well have new cupboards while we're at it." Dick scratched his arm thoughtfully. "Yep—it won't take long. Every one of these here men's been to the Doc for something and they'll do good work for you." He took a small notebook out of his pocket, sat down at the kitchen table and began to write, "Why don't you put a pot of coffee on, and we'll sit around the table and figure this thing out?"

Mississip came in from the back porch: new porch—new kitchen walls—new windows—new cabinets—new linoleum—lower the ceiling—new draining-boards—he pulled out his little notebook, sat down beside Dick and began to write. The bare branches of the peach tree squeaked against the kitchen window. Mississip looked up. "We'll put canvas over those frames while the windows are out—keep Ladybug warm while she's cookin'."

Worden came up from the basement: new fuse boxes—new

wiring—move the stove—move the refrigerator—it's a wonder the house hadn't burned down long ago—never pass inspection—it's a good thing the inspectors hadn't seen this firetrap—really ought to rewire the whole house while we're at it—people with kids ought to be more careful. His notebook was already bulging with suggestions as he sat down at the kitchen table. He said briefly, "No cream—can't have milk", added a few marginal notes, and put four spoonfuls of sugar in his coffee.

McNaughten looked out at the rain, said his rheumatism always bothered him in the winter, that only ducks like this weather: new two-inch pipe, new sink, all the lead fittings have to come out—probably the sewer connection was no good either—he didn't drink coffee—kept him awake—yes, he'd like tea.

I asked them if they would be through by Christmas.

Dick said, "Sure, sure, not a thing to worry about."

McNaughten said, "If I did this job right I wouldn't be through for two years."

Worden said, "It's up to you and the Doc—if you want to wake up some night with the house full of smoke. I can be through by Christmas—otherwise—" He shrugged. Mississip bowed low, "Ladybug, we'll do our very best and no more man can do, even for a lovely lady."

They scratched little notes on their pads, ate the rest of the cookies in the cookie jar and, finally, pushed their chairs back.

Dick said, "Did you put that there powder around like I told you?"

I nodded and pointed to the two dead cockroaches.

"It won't get 'em all—but they'll quit chasing the kids for a while until we get this here old wood out. Well, see you tomorrow." They rose and trooped out into the November rain.

Mississip arrived promptly at eight o'clock the next morning armed with crowbars, tool chests, another carpenter, and a bad cold. He asked me to turn the oil burner up a little higher—he wasn't used to this cold Nawth yet—drank two glasses of hot water and took two aspirin.

While Jake, the assistant, started to set up the workbench immediately in front of the stove, Mississip leaned against the wall and told me the number of colds he'd had since he came Nawth. He'd had cold shots too, but they didn't seem to do any good. His blood was real thin and his resistance was low. Jake took off the back door and a gust of windy rain blew across the kitchen.

Mississip shivered, tucked his scarf tighter around his throat, said he hoped the cold didn't get down into his chest or he'd be hackin' all winter and asked me whether I wanted just a regular old slap-dash remodelling job or something real artistic. Jake took out the window across from the door and began to remove boards from the intervening wall.

The children came out and complained that they were cold—somebody'd left a door open—and I turned the oil burner up to eighty. Mr Worden came in, dropped a wet raincoat over a chair, put three tool boxes down in front of the refrigerator, asked me if he could pull the main switch for a couple of hours, and went down in the basement. Mississip put a heavy pea jacket on over his overalls and coat and coughed several times. Did I have any cough syrup that didn't have dope in it? Back home he chewed slippery elm for a cough, but up here they didn't seem to have it. I got the cough syrup, built a fire in the fireplace and put sweaters on the children. The oil burner had gone off with the main switch.

Mr McNaughten came into the living room. I was reading:

> 'James James
> Morrison Morrison
> Weatherby George Dupree'

for the fifteenth time, in a vain effort to keep the children out of the kitchen. "It's all right if I turn the water off for a couple of hours, isn't it? You might draw a kettleful—in case it takes longer than I think."

I told him I usually bathed the children before lunch, and did he think the water would be turned on by that time. He patted Sally on the head, said that 'too many baths remove the natural body oils and make children catch cold' and—he couldn't be sure about the water, but he'd turn it on again before he went home. Would I ask the Doctor to bring him home another prescription for his rheumatism?—he'd taken the last capsule a couple of weeks ago and lost the box. Sally sneezed, said I'd better ask Daddy to bring her home a pill too, she had a cold. Mississip came in holding Mari's hand and said I'd better keep the children out of the kitchen, they might get hurt and was that homemade soup he smelled cookin'?

We all had a bowl of home-made soup around the dining-room table. The children were fascinated by the lunch pails and begged for bites of everything.

Mississip told all the details of each cold he had had since he came Nawth, all the doctors he'd gone to, what the man at the drug store said, and that he'd found the best thing to do was to keep a light mustard plaster on his chest all winter and have a nice hot toddy before he went to bed. He was real worried when he first came Nawth for fear he had the *con*-sumption but Dr Jim told him it was just a plain old cold. Didn't I think it was funny that doctors could find cures for all sorts of real hard diseases but couldn't do nothin' for the plain old cold?

Take McNaughten's rheumatism now, Doctor Jim said it was sciatica. He was afraid of arthritis, his brother had that and was all crippled up so he couldn't work, but this was a muscle strain. He chewed thoughtfully on a piece of celery spread with peanut butter. Personally, he'd found that if he didn't eat any bread of any kind, or anything made with flour, his rheumatism wasn't near so bad. He probably had one of those allergies everybody was talking about now.

Mari, Sally and Heidi asked for a piece of celery spread with peanut butter. He took a knife out of his pocket, cut his celery in three pieces and gave them each a section. Celery was good for kids, it gave them energy.

Jake couldn't eat celery nor cucumbers nor cabbage—they repeated on him. Funny thing, onions didn't, like they did on most people. He could eat all the raw onions he wanted to—just celery, cucumbers and cabbage. Never thought of it before, but *it* was probably one of them allergies too. He cut three chunks off his piece of apple pie and gave the children each a small wedge.

Dick was allergic to chocolate and turpentine. Boy, did he have the old painter's colic—every time he got through with a job he had to stay home two or three days to get rid of the headache. Chri—pardon me—gosh, if he ever got any real dough in the bank, he was going to be a fisherman—and wouldn't it be just his luck to find he was allergic to fish? Yes sir, just his luck. He quartered his apple and gave each of the children a section.

Yep, he had them migraines—sometimes they were so bad he

couldn't see—aw, sure, the Doctor had given him some shots and his headaches were better for a while—but Chri—pardon me—gosh, if he was damned fool enough to be a painter when he had painter's colic, how could he expect the Doc to cure him? What he needed was to have his head examined, and not for dandruff either. Ha-ha.

Milk turned sour on Worden's stomach—always had. As long as he stayed away from milk or cream he was O.K., but let him have even a piece of custard pie—and blooey! He handed each of the children a carrot stick. It was his fallen arches that drove him crazy—boy, his feet burned at night like they was on fire. He had varicose veins, too. If they got any worse the Doc was going to send him to a surgeon and have his veins tied off or something. Anyways, his sour stomach was a lot more trouble to him than his varicose veins ever had been. When you came right down to it, practically everything had milk or cream in it—and he couldn't touch a bite—not one bite—or blooey!

Dick rose and stretched. "Well, that there was good soup—nothing like a bowl of home-made soup—it sticks to your stomach. Come on, boys—let's get going."

Worden asked me if I could come down into the basement a minute—he wanted to show me something. I told him I'd put the children down for their naps and be right down.

He was standing in the wood room gazing at the fuse box. "Who put that there fuse box in the wood room?" I told him that the light company had put it there about six months ago.

"Yes, they would. Just look at that there cable, would you? What if you'd got locked in here and the house was on fire and the babies upstairs. What would you have done then I'd like to know?" *I'd* like to know how I'd *get* locked in a wood room that didn't have a door and what the hell I'd be doing down there if the house was on fire? He launched into a long complicated series of ohms, amps, loads and cables, emphasizing the terrible danger of any other electrician's wiring. He'd just have to do the whole damned thing over again. It might cost a little more than the Doc had planned, but he'd feel mighty funny if his house and kids burned up while he was at the office. "No amount of doctorin' will help then—I'll tell you."

I reminded him that doctoring, however, paid the bills, and asked him how much more it would cost. He said he couldn't tell until he got into the walls.

While we were at it, Dick thought we might as well put a couple of coats of paint on the outside of the house and paint the pantry to match the kitchen—there'd be new wood showing, here and there, which would have to be painted anyway. I asked him how much more it would cost. Hell, he didn't know—he'd talk it over with the Doc—but there was no use doing two separate jobs—might as well have it all done at once.

Mississip felt that as long as we were tearing up the kitchen anyway, we might as well have a few things Ladybug, here, would really enjoy. Like a spice cabinet, and a sliding broom closet and some little shelves here and there. He'd like to put in a long steel sash window with that view, but maybe not.

I asked him how much the window would cost—and the extra cabinets. Well—that took extra labour, but the kitchen would be real pretty with just a few extras. After all Doctor Jim wouldn't object—doctors sure had everything convenient around their offices and he knew that Doctor Jim would want everything as easy for his little lady as human hands could make it. When he got through, this kitchen would be just as homey as a Southern kitchen—and as convenient as a button.

Little lady felt sure that Doctor Jim would infinitely prefer to stay within the budget and get rid of the human hands as soon as possible. I asked them if they would be through by Christmas.

Dick said, "Well, we won't paint the outside of the house in this kind of weather, that's a sure thing but aside from this and that—sure, we'll be through."

March twenty-fifth, we were all sitting around the dining room table having a bowl of home-made soup. Forsythia gleamed yellow against the watery spring day. The children still wore leggings under, and sweaters over, their cotton dresses. I had become so inured to the constant cold winds through the house that I wore jeans instead of ski pants to do the housework.

The stove and refrigerator were now added to the boxes and bales in the dining room, and the children had long since gone back to peanut butter sandwiches and a glass of milk instead of hanging over the workmen's lunch boxes. After all, the children would cease to exclaim over the bears if they were taken to the zoo one hundred and thirty days in succession.

Mississip had gone home for Christmas. He might have hesitated to tell some of his customers that he was leaving right in the middle of a job with the windows and doors still out of the kitchen, but with a doctor's family of course, it was different. Both Doctor Jim and I would understand that in order to get rid of these colds he just had to spend a month in the warm sunshine. This dreary weather was the cause of the colds and the thing to do was to get a good baking out and get rid of them once and for all.

Mr Worden had his varicose veins ligated. There was no use in trying to work with his feet and legs practically killing him. The Doc would understand in fact, he was the one who suggested it. As long as Mississip was away, there wasn't much he could do.

McNaughten strained his back lifting the new sink. The muscle strain coupled with the sciatica was too much for him and the Doc thought he'd better have bed-rest for a couple of weeks.

Jake finished a garage for his landlady during the holidays. He couldn't work while Mississip was South anyway, and this landlady was the only one he'd ever found who was careful of his diet.

Dick put the delphinium blue in the pantry cupboards so I could see how I liked it, whitewashed the basement and took care of the children so I could go down town, but how the hell was he to know that bas—pardon me—bonehead of a Mississip was going South for a month right in the middle of a job.

They continued to eat their bowls of hot soup and discuss the spice cabinet. Mississip's face lighted with memory as he told about how the spice cupboards back home were handed down from family to family—why, they were the backbone of the kitchen.

"Yeh," Dick said, "yeh—but can Ladybug afford a seventy-five dollar spice cabinet—that's what I'm getting at. Even at a dollar and a half an hour that there fiddling is running into real do-re-mi. Chri—pardon me—gosh, you have been fooling around out there almost five months, the family's freezing to death and you talk about backbones of kitchens. Doors and windows are the backbones of the kitchen where I come from. You put them in and I'll go along with you on the gewgaws."

Mississip rose, said, "Sir, where I come from a gentleman never forgets that he's a gentleman", walked out in the kitchen and began to pack his tools. As I skirted the yawning hole in the kitchen floor, which was eventually going to be a broom closet, if I lived long enough—I recalled the Gelett Burgess jingle that Jim quoted:

'I wish that my room had a floor,
I don't so much care for a door,
But this going around
Without touching the ground,
Is getting to be quite a bore.'

I pleaded with Mississip to stay, told him I loved every inch of every cupboard, that Dick was only joking and that both Doctor Jim and I didn't care how long it took that his craftsmanship was inspirational.

He said that where he came from a gentleman didn't make fun of another gentleman, and continued to pack. Also, he was getting another one of his colds, he figured that he perspired, if I'd pardon the word, when he worked and then going out in all that rain, he got a chill—no, I'd better get someone to finish the job and he'd go on another job.

I looked at the litter of half finished cabinets, the absence of any draining-board around the new sink, the mysterious hole in the floor, which was to contain the equally mysterious broom cabinet like 'the one at home' and ground my teeth. Nobody else *could* finish the job.

If Jim thought it was so darned Gelett Burgess-y—he could just do something about it. I called him from the upstairs phone, told him these were his little workmen after all and that he would have to come home and cope with them.

At one-thirty Jim arrived, walked out in the kitchen, said, "Can you get these doors and windows in by Friday night? Fine. Everything be done except the outside painting by April fifteenth? Fine. Better get that floor in by tonight—linoleum's going to be laid tomorrow. Certainly appreciate all the trouble you boys have taken, but we'll have to get this stuff cleared out of here. Medical convention you know—well, have to get back to the office. See you later."

That night as Jim was getting into bed he said, "Funny damned thing. That blue powder apparently killed the cockroaches. Have to ask Dick what it was. You know, Mary, you can't talk to workmen all the time and have them get anything done."

I snapped that if by some miracle the workmen all managed to stay out of the hospital long enough to finish by late autumn, I'd never—so help me God—let another grateful patient drive a nail in our house again. I'd never seen such a bunch of neurotic Sickos in my whole life. All they talked about all day long was their symptoms, their diseases and their allergies. I was the one who had the real allergy—and it was to grateful patients, who threw their tools all over the house, took out all the windows and doors and then sat down to be hypochondriacs for God knew how many months at God knew what an hour.

Jim said, "Well, of course, that's your fault."

"My fault!" I screamed.

"Yes. You sympathize with them. And you are a doctor's wife. Why don't you pack up the kids and go out and stay at your mother's house until they finish. I'll see that they are out of here by April fifteenth."

I did—and they were.

# 13

## The Menopause That Refreshes

CLIMACTERIC: *Change of life, the menopause.*
COMMENT: *The effects of the menopause are extremely variable.*
CECIL: *Textbook of Medicine*

"ALLO IS THE DOCTAIR THERE—no—there is nozzing anyone can do—my 'usban is much, much, vorse—I think he iss dying. 'Ow are you and the children?"

I hooked the telephone under one ear, a trick the telephone repair man had shown me, sighed, and continued to wash the breakfast dishes. Mrs Ilshenky's morning telephone call could be depended upon to last one hour.

Her doleful, throaty Russian voice altered it's tragic inflection not one whit as she told me about the Russian bazaar—they make lods of monies, Olga sold some of her perrals—her new sable hat—not good sable like they have at home, but varm. Her children had dradful colds—probably pneumonia again—they were so leetle too—and nevair strong. She could not bear to listen to Stravinsky—the nostalgia. She finally ended with the fact that she was 'joos vine' except for her dreadful disease, would the Doctair please come over and look at her 'usban's 'eart?—and that she was so busy she would just have to hang up.

By that time my dishes were done and the vegetables cut up for the soup. Everything in Mrs Ilshenky's life was uniformly 'dradful'. The children caught cold because the house was 'like Siberia widout de volves'. Her husband's heart condition was caused by the United States, 'he is depressed. 'Is 'eart breaks because everyone speaks English'. In contrast to Mr Ilshenky's background, this determination on the part of Americans to be was no doubt unimaginative, but it seldom caused coronary thrombosis.

Mr Ilshenky was born in Russia. His father was Russian and his mother was Danish. His family had lived in Russia until he was ten and then moved to Denmark to take over his mother's estate. He continued his education in Danish. When he was sixteen and attending the Gymnasium, his family moved to Harbin, China. He continued his education in Chinese and received his Bachelor of Law degree. He met Mrs Ilshenky, a White Russian, in Harbin and married her. 'I speak only Mandarin, but he speaks, reads and writes all the dialects.'

His father, who seemed to be footloose and fancy free, then moved to Idaho. Mr Ilshenky passed his bar exams in Idaho and Mrs Ilshenky 'suffaired—imagine—six tarrible mon's in Idaho—there were no people—unly trees'. They then moved to Alaska, to make contacts for the fur-importing business. Alaska, for some odd reason, was 'vonderful—mountains—glaciers—snow—tundra—just like Russia'.

They now lived in the North-west, an area which was either 'vonderful' or 'lunly'—depending upon whether or not Mrs Ilshenky had one of her 'tarrible hadaches'. The Ilshenkys made annual trips to Paris to see some 'eenteresting gloes', to Germany 'to 'ear some music that iss not jus' noise', and to Italy for 'zum zunshine'. During those periods I could get my housework done without having the telephone hooked under one ear.

When they first came here, Mrs Ilshenky had wandered into Jim's office, under the impression that he spoke fluent Danish. For one who protested complete fatalism and thought 'Dath a release', she required the maximum of medical attention for her family. Although I had never seen any of the Ilshenkys, their diseases and habits were well known to me. Mrs Ilshenky had called me at least once a day for two years, to give me a dramatic report of her rapidly disintegrating family. Each time she asked Jim to make a house call, she invited me to come with him. 'Mrs Jay zounds seempathetic'. Jim took his usual firm stand against letting me help him practise internal medicine.

That night I opened my campaign again. "Please let me go. I won't mention illness, but I'm dying to see her house." 'Eet is a leedle 'ouse—unly twenty rooms—like camping in Mongolia—it will do until we decide which country we wish to live in. We chose it because it reminded us of Russia. But it is furnished like an American 'ouse. I am zo anxious to 'ave you see eet.'

Jim smoked his cigarette and looked off into space. "You might be able to get something out of her at that. Although I take care of the family, she won't make an appointment for herself—just looks pitiful and says she has the American Disease."

It was a huge white house, which reminded me of nothing on earth. The builder had started out with a turreted Victorian, had changed houses in mid-stream when he saw a Frank Lloyd Wright, and then his wife had apparently said, 'I like something sturdy', so he'd spattered the outside of this monstrosity with such enormous lumps of cement stucco that only deep X-ray therapy could hope to reduce the swellings. The Ilshenkys had bought the house direct from the builder.

There were two round turrets on the north and on the south with little gun-holes in each turret for windows. The turrets were separated by a long, flat-roofed centre area. The stucco lumps on the turrets were replaced in the centre area by flat glistening white stucco (the glitter achieved by little snips of broken glass and mica), glass-brick bands and huge steel-framed windows. The front door, which was large enough to be a portcullis, held an enormous Russian crest. 'Eet is not elaborate, but eet is 'ome. My 'usban' must have a quiet place to res'.' The house was about ten feet from the side-walk and on one of the busiest arterials in town.

The wail of Tchaikovsky's B Minor shook the house as Jim rang the doorbell. The door was opened by a fat little blue-eyed boy in a dark sailor suit.

Jim said, "Hi, Peter." Peter, who had 'almos' died' several times during the two years, with pneumonia, appendicitis, brain tumour and lockjaw, which had turned out to be mumps—removed a large sucker from his mouth, roared, 'Mo-ther', and stood in the doorway.

A fat black-eyed little girl appeared beside Peter. Sonya, who had 'almos' died' of polio, a broken neck, meningitis and appendicitis—which proved to be the entire crop of green cherries from a neighbour's tree removed her finger from her mouth, roared, 'Mo-ther', and stood in the doorway.

'Mo-ther' appeared, opened the door wide, and said, "At las'—you are in my 'ouse", and kissed me on either cheek. Her voice was deep, melodious, and very tragic as she said, "Let's go upstairs and see 'im before eet iss too late—'e iss dying I think." The Tchaikovsky changed to Rachmaninoff's Third. This was the first time I had ever laid eyes on Mrs Ilshenky. Because her descriptions of her trips all over the world were so harrowing, and because the only other White Russian I had known had been as sturdy as a Metropolitan Opera star, I was startled. She was slight and very beautiful. Enormous black eyes, ringed with deep black circles, black hair with a white wing on the left side, and the most exquisite black velvet hostess gown I have ever seen.

As we went in the house, I wondered why the record player was at full volume considering the fact that she had called me at noon to say she had one of 'my tarrible hadaches. The whisper of a voice is unbearable, the light is agony and the fall of a rose is sheer torture'. The shriek of Rachmaninoff's Third almost blew us up the stairs as she said, "My 'usban' loves Russian music—eet is all he has now, music and his books."

The maroon velvet-draped stairwell was dimly lit by a jewelled bowl lamp, which hung from the ceiling by three heavy brass chains. We wound up the circular stairway. "Come quickly, Doctair, Peter was playing Cossack with Sonya and they fell on the stair—they are not dad but their backs are broken", and into one of the towers.

''Usban' was lying in a huge canopied bed. He was fat, blond and very handsome, and looked extremely healthy and debonair. The bed was littered with books, there were books piled on chairs and on the floor, and bookcases lined all of the walls.

He waved a long cigarette holder and said, "I have been translating. I cannot see why all translations are so bad. Perhaps I shall cease to import furs and make translations." He patted a small area beside him on the bed. "Do come and sit here, my dear, so I can see you. Do sit down, Doctor." The music was sufficiently muffled by distance so I could just make out what he said. His accent was like Charles Boyer's when he says, 'Pink champagne for you, my dear', and his voice equally caressing. I sat down on a chair. Jim took out his stethoscope and bent over Mr Ilshenky, who waved him imperiously away with "But first let us have vodka. Tanya, my dear, our guests."

Mrs Ilshenky walked over to a huge carven sideboard and poured a white liquid into some small crystal glasses. Mr Ilshenky said, *'Salud, pesetas y amor'*, and we drank. It was like drinking flaming kerosene.

Tanya and the fat stolid children and I went downstairs while Jim examined Mr Ilshenky. The living room held three enormous maroon cut-velvet davenports. The bay windows were entirely screened by maroon velvet drapes. We waded almost knee-deep in the pile of glaring American Oriental rugs. The lamps on either side of the fireplace were little blackamoors holding jewelled balls. The record player was in a huge, carved oak cabinet as big as a hospital icebox and, judging by the volume, must have contained at least ten speakers.

Tanya turned down the volume two decibels and spoke to the children in rapid Russian. These little bridges between Russia and America said, 'Naw, we don't want to', and continued to stare at me.

"We will take them to the playroom, then", Tanya said. She led the way through a maze of rooms, each dimly lit and each furnished with Gargantuan, fumed oak furniture. The playroom, which was in the back of the house, may have originally been intended for a library.

Shelf after shelf held toys, bicycles, scooters, trains, boats, dolls, mechanical toys, slides, rocking horses—only Schwartz Toy Shop at the height of the Christmas season could have hoped to compete with it. I crossed over to the shelves of dolls and started to pick one up.

"Don't touch that, it's mine", Sonya said. She ran over and stood in front of the shelves of dolls and continued to stare stonily at me. Peter picked up a gun, which looked exactly like a twelve gauge shotgun, and might have been for all I knew, pointed it at me and said, "I'll kill you. Bang, bang, bang." Then he walked over and pinched Sonya, who promptly kicked him in the shins, and they both began to bawl.

Mrs Ilshenky said, "Leedle animals—all children are sadists." She waved a jewelled hand at them. "Play", she said, and closed the door. They promptly began to kick the door and shriek, "Let us out of here."

We went back into the living room and sat down in front of the fire. A maid produced a tray on which there was another carafe of vodka and some crystal glasses.

"You like music? I will play you some leedle Russian folk songs." She went over to the record player and put on some records. As the sorrowful voices intoned the music, Tanya translated. 'The mother is taking the children for a sleigh ride, eet is snowing, the volves come, they follow the sleigh. The mother tries to whip them off, eet does no good, the volves eat the children. She sings her lament.

'Eet is a village wedding, they sing and dance, the Cossacks ride through the village, her lover is taken away, she sings her lament.

'Eet is a work song—eet is a planting song—the Cossacks trample the bride to death.'

The record player gave a final howl and subsided.

"The Russians are a strong people", she murmured as she gazed into the fire and absent-mindedly drank glass after glass of vodka.

"They certainly are", I agreed, and tried to get up enough courage to take another sip.

She rose and put Tchaikovsky's B Minor on again.

"Eet is because they have so much trouble."

I asked her if her headache had gone. She raised sorrowful black eyes to me.

"Eet is never gone—eet is not a headache exactly—I think I mus' have the American Disease. The Doctair tells me I should come to his office and have an examination, but if eet is the American Disease, what is the use?" She turned down the record player to a low wail. "I have lived in France, in Italy, in Austria, in England, in China, in all the Nordic countries—nowhere do I hear of this disease. And now I live in the United States and everywhere I go every woman has eet."

She shrugged disconsolately.

I asked her what the symptoms were.

"All different. That is why I cannot tell the Doctair. Some of them go crazy. some of them have headaches, some of them are tired all the time, some of them get a divorce they are so nervous. I am nervous and all of them are nervous, that is one thing."

The children had apparently kicked the door down because they came screaming and fighting into the room. She spoke to them in Russian. "We don't want to", they said as they sat down across from me and resumed their staring.

A maid came in with a tray on which was a great bowl of caviare on ice, some crackers and cheese and a mound of cake. Tanya handed a piece of cake to each fat lump of a child and said, "They do not like to go to bed—eet makes them lunly."

A nurse came in and took Peter and Sonya, kicking and screaming, through a curved doorway toward another tower.

Fortunately she was a big, tall nurse. I felt that either of those big stinkers would make me nervous and both of them would cause a complete breakdown, as they bit and kicked their way toward the stairs.

"Leedle children are so *on*happy. They do not understand a world made up of tall people who arbitrarily say 'no' all the time." Tanya sighed. "If eet were not for the American Disease, I would not have a nurse but I am not strong enough to care for them alone."

There it was again, the American Disease. I told her I thought she really ought to go down to Jim's office and have a thorough examination. Then I asked her if this disease had any other name?

"Some call eet sh-ange of life." She said, downing another vodka reflectively. "W.hen the Doctair comes down we will all have some caviare."

# 14

## Betsy

CARCINOMA: *A malignant tumour made up chiefly of epithelial cells; cancer.*

MACROSCOPIC: *This specimen is a breast with skin including the nipple and pectoral muscles attached and some fat presumably from the axilla. Within the glandular area proper, about 6 cm from the nipple is a mass of firm, grey tissue, not grossly encapsulated nor well circumscribed, about 2 cm in diameter, fixed to the surrounding tissue and to the overlying skin, which is slightly retracted at this place. In the axillary fat are several small, grossly normal lymph nodes and one large node 2 cm in diameter filled with firm pale tissue and another similar large node about midway along the muscle. Sections are taken from the tumour mass and the nodes.*

MICROSCOPIC: *In the tumour mass is a diffuse proliferation of epithelial cells, the nuclei of many of which are slightly hyperchromatic or have actual mitotic figures, generally closely packed in solid masses or poorly defined cords, but otherwise without organized pattern in their arrangement, with relatively little reaction in the surrounding tissue and with free invasion of adjacent fat. Two of the lymph nodes are filled with similar cells.*

DIAGNOSIS: CARCINOMA OF THE BREAST (MEDULLARY TYPE) WITH EXTENSION TO LYMPH NODES.

A STRANGE AND INCOMPREHENSIBLE group of words which may mean—DEATH.

In this fanatic age of determined propaganda, research and alphabetical headquarters for everything, it seems inexcusable to me that any woman could go around secretly guarding a lump in her breast exactly as though she had achieved that lump as the result of an illicit love affair.

I cannot understand why the choice of a physician remains as unreasonable and personal as the choice of a mate, and why any justifiable and well-founded criticism of the chosen one is rewarded with a proportionate amount of blind fury.

It is not only difficult, it is harrowing, to be forced to sit on the sidelines, your mouth sealed with the adhesive tape of medical ethics, while an innocent says, 'I'm going to have a complete hysterectomy. Dr Chop says I have a growth and I'd better have it removed before I develop cancer. You've heard of Dr Chop, of course.' I know, and she should be told, that Dr Chop has a trail of normal uteri behind him like a paper chase. He is privately described by the medical profession as 'knife-happy—will cut anything that will lie still'.

Another innocent says, 'My uncle had leukaemia. The doctors all told him that he had a fatal form of blood cancer. He finally found Dr Shot, had treatments for six months and now he is completely cured. You know Dr Shot—marvellous, isn't he?' I know, and she should have read, that true leukaemia is invariably fatal. Uncle did not have leukaemia. Alleged recoveries are due to incompetent diagnosis. Dr Shot is described as a 'bumbling old idiot who wouldn't know a cancer cell from a spirochete and who gives shots for every thing—a neat medical form of endowment insurance'.

But the most agonizing of all, is the friend who is surrounded by competent physicians and whom fear has rendered blind, deaf and dumb.

"When did you first notice this lump (or skin change or physical change or whatever the distinctly peculiar symptom may be)?"

"Well, it's been going on quite a while, doctor—about a year I guess, but I was afraid to come to you—afraid it might be cancer."

Betsy Brandt was one of those.

Dick Brandt was our lawyer. The Patch was Dick and Betsy's farm across the lake and a refuge for the Neglected Ones. If life with father, the telephone and the little ones became too much for anyone of us, that one packed a suitcase and disappeared for two days or two weeks, to visit Betsy. The doctors spent many weekends and Thursday afternoons fishing off Dick's dock and having one of Betsy's heavenly dinners afterward. The children visited most of the summer and as much of the winter as possible at the Patch, riding the horses, feeding the chickens and drinking cow's milk.

Betsy even attended a sewing meeting of the Neglected Ones, now and then. She wouldn't come regularly, she said, because she was too busy with the farm and also she might get into the habit of talking about insides. "Everything between my neck and my knees is a mystery to me and I'm damned glad of it." She shuddered. "You're like a bunch of ghouls with your stories of operations and diseases. You come on over to the Patch—I like you better over there."

At the doctors' dinner parties, Dick was introduced so often as Dr Brandt that he threatened to wear a sign, 'I am a lawyer.' Although he got some mighty personal inside dope on the wives, he said it was a strain to be asked what he thought of hypercholesteremia.

For ten years Betsy and Dick had lived in a whole nest of doctors.

Pete Roberts delivered each of their five children. I will admit that Betsy had the minimum of pre-natal and post-natal care. She would not go to Pete's office more than three times during each pregnancy—two visits before delivery and one after. Pete realized that this attitude was engendered by a primitive fear of doctors as such, and kept track of her progress by adroit social questioning, of which she was entirely unaware.

Bob Murphy had removed Dick's appendix and set the children's broken legs. Bob and Jinny weren't at the Patch as often as the rest of us were, but they attended all the summer beach parties, and the big Christmas party known as 'Doctors' Dilemma'.

Dick Martin was the children's paediatrician. Betsy had a compulsion neurosis about the children's medical care and had them examined much more often than was necessary. Dick and Barbara made at least one house call a month at the Patch and usually stayed all night afterward.

Jim and Tod divided the Brandt stomach aches and colds with complete impartiality. Most diagnoses were made around a beach fire or the dinner table with the easy familiarity of the medical profession toward one of its own.

Along with a two-hundred-acre farm, five children and a constant stream of guests, Betsy had a career. She gave flower arrangement lectures for the benefit of the various children's hospitals around this part of the country.

She had been away on a lecture tour and we hadn't seen her for three or four months. We'd been over at the Patch, of course, to check up on Dick and the children and had found them getting along in that desolate way that families do who possess a vivid mother. Hans and Helga were taking excellent physical care of them, but when Betsy was gone she took the zest in their lives with her.

She'd written to us from Montana, sending us tickets and reminding us not to forget the Island Benefit or the stuff at the cleaners. She'd be home the night before the lecture.

The Island Benefit for Children's Hospital was an annual affair. Betsy always asked the Neglected Ones to come over and bring all the young and have supper on the beach. The doctors took the four o'clock boat and got in some fishing, and Helga and Hans took care of the children while we were attending the flower arranging lecture.

As we walked through the blazing fall colours toward the school house, Maggie said, "She called me just before she left for the trip and said she was draggin' like an old rope. Cows, sheep and pigs havin' babies all over the place and of course Betsy feels she has to be midwife to every one of them. I made my usual suggestion that she drop down and see Pete, but she wouldn't, of course."

"Probably called in at home to see that old family skeleton who's been wondering what's the matter with her family for years. He's the only doctor she ever will go to see voluntarily. Brought her into this world! I'll bet he was as surprised as she was."

Faith kicked at a log, muttered 'damn fool' and walked on.

"Of course I don't know her as well as you do, but it's always seemed funny to me that her best friends are doctors' wives," Jinny mused. "Although she was more than co-operative when Bob operated on Dick."

"And she certainly drags the children into the office at any and every sniffle", Barbara Martin added.

Maggie laughed. "As long as she isn't the victim, she's nuts for doctors. She wears us around her neck like an asafoetida bag—to keep diseases away."

The little brown school house was packed. The high expectant voices of the women 'oh'd' and 'ah'd' at the great trays of flowers from Betsy's garden, the stacks of wheat, weeds and seed pods, and the long shelf of containers that Betsy had collected.

A brown kitchen table stood on the platform, on which was a square black box lighted by two spotlights.

Betsy walked out on the platform and smiled. There was wild clapping from the audience and a horrified gasp from the Neglected

Ones. She was so thin! The black freckles stood out on her face. Her dimples made shadowed ridges on either side of her mouth as she spoke. The spotlights accentuated the deep blue circles under her eyes.

"This year something new has been added." Betsy leaned forward and placed a copper lustre pitcher on the table in front of her.

"And I'd certainly like to know what it is", Faith murmured behind her hand. "She looks like death warmed up. What in God's name is the matter?"

We shook our heads and continued to watch Betsy. "There are four of us this year, each representing a different type of flower arrangement. We are going to auction the flowers to raise the money for the new hospital beds. We need fifteen thousand dollars you know."

There was an audible murmur of 'We don't like anything but Betsy Brandt'.

Betsy smiled. "I'm sure everybody is sick of hearing me 'take a chrysanthemum'." She completed a glowing arrangement of wheat stalks, deep red chrysanthemums, a brown dock seed pod, and two orange dahlias. The women gasped as she turned it around. "If you don't have a copper lustre pitcher, a syrup jug will do." Twenty-five dollars for the Children's Hospital. It was carried away by a proud bidder.

"For a buffet supper—" Betsy took a flat board covered with goldfoil wrap and placed an empty, oval salmon tin on it. "This is an empty salmon can—nice shape, isn't it?" The audience laughed delightedly. "By the end of the season my family gets quite tired of canned salmon." Crimson and gold chrysanthemums, golden oak leaves, sheaves of wheat and five dark brown candles. The effect was casual and gorgeous, like a fall meadow in the shifting sunlight.

Betsy had always been as unaware of her personal magnetism and exquisite artistry as one of her shaggy chrysanthemums, but her usually vivid, warm voice was thin with exhaustion as she continued.

"Everything except the candles is out of the garden or the vacant lot—they're from the ten cent store. I always feel—" Betsy wavered a little and took hold of the table for support, "that I cheat if I use flowers from the florist, particularly out here where there is such a wealth of material."

There was a storm of clapping. Fifteen dollars for the Children's Hospital.

"She looks like she was going to faint. Talk about fiddling while Rome burns", Faith muttered.

Betsy sat down on the edge of the platform, near enough so we could whisper to her. "What's the matter with you? Are you sick?" Faith asked.

She sighed and drew her hand across her forehead. "Just tired. Haven't been sleeping, trains and hotels. Watch this one." She turned back to watch the lecturer.

"She's thin as a picked chicken, poor baby", Maggie said behind her hand.

A stiff-faced, high-style woman was producing a formal arrangement with twenty dollars' worth of calla lilies and a white jade vase. It was as cold and calculating as the expression in her eyes, brought only five dollars and a spattering of clapping. "You should see her house. Cosy as an ice tray", Betsy murmured.

A nervous little woman took White Jade's place. She wore a pink feather hat, a pale blue coat and an apologetic manner. With a knobbly English castor and many fluttery stops and starts, she produced a fussy pink and blue arrangement which was as unsure as her faded blonde hair and vapid face. Sympathy brought the bidding up to ten dollars again.

Betsy made the last ten arrangements which brought twenty-five dollars each and offered to help anyone in the room if they would just telephone when they were trapped with a flower, a vase, and a blank mind. She was promptly surrounded by a crush of admiring women and we sneaked out the side door to wait for her.

"What are we going to do? She looks perfectly awful—nobody's just tired who's that awful colour—she must have lost twenty pounds—her throat's all crepe-y." We turned to Maggie. "When did you see her last?"

"I was just trying to think. She called me to say good-bye—I told you that, but I haven't actually seen her since about a month before she left. She came in town to do some shoppin' and we had lunch together."

Maggie bit her lip in an effort to remember, then shook her head, her eyes wide with the unexpressed fear that was haunting all of us. "You don't really look at people you love, you know how they look.

Betsy has always been as round and brown and freckled as one of her Plymouth Rock eggs. She was a little thinner maybe—she always is in spring—but not like this." Maggie's eyes pleaded with each of us. "'I tried to make her see Pete. Her mother and sister—"

"Both died of cancer and so she is too frightened to go to a doctor and have a check up", Faith finished, each word spaced and bitter. "If she's had a lump in her breast and that old fool back home has known about it and been watching it to see if it would develop, I swear I'll kill him with my own bare hands."

Maggie grabbed her arm. "Hush, honey, here she comes."

Betsy walked toward us, her arms laden with glowing fall leaves, a sheaf of brilliant chrysanthemums, and several bunches of wheat and seed pods.

"I knew you wouldn't pay those astronomical prices for my arrangements so I brought the equipment and when we get home I'll make you each one, although you don't deserve them. Fine doctors' wives you are, wouldn't bid over two dollars for the Children's Hospital." She handed us each an armload. "You can at least strain yourselves to the extent of helping me carry them."

As we walked through the brilliant fall leaves toward the Patch, I felt for the first time that the glowing autumn colours represented a farewell to a beloved summer, not a satisfactory time of harvest and fulfilment. The trees seemed reluctant to lose each yellow leaf, and the cloud shadows on the fields looked desolate rather than protective.

Maggie clutched my arm. Her eyes were full of tears. "Mary, I can't stand it. I feel like I was takin' Betsy to see an awful sad movie where I knew the end and she didn't."

"Maybe she is just tired. After all, we just think it's cancer, because of her family history. We don't know it."

"Remember, I was a technician." Maggie said darkly, and walked on.

We stopped on the way to the house to count the children. They were dancing around a roaring beach fire, toasting wienies and marshmallows and clutching large jugs of milk. Betsy watched them fondly. "Why don't you let them stay all night?" We protested. "Oh, we can put sleeping bags around here and there. Why don't you all stay all night? I haven't seen you for ages. I've got lots of food and you don't care where you sleep."

“We’ll see how strong we are after dinner”, Faith said. “By the time the little dears have stopped eating and begun to whine, we’ll regard them with a far more jaundiced eye.”

Betsy went around the back way to tell Helga something about dinner and called over her shoulder that she was going to take a bath and for us to go on in and have a drink.

The husbands were standing in front of the fire in the living room, hefting guns and discussing pheasant shooting. A cartwheel of dogs lay at their feet and panted in the heat from the fire. Dick handed us each a hot buttered rum and turned back to draw a picture of the little back road which led up into the sagebrush. “The place is alive with pheasants, but you have to have dogs—the birds go up into the arroyos and hide.”

Tod and Jim leaned over his shoulder and watched absorbedly. Dick drew a final crooked line and leaned back. “We’ll go next week. Well, wives, how did Betsy hold out? She looked like hell when she came in last night.” He handed Bob a shotgun. “I told her she ought to stay in bed, but she insisted that the future of the hospital depended upon her putting a seed pod in a salmon tin today.”

“She was wonderful. She always is. They don’t even glance at anyone’s arrangements but hers—let alone pay twenty-five dollars for them”, Faith said. We were quiet as we sipped our drinks, each haunted by the thought that we should have been able to say or do something that would have made Betsy have a physical examination.

Betsy came downstairs in a new hostess gown which Dick had given her for a homecoming present. It was black velvet with a deep heart-shaped neckline. It accentuated her pallor and made her freckles and her lipstick stand out, but it had a full skirt so she didn’t look quite so thin.

Pete eyed her. “How much weight have you lost, Betsy?” She didn’t know, fifteen or twenty pounds maybe. She was glad for the first ten, but could see that if she kept on at this rate she would be ‘like Augustus who wouldn’t eat his soup’.

“Here, eat this.” Pete handed Betsy a cracker with some cheese on it. She waved it away. “Can’t. Everything I eat makes me have a stomach-ache.” She sighed. “I’m probably turning into one of those neuros you all talk about—but I can’t remember when I was last really hungry.”

Pete said, "Eat it. I like my women round and dimpled."

Betsy obediently opened her mouth and ate the cracker. Then she said, "But don't worry about the dimples—I even have a new one to show you." She pushed down the corner of the neck of her dress and showed Pete a strange indentation which looked like the hole in dough after you have poked your finger in it.

"How long have you had that?" Pete asked. His voice had lost the lazy, teasing quality and was his formal examining-room voice. My heart dropped and I held my breath.

"I don't know, six months or so. I showed it to Dr Stubbins when I was home and he said it would bear watching—but then, he says that about everything. He's watched us all for so long it's a habit I guess."

I looked over in time to see Faith mouth the words, 'Incompetent, murdering bastard'.

"Suppose you come in to the office in the morning, Betsy. Bring her around ten o'clock, Dick." When Pete uses that tone we all do exactly what he tells us to, all except Betsy.

She stuck out her chin. "Tomorrow's Sunday and I haven't even unpacked. I'll come in some day next week." Betsy looked around to be met by the aloof, impersonal expression on each face which meant perfect medical agreement with the doctor. With an exaggerated sigh, she continued, "And don't tell me I look like the devil. I know it. I haven't closed my eyes for days nor eaten a mouthful of decent food. You know what those fall flower trips are. The trains were a crawling mass of mothers, babies and children, all tired and cross, not to speak of dirt. And the flower groups all wanted something dainty in orchid or pale blue. I don't see how people exist in a country which has no evergreens and no winter-blooming flowers. I'll be all right as soon as I've had some rest."

We waited as silently as a jury for Pete to outmanoeuvre her. "Next week would be fine, Betsy, but I happen to be solidly booked with paying patients." He grinned. "My doctors' wives and other non-paying patients, I prefer to take on Sunday whenever possible."

During dinner, I presume because we were all of, or associated with the medical profession and trained not to quiver or to speak our minds, we concentrated on news of the Patch, developments in the children and other non-essential familiar things. Betsy said that she supposed as the children got older she's have to stop these junkets around the states. They were already at the stage where they wouldn't obey Helga without arguing.

Maggie promptly became hilariously, heartbreakingly funny. The boys were little angels when she wasn't home, but let her put one foot in the house and they were so mean and ornery and hateful she just wished it was the good old days of a thousand lashes. She doubted if the state would even let 'em in the reform school when they got bigger. Her house was a pigsty, looked like a tornado had struck it and her flower arrangements—Pete accused her of stuffin' 'em in a bowl and sittin' on 'em.

Betsy ate a few mouthfuls of food and the dinner was finally over. Faith offered to round up the children and separate them into families in a vague sort of way. Although, God knew, she'd just as leave have any others as hers, but it wasn't fair to the recipient. Hers were healthy demons all the time.

"Why don't you let them all stay?" Betsy asked. Faith said, "Oh no. A medical examination and a dozen or so hellions is more than any strong woman should have to face in one morning—let alone one who has had to arrange flowers." She left to get coats and hats together. I rose to follow her, ostensibly to help, but actually to get out of the room. The atmosphere of leashed fear was so great it was almost tangible.

Maggie shook her head at me. "Speakin' of hellions, I told mine and Faith's and Mary's, in a too maternal moment, that I'd take them to the Zoo tomorrow. Why don't I take them all, and then you can come back to my house and have ham and Spoon bread?"

Barbara and Jinny were leafing through magazines. They looked up at Maggie. "Can't do it—visiting doctors—taking them up to Mount Rainier." It was Maggie's way of seeing that Betsy got to Pete's office. I told her Faith and I would take the children to the Zoo if she would cook the dinner. "Betsy, you can come direct to the house from the office and I can tell you all the gore you've missed by bein' on that trip", Maggie said.

"At the risk of seeming ungrateful, I'd much rather stay home in bed tomorrow, but as long as Pete's making me come into town, I'd love to have dinner with you. Dick can drop the kids at your house on the way to Pete's office." Desultory, familiar plans which we dovetailed with the ease of long experience. Betsy reached over to pick up a cigarette and Maggie leaned back with a sigh of triumph.

Sunday was just as we'd planned. Betsy had her examination and we all had dinner at Maggie's. The confusion with all the children kept us from showing our fear. Betsy left early with Dick to go to the hospital for observation, and we left immediately afterward.

Monday they took her to surgery. Betsy was in the hospital all winter. She begged to be taken home to the Patch in March.

"I have to see my hyacinth bed with the flowering peach tree at the back of it. I've never seen that bed in bloom. Please, let me go home."

Pete had to tell her that the agony of seeing her suffer wouldn't be fair to the children.

After that she gave up and stopped fighting.

Betsy died in April.

# 15

## Never Mind Over What's the Matter

PSYCHOSOMATIC MEDICINE:*Pertaining to the mind-body relationship.*

THE FIRST WEEK OF MAY brought the doctors' wives out of their long winter hibernation of medical meetings and school lunches. Blankets blew in the soft spring wind, painters' scaffoldings hung like bibs on their houses and their telephones rang constantly with colds, hay fever and arthritis, induced by similar activities in the homes of the patients.

White sailboats were strewn over the lake like far-flung pocket-handkerchiefs. Drifts of flowering trees lured the wives out into their gardens and winter's accumulation of dirt forced them back into their houses.

Record players, turned up to full volume, roared accompaniment to the beating of mops, the hum of vacuum cleaners and the slap of paintbrushes.

Daphne and hyacinth replaced the Garden Club's winter flower arrangements of seedpods and sage, and their haunting fragrance combined with the acrid, clean smell of turpentine, caused further restlessness in the hearts of the Neglected Ones.

Sheer physical exhaustion forced occasional brief pauses in this feverish activity, and complaints hummed over the wires like storm warnings.

'I'm so worn out I can hardly creep. HE won't pay any attention to me, so I think I'll just go down and be checked up.'

Symptoms contributed by the patients and by the calls to one another, were strung as lovingly as an Add-a-Pearl necklace on the long chain of inquietude. Slight migraines (due to the smell of paint) were not alleviated by gynergen, which HE suggested. Lower back pain (due to setting out three flats of perennials) which was not exactly a sacro-iliac as HE thinks, wasn't even touched by an infrared lamp. 'HE thinks heat will cure anything I have from athlete's foot to Vincent's.'

Fishing tackle and tide charts littered the doctors' desks and patients crowded the waiting rooms. The reports on the checked-up wives were pungently uniform. Avitaminosis.

'You know what he did. Same thing he did to you probably. Opened his right-hand desk drawer, handed me a bunch of vitamins and told me to get outdoors more. Then he showed me his new spinning reel. I'm so sick of having absolutely no medical attention or attention of any kind for that matter, I could kill myself.'

Opalescent mists drifted over the lake and the nights were soft and warm. It was spring.

Faith gave the first dinner party for Dr Randolph, a visiting psychiatrist. He was a classmate of Tod's and had arrived to give a talk on psychosomatic medicine. Faith's pearl was the lower-back pain. "I'm remodelling the basement, among other things, so Tod—with his usual low cunning—has asked house guests. I'm too exhausted to speak, let alone protest—so you have to come to dinner Friday. Seven—no, but you might bring some bourbon."

Friday, at seven-thirty, Jim was dressing and I was picking up his unsterile garments as they fell to the floor like petals from his limp hand. He meandered over to the window, laid a maroon tie along his arm and surveyed it critically.

"This Randolph's a smart cookie." He smiled reminiscently. "You'll like him."

"I'll never get to see him if you don't hurry. It is now seven thirty-five."

He sighed and wandered back to the tie-rack. "Did you give my blue plaid tie to the Good-Will? It's the only one I like."

"No, it's right there under the blue stripe."

"Where? I don't see it. How's your rash?"

"All over me and don't tell me it's an allergy."

"Maybe it's an accumulated allergy to doctors."

He finally located the blue plaid tie from an impenetrable maze of six ties, and began to stuff his pockets with notes, old insurance receipts, a pocketknife and a comb.

I suppressed a desire to scream, "Don't make your pockets look like a ski pack. We're only going six blocks", scratched my raw arms and looked moodily out the window at the delicate chartreuse dogwood blossoms against the glittering spears of the Cascade Mountains.

I turned back just in time to see him stuff three half-empty cigarette packages and two clean handkerchiefs in his hip pocket. He turned toward me with a bright, anticipatory smile. "Don't stand there dawdling, come on—it's late."

"Is Doctor Randolph attractive?" I asked idly as we drove past gardens blazing with azaleas, rhododendrons and flowering quince.

"Didn't notice, but he certainly speaks well. Sound, too." He chuckled. "Some of his case histories are funny as hell."

When we got to Faith's, I went straight into the pantry with the bottle of bourbon I'd promised. Faith was mixing old-fashioneds with her usual laboratory technique and equipment. She looked up as I came in. "Hello Mary, this is Dr Randolph."

I wondered how Jim could not have helped noticing this man. He was very tall, had white hair, which stood up like a dandelion seedpod, and his jet-black eyebrows met across the bridge of his nose. Smoke came from his nostrils as from a dragon while he spoke to me, and he had a tic on the left side of his face which twitched with every heartbeat. Faith looked slightly flustered as she returned to her millimetric measuring.

Dr Randolph's face creased with amusement as he watched her. "It is a ritual when Faith mixes a drink, is it not? May I mix them for you, Faith?" He had a deep early morning voice, so that everything he said sounded intimate.

"Thanks no, everything's under control." She started toward the icebox. Faith is tall and slim, intelligent and well co-ordinated. She was a nurse in some enormous Eastern hospital before she was married and she puts all her skilful organizing technique into running her house. Her days mesh as perfectly as an assembly line and most of her telephone calls from the other wives begin, 'Faith, how do you—?'

"I think of a nautch dancer when I see you walk, Faith." Dr Randolph's voice was silky. "It is the perfectly controlled twitching of your hips. Walk for me, Faith, while I mix the drinks for you." I was too astonished to move. He continued to play high notes on his reed pipe while Faith stood as still as the cobra and allowed him to take the ice trays.

"If you were in India, Faith, you would be the most alluring dancer in the harem—rather than the most efficient housewife of your acquaintance." She winced as he added a grain or so too much sugar to each drink, but her 'Nonsense' was weak with pleasure.

I was going to love this man. He smilingly included me in the game. "The efficiency fetish of the American woman usually denotes frustration—however, even an American girl cannot completely submerge the dancer, so Faith walks with a dangerous lilt in her step." He leaned closer toward her. "Be more of the nautch dancer, Faith, it is in your heart." Faith's cheeks became quite pink as she put the drinks on a tray. You could almost see the conflict going on in her mind. If she moved, she nautched, and if she said her usual brisk 'Let's get going, our guests are not camels', she was denoting frustration. Dr Randolph picked up the tray and walked ahead of us, tactfully solving her problem.

My whisper was urgent. "How long is this Mephistopheles going to stay here?" I wanted to know about me.

"A week or so. His wife's with him. Now where in the devil did I put the cocktail napkins?"

The guests were congregated on the terrace and Tod was explaining Faith's camellia bed. Here was no nostalgic Southern riot of bloom, but the shining precision of a laboratory. Each bush held its full quota of tremendous blooms and each shining green leaf was wormless and bugless. Maggie was ecstatic.

"Faith, I don't see how you do it, but then I don't see how you do most things, honey. At home the camellias are all over everything, but they look real raggedy. Of course, I can't even have a good crop of weeds, the children stamp everything down the minute it sticks its head up."

"The children don't play in this part of the yard, of course", Faith began, and then gave Dr Randolph a sidelong glance. "Good varieties and spray—the climate—" her voice trailed off.

"How's your back, honey? I meant to ask you when I came in." Maggie's voice was courteously solicitous.

"My back? Oh fine—I haven't thought about it much. Just gardening probably."

Dr Randolph walked over toward Maggie. It looked like it might be her turn, so I followed him.

"How many children have you, Mrs Roberts?"

"Three boys fundamentally, but millions by ten o'clock in the morning—all shoutin' and shriekin' and runnin' through the house. We've had painters all this week and naturally children can't stay away when anything fascinatin' like paintin's goin' on. Have you any children, Dr Randolph?"

"No, we haven't."

"Well, mine are just fiends. Oh, I really have fun with them except when I have somethin' goin' on, and then I could scalp them all. They've been gettin' in the paint and spillin' it on the rug—" she went on with a laughing description of pure bedlam.

"Children have an immediate and untrammelled reaction to beauty and personal magnetism that I find very interesting to watch." His eyes caressed Maggie's charming, vital face. "I'm afraid you'll always have crowds of children, and adults as well, Mrs Roberts, you'll just have to dispose of the painters."

Maggie was used to the charming flattery of Southern men, but this calm assumption that her dangerous person caused her household havoc was a pleasant new idea.

As Dr Randolph walked over toward Dorothy, Maggie took Faith's arm. "Faith, that Dr Randolph's real dangerous. Are you sure you're safe with him in the house?"

"Not in the least, and it's a pleasant change." Faith raised her voice to include the group, "Shall we have dinner?" Her hips switched like a clock pendulum as she walked into the dining room.

Dear old too-familiar faces Faith and Tod, internal medicine; Dorothy and Bill, surgery; Maggie and Pete, obstetrics; Mary and Jim, internal medicine with the delightful and stimulating transfusion of new blood in the form of Dr Randolph and Betty, psychiatry. The wives' eyes shone with the hope that here at least there would not be the usual melodic line of incomprehensible medical terminology with a *sotto voce* accompaniment of house cleaning and children.

Dr Randolph sat next to me, and Betty sat across from me and next to Pete. Betty was the antithesis of her husband. Short and warmly round, she was effortlessly frank and amusing. Pete's dimples were their most deeply appreciative as he listened to her. 'Read pinchy-bust for satyriasis, selfish pig for introversion, life of the party for extroversion and spoiled brat for infantilism, and you have my job.'

"Have you always done personnel work?"

"No, I stayed home hoping to be pregnant until I almost

produced pseudocyesis. Then I went to work in an aeroplane factory. Personnel, of course, is their grave problem. I'd been listening to Paul for fifteen years, so I thought I probably could qualify, and I did."

"And now?" Pete's eyes were gleaming with appreciation of this healthy, nerveless wife of a doctor.

"Now I am the Personnel Manager. Perfect job for a woman. Monkeying in other people's affairs and getting paid for it." Pete's laugh was explosive. "I've got a long list of potential assistants for you, whenever you need them", he said.

Dr Randolph turned to me. "Faith tells me you sold radio advertising before you were married. The adjustment of sublimating your personality must have been difficult."

Just as I found myself eagerly starting to tell him how white I'd been about the whole thing, I caught Jim's amused expression. He lifted his quotation eyebrow. 'The secret of being a bore is to tell everything.'

I could almost hear it. I swallowed the cud of life history, remembered that Dr Randolph was a Menninger product, and prepared to be impressively psychiatric. I asked him to tell me exactly what the term 'psychiatric consultant' meant.

Dr Randolph blew a gust of cigarette smoke through the mashed potatoes he was reflectively chewing in an original but probably well-adjusted manner. Then in a lullaby voice just a notch above 'Once there were three bears . . .' he began.

"The psychiatrist as consultant to a firm employing large numbers of employees attempts to play the role of the medical man who is interested in correction, amelioration, or elimination of the problems of the individual man. This attitude has heretofore been quite foreign to the mass production, profit system. He must, therefore, play this role in a milieu set up to ignore the personality problems of the individual as long as the group functions profitably."

He grinned as my eyes began to glaze with medical incomprehension, and the narcotic effort of his mellifluous voice. "Let's put it this way. Executives in enormous firms become so important that they have very little to do but brood about nebulous things. They eventually become introspective, so they pay a psychiatrist huge sums to give them an *alter ego* on which to blame their personality peculiarities, and to prevent them from ramming square pegs into round holes from an employee standpoint. Is that better?' His eyes glinted wickedly.

"It's more my mental level", I said.

"It hasn't as much personal application perhaps. Then, too, no matter how vitriolic the dissatisfied wives of these executives become, I furnish a protective colouring of psychiatric terminology. 'Emotional instability' hurled at an angry wife, is a lot more satisfying than 'yah-yah-yah', and it leaves her with a sneaking hunch that it might be true."

Dorothy Jenkins broke in eagerly, "What does psychosomatic medicine mean exactly?"

"Psychic symptoms can, and often do, cause somatic trauma. When the cause of the psychic disturbance is uncovered, the physical symptoms disappear."

Pete broke in, "Occasionally we see cases of pseudocyesis where the patient has actually been capable of swelling the abdomen to simulate pregnancy."

"She wasn't a doctor's wife or she wouldn't have had to simulate pregnancy—she'd be pregnant." Maggie patted her swelling stomach fondly.

Jim made a determined effort to keep the conversation in the clear eddy of medical discussion.

"I had an interesting case of hysteria this year. The early predomal symptoms were the usual headache and tiredness. The final symptoms were muscle hypofunction and then partial paralysis. There were certain inherent deficiencies in this patient's background which, up until her parents refused to let her marry this boy, had not produced any chronic psychological inaptitudes. However, the psychic disturbance was so great that, coupled with the emotional depletion of endocrine reserves, it caused a partial neuro-blocking of vasomotorimpulses which finally resulted in paralysis."

Jim is past master at the telling phrase when he is sympathetically reviewing a case in which he is vitally interested. But let him retell this case to doctors, and he carefully removes any colourful shreds of marrow from the bare bones.

I began the laborious reconstruction process. "Tell about her old stone-faced father first, Jim."

The rhythm of Dr Randolph's facial tic quickened with interest. "It failed to fall into a diagnostic pattern?" he asked.

“Not so far as we could tell. There was the usual history of vague headaches, anorexia, diarrhoea, polyuria and physical exhaustion. She was a nurse, so she attributed these symptoms to anxiety and strain due to her duty on the psychiatric ward.”

“Jim, *please* tell it so we can all understand it. Tell about her granite pylon of a mother.” It was like removing a beard with a stone instrument, hair by hair. The Norwegian nurse was on the psychiatric ward—the Italian doctor was a medical resident. She apparently admired his drive and ebulliency as much as he was fascinated by her blonde braids and aloof manner. They had the usual dates, against the hospital rules, and, as this was her first dereliction from duty, she began to have headaches. Her family placed a sea wall of objections in the way of marriage, stemming primarily from the fact that an Italian couldn’t possibly originate in a Norwegian fjord.

His family contributed to this resistance by pelting the Norwegians with bottles of excellent wine, crates of berries and many telephone calls protesting Italian good will. You don’t buy Nordic friendship, and they remained adamant.

During the resultant impasse, intense muscle pain, hypofunction and eventually partial paralysis developed in the obedient nurse. After careful examination it was determined that subconscious rebellion, rather than somatic trauma, caused the dysfunction and the Norwegians were persuaded to relent in order that their daughter might walk again. They were of the ‘if you’re not bleeding, you must be well or disobedient’ school of medicine and this feat took much stern medical persuasion.

The wedding reception was held in an impersonal hotel halfway between the Norwegian district and the Italian quarter. On one side of the room, the Italians waved their hands, drank innumerable toasts to the bride, to the groom and to one another, paid extravagant compliments to Jim and promised their beloved offspring their cars, their houses—anything and everything to make their *bambino* happy.

The Norwegians stoically inhabited folding chairs on the opposite side of the room and gazed with glacial eyes at the ‘Wops’. Occasionally they vouchsafed a reluctant ‘Yah —she iss a good girl.’

Faith said, “She should have waited until after she married a doctor to get paralyzed. She could have used it then.

Betty Randolph’s shrewd blue eyes rested speculatively on Faith. “Avoid the issue as I do—get a job. It lowers the perfection requirements of the so-called 'lost' American woman."

"It seems to minimize frustration after forty." Dr Randolph gazed fondly at Betty. "No fancy terms for her, no long and unsatisfactory personal analysis. She merely applies the tenets of a good digestion and cheerful disposition and seems to be a huge success."

"It's certainly simple. If a welder shyly confesses she is going to quit because she yearns for Ole, I give her a job next to Ole—and the rest is up to her. If Jerry longs to pinch Mable, they are both given a job way up in the scaffolding and Mable either gets used to being pinched or falls off. Satyriasis in a factory is relatively easy to handle."

Most psychiatrists I have seen look as though they could use a little of their own sulphur and molasses, and Dr Randolph, in spite of his siren quality, was no exception. He was under a terrific tension and it was very obvious. He smoked continuously, wafting great gusts of smoke through each bite of food. He was charming and suave and undoubtedly one of the top men in his field, but he was at least as maladjusted as the rest of us and did have a definite facial tic.

"Did you finish your analysis with Menninger?" I asked. Betty grinned at me as Paul Randolph prepared to dart with consummate agility around the point. "Not quite, a year or so more. Probably have a chance to complete my analysis next year." Every time I meet an analyist, sooner or later I sidle up to him and ask him if he's finished his own analysis. Nine times out of ten he lacks a year or so of completion and he is always going back to finish up at some future date. It seems to be something like achieving charm—each year it gets better but the best is a mirage which is always just over the next hill.

Betty broke in. "*I'm* finishing his analysis. If he'd stop smoking so much, go fishing, and quit playing with coots all the time, he'd be all right. It's just as though he were continually living in a swamp where everything is dreadfully distorted. What he needs is what every normal human being needs—fresh air, sunshine and a couple of weeks in a factory. There are no complications there. Work a little, complain a lot and covet everything in a sweater. Avitaminosis—no less."

There was a howl of derisive laughter from the wives. Avitaminosis. Almost in unison they told their stories. Sciatics, migraine, nervous indigestion, bursitis, rashes, all due to avitaminosis. Psychosomatic medicine was what they wanted.

After dinner Dorothy brought her well-muscled little body over for Dr Randolph's soul salve.

"Could my sciatic be psychosomatic? I've practically lived outdoors all my life, and now I can't sleep on my back at all. And don't suggest B complex. My stomach rattles I've swallowed so many B complex tablets."

The soft spring night was filled with the haunting Chopin Second Concerto. Stock and iris and the smell of wet earth clutched at your throat from every side.

"This amazing country!" Dr Randolph drew in a deep breath. "You ski, Dorothy. You know, effortless precision in sports always reminds me of a concerto. The tremendous etched background of the mountains and the lovely breathless flight of the skirt—so like a masterfully executed cadenza."

Dorothy gave a gusty sigh. "How can I possibly ski when I have children hanging on me all the time?" Her voice was almost tearful at the picture she was creating of herself.

"Take your children with you. Let them watch you ski. They will then know the poetic, creative side of their mother. It seems only fair to them. You will always be a winged thing in their minds as well as a haven."

Dorothy's face became radiant as she listened and Bill's face had an unsure, husbandy look.

Dr Randolph turned to me. "Mary, do you find that your tremendous vitality has a sufficient outlet in merely being a housewife?"

I said that merely being a housewife, as he so quaintly put it, required twenty-four hours of unremitting labour to maintain even a stationary place on the treadmill. He, for instance, was not required to be a lawyer, a sales manager, a purchasing agent and an accountant, not to speak of hundreds of little graceful attributes which he was urged to acquire as additional personal charm.

The Randolphs were entertained all the week they were here, and the doctors did not protest or think up medical meetings. As a farewell gift, Faith received Schonberg's *Transfigured Night*; Maggie, Debussy's *Children's Corner*; Dorothy, *Night on Bald Mountain*; and I, Khachaturian's *Concerto for Piano and Orchestra.*

During the days that followed there were a couple of psychic tremors. Faith called to ask the formula for peanut butter cookies. "Speaking of cookies, have you seen Maggie?—neither had I until yesterday. I wish you'd been there—a pup tent in the living room, little boys tearing in and out like wild Indians, Maggie baking cookies and handing them over before they cooled—oozing magnetism with every cookie. Dr Randolph should have told her that a firm hand beats personal magnetism any day in the week to my way of thinking."

Maggie called to ask us to eat chicken hash Sunday night. "Although goodness knows if you'll get anything to eat. Faith was over here yesterday morning flipping her fanny like a Shetland pony and bossing the daylights out of me. She brought a couple of Schonberg's recordings that are all squeaky and bangy and have no tune and told me if I'd concentrate I'd learn to like 'em. She'd better concentrate on givin' those children of hers some lovin' care—that's what she'd better do—tellin' me I had no business takin' care of Dorothy's babies."

"Where's Dorothy?" I asked.

"Spring skiin' with the older two. She just keeps goin' higher and higher up in the mountains like a goat. Bill's goin' to have to shoot her to get her down. What did that old Paul Randolph tell you, honey?"

"He suggested a creative outlet for my energy—said it would be the best thing for Jim's ulcer."

"What energy?" Maggie snorted and hung up.

Sunday night at Maggie's we were waiting for the men to come home from the golf course. Faith was making old-fashioneds while Maggie and I were getting supper on the table. Faith turned and asked Maggie for the bar sugar.

"There isn't any bar sugar nor any other kind. I used the last grain makin' cookies. The last, may I add, that I'm ever goin' to make. From now on I'm buyin' hard tack by the bale and throwin' it to those devils through the bars of strong cages." She slammed the oven door and turned and faced us. "This afternoon after I drove Dorothy's little demons home I walked in this house, grabbed the boys by the scruff of the neck, banged 'em on the head and put 'em to bed where they're goin' to stay till they mind their manners. I sweah—ever since that creepy old sweet-talkin' Doctor Randolph told me I had personal magnetism, I've just acted soft in the head. This house has been just like feedin' time at the Zoo, and Pete barely speaks to me."

Faith put a meticulously measured seven-eighths of a teaspoonful of maraschino juice in each old-fashioned glass and turned to me. "And how is your id?"

Id, as far as I was concerned, was short for idiot. My unleashed energy had created little dresses for the children which they were too sharp to even try on, let alone wear. I'd created so many new dishes that the whole family either looked furtive or hid when they were called to dinner; Jim gulped soda by the handful and threatened to eat all his meals at the hospital. I'd created so much havoc in the garden that even the oldest and sturdiest shrubs were drooping or dead. I'd say offhand that I'd created confusion. Other than that 'id' was just dandy and how was hers?

Just at that moment Dorothy appeared in the kitchen doorway, beaming and on crutches. "Sorry I'm late, but I had to get this ankle taped up. It's not broken, just a bad sprain. Maggie, you were an angel to take the babies. I had the most divine time; the children are both doing Christies. I'm so thrilled, my dear!"

Faith handed her a drink. "How did you sprain your ankle?"

"Well, my dear, it was the funniest thing. There was this Swiss ski teacher—a terrific skier and a divine dancer. We were doing the Swedish polka; he whirled me over his head—and sprained my ankle."

"Nautch", Faith said and raised one eyebrow at me. "Did you get that gorgeous tan skiing with the Swiss?" Faith examined Dorothy's arms enviously.

"Heavens no! I couldn't begin to keep up with him. He took the children off early in the morning and they skied with him all day. I practically never saw them. I skied once or twice before I sprained my ankle, but I got so stiff, my sciatics nearly killed me. There were a lot of Austrian and Norwegian jumpers up there—we played records and sat on the sun deck all day long. Oh it was heavenly. The mountains were the most gorgeous things you can imagine!"

Faith carried the cocktails into the living room and we followed her. She put the Schonberg on the record player, listened attentively for a few moments, shook her head, and turned to Dorothy. "Skiing is largely a matter of practice and control, isn't it?"

"Oh definitely. I'm too old just to swoosh down the hills like I used to, and too impatient to bother to learn the new techniques. I'll leave that to the children."

Faith said, "I should think if you took a few lessons and practised—"

Dorothy interrupted her, "You'd ski divinely, my dear, with that brain and that body. You'd be terrific!"

"And with free medical care to mend your broken bones you can't lose!" Maggie added darkly.

Faith walked over toward the record player. "Who said anything about skiing? It's the child care and the sun deck that arouses my sporting blood." She turned off the Schonberg. "My God, that thing's hideous! I've listened to it about fifty times and it's just plain ugly." She searched through the records and put on 'Whispering'.

"There, that's more my mental level. You know, after having Doctor Randolph and his bumptious Betty in the house for a whole week, I think I'll just keep my psychic quirks—Tod's used to them now, so what the hell."

# 16

## It is Out, Isn't It?

MEDICAL CONVENTION: *I am torn between two and I give them both to you. 'Arbitrary custom' and 'Extraordinary assembly'. You can take your choice.*

WHEN YOU HEAR a Doctor's wife say, 'Bill's gone to St. Louis to a medical meeting. No, I've never been there. Oh yes, he asked me to go, but there's the spring cleaning, and the P.T.A. tea, and the garden's alive with slugs', don't jump to conclusions.

She gets cabin fever just as often as you do, her motto is also 'Do I care where it is?—it's out, isn't it?' But she has learned the hard way that waiting is pleasanter in the familiar surroundings of her own home than it is in an unfamiliar hotel bedroom in a strange city.

Periodically we all forget this and start badgering our husbands to take us with them to a medical meeting. Hope springs eternal, and we know that this time it is going to be different.

Early in the fall, Maggie and I decided that we wanted to go to the A.M.A. We planted little suggestive seeds all winter. As each one withered in the clay of long familiarity, undaunted, we borrowed seeds from other Neglected Ones. 'Tell HIM that you and the children get on each other's nerves less if you have a vacation', Barbara said. 'That one worked with Atlantic City.'

Jim said what about his nerves and Pete said he would not deprive the boys of Maggie's personal magnetism even for a week.

Barbara suggested a good big fight, with packed suitcases left in various strategic places. 'Don't forget to leave them where HE'll stumble over them—otherwise of course, HE won't notice.' That seed had produced her trip to Chicago, although she thought for a while that she might have to go home to her mother for good. The fight was a little bigger than she'd planned.

Faith suggested the seed that took root and, oddly enough, it was the truth. 'Why don't you tell HIM that you want one week of HIS undivided attention? Sort of a second honeymoon only you don't have to be nauseating about it.'

Maggie and I called each other hourly, planning days of luxury followed by orgies of nightlife—when Maggie wasn't brooding over the possibility that she might not be able to get childcare and would have to stay home.

Our family was blessed with Sumie, the little Japanese girl who came in after school to do everything better than I would ever be able to. I thought her efficiency, charm and remarkable influence on the children, was a question of being Nisei, or second generation. Jim recognised it for what it undoubtedly is—the excellence of Japanese home training plus a brilliant mind and a sound body.

I called Jim so many times at the office that Jean took to telling me that he had a patient and could she take the message.

Finally, I settled down to find out what this A.M.A. was we were so hell-bent on attending. The report went something like this: An A.M.A. is an enormous convention. There are only five or six cities in the United States with sufficient hotel accommodations to house the members; fifteen to twenty thousand doctors attend. An A.M.A. is like a twenty-ring circus with as many as thirty important papers going on at the same time.

The scientific exhibits, dealing with the progress of the various branches of medicine, fill one-half of a huge auditorium. The other half is dedicated to the technical exhibits furnished by the pharmaceutical firms, medical publishers and producers of food. Jim said idly that he thought I would enjoy those exhibits. They would remind me of the good old days in advertising.

No doctor can possibly attend more than the small section of the sessions which refers to his speciality. The doctors who can manage to attend an A.M.A. usually do so, but in order to leave the necessary skeleton staffs at home to care for the sick, they can't all go every year. To be asked to give a paper is a signal honour and requires terrific work.

The convention serves a valuable dual purpose. The doctor is brought up to date on all new medical procedures, the latest developments in equipment and technique, and has a chance to see and hear the outstanding men in his field. He returns to his own practice with renewed interest and a sneaking hunch that although he hasn't had a chance to study as much as he would like to he is not as far behind as he thought he was.

One wife said she was glad she went to St. Louis; it was the year her mother was so sick and the time passed very quickly. Another said she adored the Chicago meeting, an old beau and his wife were marvellous to her. She only ran into her husband quite by accident an hour before the train time home.

The older, more experienced wives had a uniform recommendation. If we felt a compulsion neurosis to go, we'd better stick with the Women's Auxiliary. It was quite exhausting, but you did see the city and anything was better than brooding in a hotel bedroom, waiting for husbands who never came.

By this time I was so wrapped up in my mental picture of a second honeymoon that I gave Maggie a glowing description of San Francisco. I attended an advertising convention for a giddy two-week period a couple of years before I was married, and I had a vivid memory of a city as deftly enchanting as a sophisticated woman; of my large, comfortable hotel room and the cordial note of welcome with the enormous box of roses. Of the view from my window of misty lights and the Bay veiled and subtle. Of intimate little restaurants which served wonderful food. Of perpendicular hills and cable cars filled with gay, busy people who swung on and off with suicidal carelessness. Of the advertising convention itself, glittering, mammoth and roistering. Of rushing back to the hotel to change my clothes and finding, no matter what I wore, that I boiled in cotton during the day and froze in fur after four o'clock although the San Francisco women wore suits all the time, looked as crisp as eyelet embroidery, and seemed perfectly comfortable.

I ended this Chamber of Commerce eulogy with the fact that *I* certainly wasn't going to stick with the Women's Auxiliary. That any fool doctor's wife who preferred to tag along with a herd of women, when she could be alone with her husband, deserved to rot in her hotel room.

Maggie asked me what made me think THEY'D stay with us just because we were in San Francisco. After all, it was a medical meeting. She was a little bitter because her child carer was being coy and unsure about staying with little boys. 'Although what she's screamin' about I don't know. She only has to stay a week and I have to live with 'em all year long.' It was a trying time.

We decided to borrow suits from the Neglected Ones who were not going. With the heterogeneous enthusiasm of a Salvation Army drive, we rushed from house to house, snatched what was not actually being worn, carted it home and divided it up. By careful selection we finally succeeded in ramming our borrowed suits into six borrowed fortnighters—three for each. Jim and Pete were firm. This was not a safari into the Gobi Desert, but one week in San Francisco. We could take one small suitcase and an overnight bag. Sumie packed the same number of suits into one fortnighter and then went over to Maggie's and did the same thing for her. Then she produced an older sister to stay with Maggie's children. 'We have little brothers, we are used to little boys.'

One hour before train time, Jim came home, filled his fortnighter with papers, books, lantern slides and A.M.A. *Journals*, stuffed four shirts and a toothbrush into an overnight bag, and was ready to leave.

The moment we got on the train, Pete and Jim settled in one section, opened their fortnighters and began to sort and to drop papers, and to ignore us completely.

Maggie said, "Let's not wait for them, let's go in the dinah and eat everything on the menu. Just imagine one whole week of a real creamy hotel and somebody else's cookin'."

In the diner we discussed what we thought the A.M.A. would be like. Maggie remembered staining slides and fixing museum specimens for every doctor in the hospital for six months before an A.M.A., working until she was blind as a mole. It stood to reason that if every technician all over the country was doin' that, there must be hundreds of miles of slides, not to speak of acres of museum specimens. She just had a good mind to spend one day at the medical exhibits, if only to prove to herself that she'd rather be married.

I definitely wanted to spend one day at the technical exhibits. Why, at the advertising convention beautiful models stalked around scantily clad. Named bands played at both ends of the enormous auditorium. Machines, their motors throttled down to a refined murmur, washed or ironed or cooked or mowed. There were athletic contests and World Champions littered the place like peanut shells. Purple velvet, gold braid, and tremendous baskets of flowers made the auditorium seem like a cross between a king's coronation and a gangster's funeral!

Maggie chewed and looked thoughtfully at me. She hoped I

wouldn't be disappointed but in her estimation doctors sure gave the old kiss of death to everything they touched.'

"Nothing bothers real merchandising", I said loyally. "You just wait until you see what an untrammelled advertiser can do."

Maggie knew one thing, she'd made Pete promise on a stack of Bibles that he'd take her dancing to a different place every single night, meeting or no meeting. She'd never been in San Francisco, but this was one time when Pete's patient Griselda was goin' to turn into old Slough Foot Sue right in front of his eyes. She was goin' to pretend every minute that Pete was still datin' her and takin' her dancin', and she was goin' to be plenty hard to get—but plenty!

I wasn't so sure about dancing every night, considering the fact that Jim had never willingly touched toe to dance floor even before we were married, but I was planning to see two or three good shows, spend quite a lot of time at the Top of the Mark, and concentrate on having breakfast in bed every single morning.

We spent the rest of the trip in the diner, except for a few brief forays into the women's dressing-room to experiment with make-up suitable for night clubs.

As we neared Oakland, Pete and Jim began to show restrained excitement. They jumped off the train into a *mêlée* of doctors and hailed this one and that one with wild enthusiasm. That is, it was wild enthusiasm for doctors. Maggie and I stood against a pillar waiting for the luggage, and watched the doctors' wives trail up the ramp on to the ferry like animals going into the Ark. Two yellow ermines, two minks, two silver fox capes, an oddly mated squirrel and otter, a leopard and what we feared was real sable.

"I'm beginnin' to feel underprivileged", Maggie said clutching Dorothy's blue suit around her and looking, for the first time, at the way it hung. "And if that's the Women's Auxiliary, I hope they're goin' to be hotter than a fox the whole time they're here."

I undid the lower two buttons of Faith's brown suit, It had been fairly snug around the middle when I put it on, and the time spent constantly in the diner hadn't loosened it any. "Oh well, we can always pretend we're hen medics and are here to improve our minds. Come on, here are the bags."

In the taxi we discovered that we were to be in different hotels. 'What about breakfast in bed?' we wailed. 'And what about waiting for you to come home from the meetings?'

Pete and Jim looked distinctly pained. The hotel reservations were made months ahead of time, the specialities confined to one hotel as much as possible. The hotels were right across the street from one another. Pete suggested that if worst came to worst, one of us could always get dressed, go across the street to the other's room, get undressed, get into bed and then order breakfast. This coming to the A.M.A. was our idea, not theirs. We dropped Pete and Maggie at the St. Clemens and went across to our hotel.

The Fairfield was a small grubby edifice, crouched between two more imposing buildings. The long bay window facing the street exposed a rubber plant and two morose gentlemen asleep in Morris chairs. As we walked through the revolving doors, we found that the lobby was entirely missing.

Carpenters and plasterers hung precariously over what had once been the desk area and roared 'hold'er' to each other. The switchboard operator, sitting in a strange little island in the midst of saw horses, table saws and mounds of canvas covered furniture, was murmuring laconically, 'Fairfield, sorry, no reservations, sorry, you might try the Medical Registrar.' The switchboard's exposed back faced the entrance. It writhed and blinked as she spoke. The desk clerk, minus any desk other than a couple of apple boxes and an oak table, was explaining to a whining guest that he thought the elevator would be running again by six o'clock. He couldn't promise anything definite, what with the remodelling and a damned medical convention.

Jim told me to stand by the luggage, picked his way over to the apple boxes, and said something to the desk clerk. As he spoke he turned and pointed at me and shook his head. The desk clerk leaned far forward, looked me over carefully, and said, "Oh. Well, we can take her up in the freight elevator, Doctor. It'd be better than having something happen in the lobby."

Jim said, "Fine, thanks", took me tenderly by the arm and ushered me across the lumpy canvas and into the creaky freight elevator. An aged bell-hop followed with our bags and stood as far from us as possible, eyeing me nervously.

When we got in our room, the bell-hop dropped our bags, opened the window a quarter of an inch, turned the radiator on and off, swiped at the bureau, muttered that the radio worked by putting in a nickel and dashed out the door without a tip.

"What did you tell the desk clerk about me?" I asked. Jim grinned. "He said our room was on the twelfth floor. I just said I was afraid the stairs would be too much for you in your condition, added that I didn't dare leave you home and he drew his own conclusions. Now, now, better start unpacking and I'll go and see where the fire exits are."

I stood in the middle of the room for the simple reason that I was afraid to sit down on anything. A lipstick-stained Kleenex was crumpled on the bureau beside a dirty comb with a few hairs still clinging to it. The air was thick with the mingled odours of disinfectant and stale cigarette smoke. There was an electric-blue velour chair with a dark spot where many greasy heads had rested.

The beds were covered with soiled peach-coloured rayon bedspreads pulled crookedly over lumpy blankets. For the first time in my life I looked to see if the sheets were clean. Under the glass topped surface of the bureau were rules covering everything from the Mann Act to outright burglary. The wastebasket had not been emptied and the room made you uncomfortably aware of every sordid occupant that had ever been in it. As a place to wait for Jim, I infinitely preferred any lavatory in any station.

Jim came back and said the fire exit was to the right, the elevator was running again, although it looked kind of rickety to him, that he'd found a maid in the hall who had promised to clean the room, and how about taking a bath and changing my clothes so we could go out to Civic Centre and register.

We picked up Maggie and Pete and went out to the Auditorium. Hundreds of doctors milled around the entrance and streamed in and out of the building. Maggie gave a shout of joy and embraced a charming looking older doctor. "Mary, this is Doctor Mac—the one I used to make the slides for. Is Doctor John here, too?" Dr Mac pointed to a group of St. Louis doctors to whom Pete and Jim were talking and Maggie disappeared into the centre of the group. Doctor Mac followed her fondly with his eyes. "We've never had anyone like Maggie. Boy, was she a wizard! Only lacked six months to get her master's degree you know. Photomicrography and slides were always perfect. We certainly miss her at the hospital." His expression held the impersonal medical admiration engendered only by a flawless technique.

For some reason, Maggie as a technician had never occurred to me. I was perfectly accustomed to having every male cast an admiring and often covetous glance at her whenever she walked into a room, and always waited with fiendish delight for the surprised, hurt look which followed an excess of enthusiasm accompanied by an error in judgement. Maggie was like a porcupine, she looked smooth and sounded gentle, consequently they were never prepared for the suddenness of her verbal quills. She came back to us, stood on tiptoe and whispered to Doctor Mac. He grinned and nodded and they disappeared into the building and came back proudly bearing two badges. 'Dr M.Jay, Exhibitor', and 'Dr M. Roberts, Exhibitor'.

Maggie was glowing. "Dr Mac got these for us, bless his heart. Now we can get in to see the scientific exhibits; lay people aren't allowed you know. I can hardly wait to see Dr Mac's coloured microphotography on the cervix." I watched for the usual conspiratorial wink, but it was missing. Maggie *wanted* to see his exhibit. I was thoroughly shaken.

We had dinner with the St. Louis doctors. Maggie talked medicine all during dinner. Then she announced she was going to bed, so she could get up bright and early the next morning.

Jim went on to a meeting and I went up to our room. It had been cleaned after a fashion. A towel hung over the greasy spot on the chair, the bedspreads were now orchid rayon and folders saying welcome to California were on the desk. I took a book and got into bed and began to answer the telephone. It rang steadily until eleven o'clock. Every call was for Jim and from strange doctors. At eleven o'clock I turned out the light and went to sleep.

The next morning Jim left before eight o'clock to meet Pete. I was just trying to decide which luxurious breakfast in bed I'd order when Maggie called. "Hurry up and get dressed, honey. I'll meet you downstairs for breakfast. We've got to get out to the Auditorium. The exhibits open this morning."

During breakfast she kept up a bewildering chatter about iron hematoxylin stains *versus* sudan one, two and three, and eosin methylene blue. Worst symptom of all, she had on her own suit. I felt I'd given birth to a changeling.

The entrance hall of the Auditorium was the first major shock. Instead of the advertising convention's sheaves of flowers, shimmering satin hangings, fountains of perfume and importunate programme sellers, the A.M.A. had covered the walls with a wrinkly black material which hung limply like an old Halloween costume and smelled of formalin and dust. The programmes were piled on little oak tables presided over by stern young men.

There were rows of small windows like bank tellers' cages, each manned by a quietly efficient registrar. On the right wall hung an inconspicuous sign, black lettering on white cardboard, which read, 'Scientific Exhibits'. On the left wall hung a similar sign reading, 'Technical Exhibits'. In spite of this forbidding atmosphere, the doctors were practically knocking each other down to get in.

An attendant under the Scientific Exhibit sign looked at our badges and nodded permission to enter. The right side of the Auditorium had been divided by means of screens into gloomy, dark cubicles. Around the walls of the first cubicle were a series of small oak tables presided over by the exhibiting doctors. As my eyes became accustomed to the murky gloom, I realized that on all the walls there were lighted photographs, some in colour and some in black and white, of brain tumours. On the wall behind each exhibitor's table were signs indicating the type of the exhibit, intricate graphs and charts.

"Isn't this exciting? I told you it was like a State Fair", Maggie said happily as she bent down to read the lettering on a table full of jars. The exhibiting doctor smiled deprecatingly and fumbled with a box of slides. Maggie picked up a jar and handed it to me. 'Beautiful, beautiful!' The contents of the jar was not remotely like Ma's Prize Pickles. It contained cross sections of brain tumour, in varying shades of revolting pinkish grey. I quickly handed it back to her. "If that isn't the prettiest old brain and what a tumour. Never seen a neater. You must be awful proud of this exhibit." The doctor looked pleased and shy and I could almost hear him say, 'I'll give you the recipe if you like.'

"I feel like a regulah old fiah horse", Maggie said and asked him to explain the long list of cerebrocranial injuries on the chart back of his table. I wandered into the next enclosure and stood rooted to the spot! The whole far side of the room held an enormous lighted cabinet. Some literal-minded medical Madame Tussaud, not satisfied with graphs and lantern slides and specimens had made life-sized pink rubber people! Not whole people, but parts of people! Half of a head with a bulging Cyclops eye. Next to it a head, the scalp of which was raised like a butter dish so you could see the tumour at work on the brain. I walked over in a mesmeric state of horror and touched one. It gave slightly like a magic skin doll. Maggie had followed me and was absorbedly reading graphs of personality changes, physical changes and the all-too-discouraging fatality percentages which were in large black letters on the wall beside the cabinet. "I sweah, the progress in brain surgery, even since my time, is the most amazing thing. Imagine bein' able to see that wonderful progression in the growth of a tumour."

She pointed to a lower shelf where there was a whole set of pink people. The first one looked merely surprised, the second surprised and worried; the third, surprised, worried and pained. Through a series of twelve he got steadily worse, until the last was Bela Lugosi just as he jumps out at you, only the top of his head was on another shelf—a trick Bela should try some time.

"If you think these are good, just wait till you see the movie. The exhibiting doctor said it was excellent."

"I can hardly wait", I murmured, averting my eyes from a cerebral tumour as large as an Easter bonnet, this time on half the head of a pink rubber female with one raised eyebrow. Maggie flitted ahead of me to a series of museum specimens mounted in oval glass.

As I followed her I tried to get hold of myself. There was no reason why I should hate these things so. After all I was a doctor's wife and I should have learned, by this time, not to apply everything I saw personally. I should cultivate the aloof, scientific desire to observe and learn, beginning with the fact that I was looking at diseased organs, not repulsive insides. I mentally held my nose and dived into the next room.

It was a cancer exhibit. At the end of half an hour, I was a seething mass of shooting pains and the only cancer I didn't have was cancer of the prostate.

I was so whipped by this time that I positively leaped at the chance to hear a lecture on fractures and fracture splints. As we followed a long queue of doctors into the lecture room, Maggie told me that this was the opportunity of a lifetime. That Dr Hanson was so famous for giving the most brilliant lectures that even Pete was taking time off to hear him. She'd read a lot of his articles and of course was familiar with his splints, but just imagine seeing and hearing him!

When the lecture auditorium was filled to S.R.O., a long, angular doctor ambled out on the platform and smiled hesitantly. He then called to the back of the room and asked another doctor if the slides were ready. There was a loud crash followed by muttered curses and a voice said, 'I think so. I've dropped them but—"

Maggie giggled. "Now watch. He's helpless without his nurse hoverin' in the background to pick them up."

There flashed on the screen:

latipsoH ycreM
sesaC 005

The lecturer said, "That slide seems to be backward, Doctor."

There were more muttered curses and 'Mercy Hospital—500 Cases' was substituted.

Dr Hanson spoke well and authoritatively of hip fractures in the aged, of the attendant deaths from shock and the prevention thereof. A little old lady was shown lying in bed in a Hanson Splint and then three weeks later—she was shown in a wheel-chair hanging from the ceiling!

"That slide seems to be upside down, Doctor."

An old man was shown lying in bed in a Hanson Splint and in two weeks he had progressed so far he had turned into a little coloured boy!

"That slide seems to be misplaced, Doctor."

Maggie and I were having muffled hysterics but the hundreds of doctors in the auditorium were sitting on the edges of their chairs, listening with rapt attention.

Dr Hanson abandoned the slides and continued to tell of thousands of hours of patient work on fractures. As we left the lecture we heard on all sides, 'If I never hear anything else—that's the best damned paper I've heard in years.'

"Why didn't his wife or his nurse arrange those slides and give them to that doctor all ready to be shown? Of all the dough-headed tricks to leave him alone at a time like that", Maggie snorted. "Come on, honey, I'm starvin'. We can come back after lunch and see the brain surgery movie. This is lots more excitin' than goin' on tours with the women, don't you think so?"

During lunch she chatted happily about the dear old days in the hospital, how brain tumours sort of sneaked up on you, like an overdraft at the bank. Why, she could remember one patient, she looked sort of like me only her hair was redder, she just got more and more excitable and when they finally did operate, they found a hemangioma as big as an apple.

She'd sure be glad when they advanced to the stage where most of their patients didn't croak though. It was hard on a brain surgeon to have practically everybody die.

I suggested that it might be hard on the patient too, particularly if his brain tumour started with a hell of a headache like the one I had; and why didn't we walk around in the fresh air an hour or so before we took on the movie? Maggie reminded me firmly that we mustn't forget that we were very fortunate to be able to see these scientific exhibits. That most lay people never poked a nose inside the door. I said tartly that I was beginning to see why.

The cubicle in which they were showing the brain surgery movie was jammed and we had to lean against the wall in a far corner. We had missed the first part showing who was operating and at what hospital and arrived just as the patient was being wheeled in. He was described as suffering from a tumour on the brain, in the region of the temperosphenoid lobe and as a result his right hand was paralyzed. As the surgeon began to administer the local anaesthetic, the several assistant surgeons moved forward slightly, their eyes intent and watchful. The operation was described as taking from three and a half to four hours and the patient to be dozing most of the time.

As the surgery progressed, slowly and carefully, the holes bored in the skull, the bone cut with the saw, and the tumour drained, each process was explained. At the end of the operation, the patient talked cheerfully, shook hands with the doctor with his previously paralyzed hand—and was healed.

It was the most dramatic movie I had ever witnessed.

Maggie looked at her watch. "Lordy, we promised to meet Pete and Jim at four-thirty, and it's nearly five now. We've got to get out of here."

When I got back to the hotel, there was a box of gardenias on the bureau and a note from Jim saying, 'See you at the Top of the Mark.' I was so bemused by the surgical movie that it seemed almost irreverent to go gallivanting off for cocktails. However, the smell of the wet gardenias helped to restore my original idea of the trip. As I rushed into my clothes, I planned a lovely tender hour alone with Jim at the Top of the Mark while we looked out over the misty lights of San Francisco and I convinced him that there was still time to switch to brain surgery.

As Maggie and I stood at the entrance of the cocktail lounge, she hissed, "There they are over in the corner. If they tell me she's a doctor, I'm goin' to kick 'em both."

A tall, dark woman sat between Pete and Jim and she was snuggled in what we feared was the *real* sable coat!

As we walked toward them, she threw back her head and laughed, showing perfect white teeth and deep dimples. She looked and smelled dangerous and was introduced as Dr Miller.

Maggie's face promptly lighted with the worshipful look an adolescent gives a movie star. "I've been following your articles on diabetes in pregnancy—but I sure didn't think you'd look like this."

Jim and Pete obviously didn't either.

I hadn't read the articles, and had a strong tendency to tell her to make up her mind, to be either sultry or smart. I asked her, rather bluntly I'm afraid, if she was married. She said yes, but that her husband wasn't a doctor so she didn't bring him to the A.M.A. meetings. They were awfully difficult for a lay person. After all every moment was taken up by meetings. Her husband didn't seem to enjoy them.

I listened to the avid medical conversation and wished she'd brought her husband.

Jim and Pete and Dr Miller went on to a dinner meeting saying gaily that they'd see us later, and Maggie and I had dinner at her hotel. I just happened to mention that so far the whole A.M.A. reminded me strongly of an article I had once read entitled, *'If You Knew You Had Only Six Months to Live—What Would YOU Do?'* Maggie got haughty and said she thought I was downright sacrilegious and to stop acting like a Yankee. We finished dinner in a cold silence and I went back to the hotel.

I leaned my hand on the window ledge of my room and looked at the tiny glimpse of the Bay between the grimy buildings across the street and felt forlorn. I thought of the last time I'd been in San Francisco. Of my carefree newspaper friends. Of the time we had gone down to Fisherman's Wharf at one o'clock in the morning and eaten frogs' legs.

The thought of the frogs' legs reminded me of the pink people and of brain tumours. I shifted my position and felt a prickling sensation up my arm. 'Probably the onset of the paralysis which is the beginning of a brain tumour', I thought dispiritedly and went in and turned on the bath water.

The telephone rang. It was Jim telling me to fix my face, he was picking me up in ten minutes and we were all going to Chinatown for some Chinese food.

"Is Dr Miller going?" I asked.

"Who? Oh—I don't know. Haven't seen her. There are about ten of us. Call Maggie and tell her we'll pick her up too. See you later."

I remembered then, from the past, that the newspapermen had drunk too much and, due to a slight street altercation which ended badly, I had had to find my way back to my hotel by myself at four o'clock in the morning.

We got in very late after wandering around the Chinese district, going to several night clubs and enjoying the thoroughly, unnerving experience of ten men to two women.

The next morning I called Maggie and woke her up and told her to hurry and get dressed and come over and have breakfast with me. It was my turn to show her the technical exhibits. As she grumbled I reminded her of the 'opportunity of a lifetime' wasting away out there without our help.

On the way out to the Auditorium I worked myself up again with a fuzzy nostalgia for the dear dead days of advertising. I could hardly wait to show Maggie the manufacturers' exhibits.

Take cigarettes for instance—I remembered droves of briefly clad majorettes, who skipped in and out among the customers, chanting the T Zone, or whatever loathsome phrase they were using then, Experience Is the Best Teacher, They Satisfy, Not a Cough in a Carload, The Pick of the Crop, and The Choice of Experience.

Everybody got dozens of packages of cigarettes and a smile exposing the whole T Zone. Nowadays when every promotion campaign began, 'Leading physicians all over the country say—' God alone knew what the advertisers would tat up for the A.M.A.

The doctors poured into the Auditorium like ants into an anthill. "Just look at them. Wouldn't you think they'd get sick of medicine?" I muttered as we elbowed our way toward the entrance.

"Oh I don't know—I think they're kind of cute hangin' over the exhibits with their eyes as shiny as kids longin' over a candy counter", Maggie said.

We fought our way toward the technical exhibits side. At a table just beyond the entrance sat a quietly dressed young man. Over his head hung a banner with the chaste inscription:

DOCTORS HAVE FOUND THIS CIGARETTE LESS IRRITATING TO THE THROAT

In a manner that could not have been more impersonal had he been passing out bank statements he looked at our badges and said quietly, "I hope you enjoy the convention, Doctor." He handed us each a small package containing two cigarettes.

Maggie said, "Oh, oh, I was afraid of this", and squeezed my arm protectively.

In place of importunate salesmen, cerise velvet banners dripping gold braid, and glittering cellophane wrapped products tied with enormous satin bows, each food manufacturer's booth was a little sterile shrine to the medical profession.

An actual working model of a milk condensing plant was surrounded by a three-deep circle of fascinated doctors. An aloof young man was explaining the mechanism.

"If that milk company thinks doctors are impressed by a little old milk plant—they should see 'em at Christmas-time around an electric train!" Maggie observed.

With a manner as furtive as though he were displaying dirty postcards, the young man finally admitted that their milk contained Vitamin D—400 U.S.P. units per reconstituted quart—and amended even that rash statement by saying the milk could be used for the new-born, the ill and the aged. "See that you limit its use to that portion of the population which cannot defend itself!" I grumbled as we moved along.

The pineapple producer's spirit was broken entirely. I had promised Maggie a gorgeous tropical oasis complete with palm trees, Hawaiian guitar players and hula girls who stopped writhing only long enough to present the panting customers with a crêpe-paper lei and a tall glass of The Drink of the Gods!

This time there was no indication whatever that pineapple juice was not originated in a drug store in Des Moines. From a glass dispenser, a young girl drew a paper cup of lukewarm pineapple juice and handed it to us with an unsure smile and no comment.

"This is just breaking my heart", I moaned.

"You can't go to the circus but you can visit your grandmother's grave." Maggie chortled. "Come on there are lots more."

"What's goin' to build athletes? Where are Dick Tracy, Terry and the Pirates and Sky King?" Maggie asked as we read the cereal companies' unadorned statements.

They clung to three facts only: (1) Cereals are suitable in every specialized diet; (2) few foods can better the nutritional contribution of a serving of cereal and milk; (3) this nutritional value is provided by virtually all cereals, regardless of grain source.

"Judging by Jim's increasing determination to eliminate all cereal products from the children's diet because they sit glued to the radio from five to six and refuse to go outdoors—they might have something there at that", I answered.

"This makes me real mad!" Maggie slammed down a folder on 'How to Bathe a Bed Patient' offered by a soap manufacturer. "What about the fourteen leadin' physicians who made fourteen drudges into fourteen dryads in fourteen days by just washin' their faces, or whatever those old liars say."

It did seem to me, as I examined 'How to Bathe a Baby', another folder which was magnanimously offered in unlimited quantities to any physician for distribution among his patients, that the soap manufacturers could be big about this. Gratitude alone should make them offer a couple of hundred thousand dollars to any physician who could write in twenty-five words or less, why he thought their soap was a mite less harmful than other brands.

"He'd probably have to be a 'leading physician' though", Maggie answered. "And they'd soon find out that no doctor can write anything in less than a million words, all of eight syllables."

The cosmetic manufacturers were represented by two firms. One whose products featured hypo-allergenic cosmetics formulated scientifically for those with sensitive skin, a far cry from 'Aphrodisiac', 'Tabu', and various other forms of bottled lust. And another who, although he had only succeeded in lowering to an irreducible minimum the sensitizing index of his face powder, stubbornly insisted that it came in a 'feast of exciting new shades'.

The drug houses' exhibits showed none of this cowering unsure attitude. They were tried and true friends of the medical profession and showed ingenuity and originality in their exhibits. After spending almost an hour looking at an authentic 1793 apothecary's shop complete with botanicals and galenicals, patent medicines and nostrums, exquisitely reproduced—we stopped in a charming lounge provided by another drug house. It was equipped with an Associated Press direct wire and several comfortable chairs and couches. A lighted fountain bubbled from a vine-covered wall (no doubt a subtle reminder that drugs bubbled from this house with equal ease), but a pleasant retreat none the less.

There were various panels showing the development of different drugs and beautiful paintings illustrating the progress of medicine. Because these exhibits were open to lay people, the comments were worded in comforting, simple phrases which gave me the warm assurance that if I did produce alarming symptoms of some fatal disease, suggested by the scientific exhibits, the drug houses would get in and pitch to allay my suffering.

"What'll we do this afternoon?" I asked, dropping on to one of the comfortable couches and lighting a cigarette.

Maggie fished around in her purse and found the Scientific Programme. "Let's see a good movie", she said as she sat down beside me. It was hard to choose from so many dandies. 'Mesenteric Lymphatics, Their Conduct and the Behaviour of Their Valves in the Living Rat'; 'Repair of Ruptured Membranous Urethra', 'Precancerous Diagnosis of the Cervix by Cytology'; 'Inter-Innomino-Abdominal Amputation of the Lower Extremity for Malignant Growths with Indications for the Extension of Its Employment'. There were a couple of hundred like that. I held out stubbornly for Ronald Colman but Maggie insisted that we might never get a chance to see these medical movies again. She clung to 'The Traitor Within' which was described as telling the medical facts about cancer in understandable terms. I refused to see anything remotely pertaining to cancer.

We compromised on 'Shock Treatment', on the very sound theory that nothing could come as a shock to us now.

The film opened with Kretschmer's belief 'that all forms of insanity come under two classes: folie circulaire and schizophrenic. The former is characterized by the alternation of moods of depression with periods of excitement, or mania; the latter by all manner of delusions down to chronic idiocy. Both forms of derangement, however, are only ordinary characteristics carried to extremes, exaggerations in consequence of some lack of control.

The patient, one Mrs B., was shown sitting in her room in a modern mental hospital with a nurse in attendance. She wore a lost, desolate expression and seemed to be completely disinterested in her surroundings. She was described as being in an acute depressive state. Convulsive therapy administered, preferably, with electro-shock, modified by curare, had proven to be simple, relatively safe, and so efficient in the treatment of depression that this clinic had used it in thousands of cases.

Mrs B. was then shown in a treatment room strapped to an examining table with a mouth gag between her teeth. A skull cap was fitted over her head and she was given what amounted to a minor electrocution. This was followed by convulsions and finally a deep sleep. Attention was called to the fact that before the use of curare in shock treatment, the patients occasionally fractured the long bones of the leg in the convulsions, but since curare had been employed, there had been no reports of injury.

"I thought curare was deadly poison!" I whispered. "Don't natives use it to tip their spears with?"

"It's a marvellous relaxing agent", Maggie answered. The importance of occupational therapy for the patient during the series of shock treatments was accented. Mrs B. was shown into a large dining room where various patients were eating lunch. Attendants in white suits stood around in strategic positions, like waiters. The only difference between this dining room scene and any other was the tendency on the part of the diners to behave the way I've often been tempted to act in a restaurant.

An old lady sitting at the end of the table, tasted her coffee, made a grimace of distaste and poured it over her hair. An attendant promptly brought her another cup of coffee. There was a close up of Mrs B. languidly picking a bun to pieces and listening to the animated conversation of the woman across the table. Suddenly she got bored and hurled her plate at the talker, a subconscious desire I've often entertained. She was given another plate and continued to eat her dinner. It was more and more apparent to me that involutional melancholia was merely a medical term for a woman with the courage of her convictions.

Mrs B. was given shock treatment for successive days and was shown each day with an increasing interest in her surroundings.

After several shock treatments she was shown playing bridge, with, as far as I was concerned, a normally sullen expression. Maggie murmured, “Who does that remind you of, honey?” Suddenly the patient dived under the table and chewed up the four of diamonds, the only practical solution of what to do with it that I’ve ever witnessed. Chewing it instead of leading wasn’t cricket in their league either, and the nurse quietly presented Mrs B. with another four of diamonds. This time she led it and sighed.

At the end of a month the patient was waiting for dismissal. She was laughing and talking, apparently normal and well.

I turned excitedly to Maggie. “There, but for the grace of God, go you and I. They ought to show this movie in every city in the country. People wouldn’t ever be afraid of mental illness if they could see this.”

Maggie shook her head. “You just like it because of your bridge game. It would never be a box-office hit as long as about sixty per cent of the population are committed to an institution at some time of their lives and the other forty per cent are teeterin’ on the edge. And if everybody doesn’t stop talkin’ about the atom bomb, we’ll all be on the inside lookin’ out.” She shuddered. “It’s comfortin’ to know that goin’ crazy isn’t a permanent thing like it used to be, but a movie like that gives me the creeps just the same. Let’s go home. I’m so sick of medicine I could scream.”

An hour later we were sitting in Maggie’s room waiting for Pete and Jim and drinking tea. Maggie kicked off her shoes and rubbed her feet. “My feet hurt worse than they evah do from house cleanin’.” She looked around the room and sighed. “And this place is even littler than the Incubatah was. I don’t know what possessed me to want to leave home. Oh, the exhibits were interestin’, but I keep thinkin’ of that old paediatric exhibit with all those foreign objects removed from the lungs of children, and wonderin’ if the boys are swallowin’ little fryin’ pans and bobbypins and all that stuff.”

I certainly wished that I’d never come. The technical exhibits had depressed me as much as seeing an old love who had developed wattles and a bay window, and as far as being alone with Jim was concerned—at home he at least had dinner with me.

“You know another funny thing”, Maggie continued. “When I

was a technician in the hospital back home, the patients as people didn't mean anything to me. I saw only the tissues after they came to the laboratory, and they were just so much work that I had to get out before I could have dinner with Pete."

Pete came in and threw his hat on the bed. "How would you like to go to Los Angeles, Magnolia? We could take the Lark tonight. There's an obstetrician down there I want to see, and after I've spent an hour with him, we could go whipping around the City of Sin for two or three days!" He turned to me. "I asked Jim but he said he had other fish to fry."

"It would be fish", I said bitterly as I went out the door. It was five o'clock and the misty June evening was filled with the sounds of busy people going home. Automobile horns mingled with the clang and bump of cable cars. The traffic from Market Street was muffled by distance to a deep drum roll. The fog softened the neon signs and made each unfamiliar street vista as tantalizing as little snatches of conversation. 'If Jim could only get away . . .', I thought and glared at a woman who was clinging to her husband's arm and smiling up into his face.

Some day I was going to spend two weeks with Jim in San Francisco, preferably when the A.M.A. was in Atlantic City. Some day I was going to spend two whole weeks with Jim and I didn't give a damn where it was. The children had something when they muttered rebelliously that some day they were going to work in a candy factory and then they could eat all the candy they wanted to.

When I got back to the hotel, Jim was taking a shower and singing, 'Marie, the Dawn is Breaking.' The pleasant sounds of splashing and slapping accompanied by roars of song merely served to remind me of home.

He came out of the bathroom, clad in slightly damp shorts and a Turkish towel. "Where on earth have you been? I've been waiting for you for over an hour."

I answered that I had been watching the life squeezed out of my old friend, advertising, by the boa constrictor of medicine, had seen a movie entitled, 'You, Too, Can Have Shock Treatment', or how to be electrocuted in six easy stages, and hearing that Pete and Maggie were deserting me and taking the Lark and going to Los Angeles.

Jim began pulling things out of the bureau drawers and throwing them on the bed.

"I hired a car. I thought you'd rather drive down the Coast and sit on the beach for two or three days. You said—"

"That I wanted to be alone with you, and I do."

THE END